The Turner trilogy

Book One

On Davidstow Moor

A chapter-less and free-wheeling, romantic Cornish odyssey

Email: mdphillips1856@yahoo.com

The Trilogy follows events from 1942 to 2032

A generally accidental entanglement of lives;

lived between,

London, Sussex, Cornwall and Germany

"All rights reserved. No part of this book may be reproduced in any form or by any electronic or mechanical means, including information storage and retrieval systems, without written permission from the author, except in the case of a reviewer, who may quote brief passages embodied in critical articles or in a review. Trademarked names appear throughout this book. Rather than use a trademark symbol with every occurrence of a trademarked name, names are used in an editorial fashion, with no intention of infringement of the respective owner's trademark. The information in this book is distributed on an "as is" basis, without warranty. Although every precaution has been taken in the preparation of this work, neither the author nor the publisher shall have any liability to any person or entity with respect to any loss or damage caused or alleged to be caused directly or indirectly by the information contained in this book."

"This is a work of fiction; names, characters, places, and incidents either are the product of the author's imagination or are used fictitiously, and any resemblance to actual persons, living or dead, events, or locales is entirely coincidental."

Contents

Page 1- Title and description

Page 5- Before you begin

Page 7- On Davidstow Moor

Page 219- And to conclude

Page 221- Others who lent words & a Glossary of terms

4

Before you begin:

If you can, have a few days in Cornwall while you read this; I was there best part of a summer to find everywhere I wanted for the story.

If you read it somewhere else the chances are you will then have places in your head you want to go and find, so I suggest you get yourself onto that long road west... where every up is like climbing to the clouds and every down like falling to the sea; where feet are yards and yards are miles and miles take in horizons and the sky.

Yes if you can get yourself down there, go west!

If you can't head west, I hope it does a pretty good job of transporting you there to the moors in 1971; and to the old airfield in wartime 1942 when floated that way.

Many of the people you find and follow are at stages of their lives in both parts of the story, as it flows back and fourth between wartime and hippy times.

There is a glossary of terms at the back, as you may find odd words or phrases needing explanation.

Also where the story stops... you will find a brief account of where things went thereafter in their lives.

6

On Davidstow Moor

On the moor you are always in the sight of a buzzard.

On most occasions he or she is not even remotely interested in you, but they can still see you; and whether in foreground or infinity their visual image is pin-sharp.

What the buzzard cannot do is make much sense of why you are there, as when compared to their high and simple world where choices range between eat and sleep, or eat then mate, or fly then rest, our lives would seem a plethora of wasted time, and spent on nothing worth spending time doing.

They sail on across the high green slopes unconcerned about people and their lives below, so that even in the war where giant growling birds pass with smokey air and grey glancing faces through thick glass… it is soon another sight they can ignore and get good at avoiding.

It is later generations of the same family of buzzards that carry us to the wartime airfield at Davidstow, where now twenty five years of winter storms have had their way with kitchens and crew rooms and vehicle sheds.

In this ragged array of buildings so many lives had found arrivals and departures as we are going to later see, but just for now a swallow skips and turns in the gusting moorland wind; although it seems hardly worth the wind's while… as curlew throws its high lament across the altitude of air.

It hardly seems to justify the trouble it clearly requires; Tugging fastidiously at cracked corrugated asbestos like some short-tempered and badly prepared scrap merchant; at least tugging the bits that still hang dull but determined to the tired roof timbers, and to rusty steel pipe lighting conduit, all making ragged whistle and dull rattle overhead.

The sun-shot summer swallow skims: though it hardly seems worth the wind's trouble to help her skip the gale ripped roof that blossoms wide where tired roof timbers open their arms to the sky; and where she could if she had a mind to fly straight through… perhaps she is still using last summer's mental map, one that does not include the revisions of one of the subsequent winter storms; but skip the absent roof is what she does, and with no more than a fleeting glance at the old cracked kitchen sinks and rusting ovens within, then they dive to the nibbled turf, both swallow and wind.

    The sheep that graze here on the nibbled turf, and bum to gale with wool tugged forwards, look ironically like someone trying to pull an awkward tight-necked pullover off over their head; and if these sheep were seen sailing aloft against a blue sky, they would look like miraculous four-legged clouds treading a path against the prevailing wash of air.

    Huts and huts and yet more huts; too many huts to ever guess or tell what they were all for.
    Were these maybe for food and cooking pans and things, or these for stores of bedding, or disassembled beds.
    The vehicle sheds were easy to discern, with rusty bolts lacking massive hinges jutting abandoned high above the floor; and a sultry grime of gritty grease on concrete beneath where oily bellies would have hung… now some whistling windy openings have no doors and only swing an invisible gulf of Atlantic air, because when the war finished, night time sorties of local farmers saw huge doors pass away to farms, where tractor sheds and combine barns can sleep now more secure.

    The peri-track, a taxi-way around the almost infinite edge of the airfield; in places so long and straight and far away that it might be thought a runway on its own. But those are longer and straighter, and even further away.
    The peri-track is a route of past, and the conduit of many lives round here: lives that built it in the war with urgent rush and pressure to repel 'The Hun'.
    Pilots who manoeuvred large cumbersome growling birds, and setting out on freezing gusty dawn patrols that all began along its 'lost alley', would often blink askance and imagine that somewhere they passed a sign; *'abandon hope all ye who exit here'*; and some would later know it to be true.

The peri-track is today a sort of road to farms and other homes across the moor, and if you look along its length you can believe that wind or time has warped it; as if returning light-years bend the distant dream that was its past.

And here comes also as of light and streaking fast, to spread her blue and white and red along the grass, our swallow; as she goes away across the turf a distant figure heads towards, though at first he is only small and visible from the waist up.

This airfield is so huge that perhaps he is foreshortened by being over the curvature of the earth to our eyes, and must climb the horizon before he can grow towards us.

As he comes his arms gesture out each-way like might those of a fanatical botanist pointing at flowers, and head to both sides oscillates, but nearer now we see he has two dogs and nor is he much of a botanist really; his arms do not point to indigenous species or to dismiss recent foreign impostors; rather they rally and direct his flying beasts that helter-skelter to and fro.

The minutes pass, he does not come to us; we only see him as a spec that grows and sharpens, passing by a furlong out; yet all he does not pass: across the airfield road there is a parked red car, and not abandoned, and soon enough this striding figure who is probably some sort of shepherd, halts and leans toward window:

"Mornin' Joe, you got the bes place from this tugging wind I reckon. Though to be honest it's not got half the edge as it was few days ago."

"You're right there Marlo… though I would have thought you were too young to start feeling the cold yet."

"Perhaps, but it whips across those runways pretty thin out there; my dad used to reckon it was because you were so far from any sort of cover, said it made you feel sort of abandoned and unloved."

"Yeah right enough, I reckon he knew his stuff out on these moors did Cliff… think you'll still be out here when you get to his time Marlo?"

"You kidding Joe, I'd rather have my testicles lashed with stinging nettles! No mate, if I can't get straight all the way to London, as soon as I get sorted I'm off to get a place in Launceston... and to do some serious shagging!

"That doesn't mean getting a place with Ginny either, it means somewhere that I can come and go from as and when I like... yeah, I mean to bring girls back to."

(And just as much it means to Marlo, somewhere he can emulate and try living out the life of his guitar-wielding hero Jimi Hendrix.)

"Oh I go all the way with you there Marlo... I reckon there is nothing more wonderful than finding out what all those different women feel like; there are some that are soft and spongy, some that look all big and hefty and over-fleshed like, but turn out firm and resilient to the touch... then you get these long skinny birds who appear not to have an ounce of decent flesh on them, but if you feel around enough you'll find something to hang on to.

Then suddenly there'll be one who just has everything that none of the others had."

"Blimey Joe, I had no idea you had ever seen that much action, I thought before you got married you'd had a pretty quiet war in your forge down there in Camelford."

"Yeah for me that's right enough Marlo, though for one brief period I was luckier than probably any man on earth; but most of the time I got to grips with bugger-all worth hooting about; unless you count my Claire, Marlo... and even that was pretty few and far between."

"Well all my life she's looked the same Joe, but I dare say she was a cracker when she was young. Which one was she of the ones you just described to me?"

"Oh none I reckon, truth is Marlo I was suddenly thinking about when I said 'for a brief moment I was the luckiest man'..."

Joe looks away a moment... His eyes have the reflexive inward shine of distance, and the flickered candle glow of past.

Then realisation of his hanging silence jerks him back from something he might speak of if he could; he lifts his head to find words and his lips form shape, then a rising peeling curlew climbs from field beyond the boundary fence, singing out tloo tloo tloo roo roo roo, and gives him leave to look away, and pause for time to find his words.

"Yeah the truth is Marlo... that I didn't get to grips with much of that stuff myself at all; sure my mates were on it left right and centre, especially the ones with any sort of a uniform... you know, back on leave and stuff; I felt a bit out of it being in a reserved profession; you don't look much to a girl strutting around in a leather smithy apron.

"No the truth is that most of how all these different girls feel like under their clothes is what I've gleaned from other blokes along the way.

"There were a few odd moments that gave me an inkling; out with our crowd and all the girls had had a beer or two... ah you know the sort of thing Marlo, they'd move from one lad's arm to another to more easily chat with a different girl, that's assuming they were not some sort of proper item with someone.

"Perhaps they would be turning to jabber backwards as you all went along, to better catch the words of a friend, and so they would turn and push against you, and you could feel the sort of stuff they were made of... if you know what I mean Marlo!"

"But you make it sound like you weren't getting your fair share from, em... sorry Joe, her name's gone."

"It was Claire, Marlo."

"Yeah thanks, from Claire."

"That's about the size of it; she and her Mum were strict chapel-goers; you got nothing more than a cheeky smile a squeeze and a peck on the cheek until you had sprinted away from the Altar married and with your bollocks bulging in desperate anticipation.

"Her Mum, and bearing in mind that they were as thick as thieves, her Mum said no wedding or children, or even space for a bit of hanky-panky till after the war. Believe me young Marlo, it was tie a knot, not with the girl of your dreams, but in your knackers time."

"Ah flippin' heck Joe, that must have done you in; I mean to take her out and be close to her etc. but not actually get to grips with her at all… and with nothing but a Blacksmith's forge and a pair of bellows to take it out on!"

"You've got it on the nose there Marlo… my mates reckoned I could bend a horseshoe with my bare hands during those years; and first thing in the morning after I had been out with her I reckon I often did."

Marlo chuckles while he is digesting the image of a man driven by unrequited passion to desperate lengths to slake his desire.

He glances across at the dogs which are snuffing and yapping into rabbit holes along the stone wall of the airfield's perimeter… thinks about how often he sees Joe's red car parked somewhere near the threshold of the deserted main runway, while from inside he gazes towards the old ruined buildings.

He would like to ask him outright as to why he returns so often to this spot; but he senses something private is behind Joe's presence here.

If Joe just loved the climbing air or the distant blue of the sea that glows luminous beyond the patchwork of falling fields, surely he would occasionally wax lyrical about it; he would at some time before now have maybe said how he only feels alive when he can taste all this stuff; the flavour of mushroom spores and stone walls, or the dandilion'd fields that climb towards the windward end of the main runway.

He has never said a thing.

If there were something that had half courted questions, Marlo would have jumped on it like the Gestapo. It feels as if he has for so long thrown a few words towards Joe as he ambles past or lingers with his dogs, that although he would love to say, *'hey Joe, this is the third time this week that I have seen you parked on this spot. There's something about it isn't there, tell me what you are seeing here?'* The time when he might more easily have asked that question has fallen beyond him.

It would hang unnaturally if now he threw in some searching thought. It would seem pitched to probe Joe's privacy, even if there proved subsequently to be nothing private to divulge.

Here something of routine kicks in:

"Are you heading for 'The Sun' in the next hour Marlo"

"Probably Joe… Oh I don't know, on second thoughts perhaps I would be better off without beer. I could just go back up the moor and climb Roughtor, and sit on the top meditating like a Buddhist monk for the rest of the day."

"All right you twat, I get the message… if you're lucky, and if you stop taking the piss, there may be a pint waiting in the wood for you when you get down there."

The moorland wind has settled to a softer waft, the day for once set fair it seems.

On the wind the curlew's rising 'tloo tloo roo roo drops back and re-ascends from one rung higher on its climbing scale; this fluteuous ladder of melody peels out and finds that as there's not a tree in sight for it to climb… it can only climb on the high sweet air.

Here their paths divide and Joe takes the road across the airfield and drives down off the moor through seven miles of deep-cut leafy Cornish lanes, past farms and fields with hazel trees and more than one erstwhile active and now empty, Sunday chapel… so many who once gave praise in so few miles.

The moorland wind has settled to a softer waft, the day for once set fair it seems.

On the wind the curlew's rising 'tloo tloo roo roo drops back and re-ascends from one rung higher on its climbing scale; this fluteuous ladder of melody peels out and finds that as there's not a tree in sight for it to climb: it just has to climb on the high sweet air.

Young Kiwi Chris the barman blasts antipodean nose out back, and checks kerchief to see if any brains have flown the nest.

"Hey, good on ya nose, that seems to have shifted things."
Now one or two of lunchtime's lurks are drifting in, and calling out in urgent tone:

"Yeah come on cobber, a chap could die of thirst round here, have you sneaked yourself a Sheila out the back there."
To them it's all 'Down-Under' down below, so there's no point talking about being a Kiwi.
But glassy clink and amiable murmur settles on the bar; and all they might yet achieve in the remaining day, like an over-laden barge in front of them is shoved away.
Sunbeams slope through curl of smoke across the slatted wooden floor, as the tatters of a pleasantry struggle to escape the speaking lips that think it's wasted on old William: Old William shows how wasted it was by lifting two gnarled fingers at the speaker and grinning conspiratorially sideways at another local 'wag'.
(Though what was said we never learn.)

Joe is in the middle of the bar below the sharp nosed fox whose resentfully accusing head stoops keenly down.
'Rufus' often gains revenge for that day up in the gorse nineteen years ago, having fled a thicket of broom and rosebay willow-herb on the sunny slopes of 'Brown Willie', then was hounded out of reach of hole, and wound up glaring from a wooden plaque.
His revenge is that his nose once soft and eagerly searching moorland air now is shrunk and hardened like a giant baked sultana. Any unwary six-footer over-eager to imbibe, or leaning out to show Chris he's in earnest, gets a bitter throbbing groove in crown that shrinks him back his cheeks blown out and hissing hot!
Joe himself has always in turn felt resentful of the fox; resentful that he has never peened his own crown on its keen nose nor ever will. He stands a mere inch or so short of it. All his years he has seen tall young guys cursing with their cheeks blown out and hissing hot, and grinning round and down at the little guys who are safe from it.
He wants to walk in and receive that throbbing groove. He wants to stagger back, the victim of being too tall: but each year his old bones settle further, and his shoes wear down, and he gets further from the sharp nosed fox.

Morris Oxford's cross-plies bald and sliding slouch the bend that opens here; it swings to car park bringing Marlo, but why he pulls the hand brake and detrains still moving none can say, it always thumps the further bank. He says it saves him walking half the car park. So after trudging ten or so miles of moorland he saves twenty yards of level stroll.

His entry today isn't just to get a beer, young Marlo seems excited as he skips from foot to foot and nods in exhibition of some tasty morsel brought with him for presentation as his comrades probe:

"What's the score then Marlo, Why you seem all puckered up and eager about something?"

"You remember that bird...
Then adds glancing round all the blank faces.

"The one I told you all about a week ago; I said she was driving the vicar of Davidstow's Vauxhall Cresta... oh come on, I said I saw her coming off the road from Bude and heading into Davidstow."

"Yeah it rings a bell Marlo; but what was it about her, or what was so exciting about her?"

"Well I had just put some sheep in that field on the corner and I was still on the bank as she came round. Well she seemed to be... no, it's a fact that she was just wearing a little pair of shorts... and..."

"What shorts with nothing else at all Marlo?"

"No you cretins... I just mean that her legs were really bare; I mean all the way down... and up!"

"Well saints above is that all; what in heavens name is there to get steamed up about with a pair of legs?"

Then Joe speaks up: it seems he thinks a pair of legs should not be too readily glossed over; seems he thinks that too many lives are pursued without tactile reference to a glossy pair of legs for far too long.

He mutters sideways to young Marlo, as if he would impart some wisdom had he any to impart; as he speaks he eyes' the window and the hill far off as though confirming past.

There would perhaps have been a life for him of sleek brown legs had things been otherwise.

Indeed had things been otherwise, maybe his life could have been lived against that sort of warmth and brownness; where his strong warm hands would have worshiped like some rampant willing slave.

But Marlo is fairly keen to nod acquiescent and pull away from Joe; then with his feet re-found, get back to his own tale of this girl's movements:

"The point is that I have just seen her again, but this time she was just leaving Otterham store as I was getting out of the car to go in and buy some bits and bobs."

"I suppose that this time she was just in the bottom half of a bikini Marlo!"

"No… look give over you lot, this is important… Anyway, so when I got inside I asked Carol who it was, and how she came to be round here."

"Blimey Marlo, I hope Carol told you to sod off and mind your own business!"

"She did not! She said that the girl was working for the vicar as a sort of house girl, you know, the kids and the cleaning and whatever.

"But apparently the girl was asking where people got together either at lunchtimes or evenings; seems she reckoned she was spending too much time up there at the 'Vicarage', and had run out of things to say to the vicar's wife."

Old William wakes up and interjects:

"I reckon I could probably run out of things to say to the vicar's wife, if I said 'get down there woman' and she failed to respond; then I think our love would from that moment dwindle, and I would have run out of things to say to her!"

"Oh blimey William you do think up some crap!"

Marlo looks a bit impatient to tell the rest of his story, trying back and forth to throw a controlling eye to get the attention of all the faces that have been throwing alternative versions around.

As he thinks he is pulling them all to heel, he starts taking decent puffs of air into his lungs like a weight-lifter preparing to take the strain, then eagerly launches forth:

"Carol said that the girl was taking the vicar's shopping home in the car, then heading down here on her push-bike."

Old William re-awakes and adds:

"And push is exactly the word to describe what she will be doing when she heads back up to Davidstow again, as it must be in the region of three or four hundred feet she has to climb before she gets to level ground… but at least you'll know if she has got a decent pair of thighs and lungs on her Marlo!"

"Not when I stick her bike in the boot of my Oxford, she won't need to push at all… at least she certainly won't be pushing against pedals!"

"Oh I see Marlo, you reckon you're going to be getting to grips with her do you? And I imagine you've got this whole thing planned to the last detail.

"So which pub in Camelford will you be taking her to for a beer this evening?"

"You lot must think I'm daft, there's no way I would take her to Camelford and have all you vultures flapping off down there, and beaking down the crack in my arse; it would at least have to be Padstow or Wadebridge, or probably even Lands End to get clear of you lot.

"Anyway, it hadn't even crossed my mind that she could be looking for a date if she turned up here.

"As far as I could gather she just wants to see where people hang out round here."

"Oh blimey Marlo, it's like looking through a shop window with you. You're motives are so transparent whenever you're angling toward something; you must think we're the biggest bunch of 'grippers' on earth."

"Don't be stupid, of course I don't… well actually I do; but either way, it doesn't really bother me if she turns up or…"

(Guess who has just walked through the door.)
Everyone stops and turns. Then realising everyone has stopped and turned, turns away. As everyone has turned away each decides they can turn back to look and finds that almost all…

The girl feels as if she has screeched to a halt at traffic lights that are alternating red and green, and green and red in random parallel.
So she stands.
She stands with her knees a little inward pointed, as though she were ready to leap to left or right, or even lunge into a backward flip as prelude to raining karate kicks on her foe.
Though standing there actually just says, hello.

Young Kiwi Chris smiles glad to see a Sheila in the camp, and counting off the dog-eared days that he has had to nurse this motley crew; nor does he even ogle at her knees, but reaches to the ladies' glasses and with tilted enquiring brow says with as much age and authority as he can muster at seventeen,

"yes my love, g'day"
then where her smiling eyes alight on his adds,

"Good to see you at 'The Sun', so at risk of incurring the wrath of my old man, this one's on the house."

The girl smiles with gratitude and whirls her head round in a circle. Why does that small momentum make her light cotton skirt flip up as in some conjurer's trick, *(though scarcely a couple of inches)* and gravity seem to take an age to bring it back down her smoothly contoured thigh *(point seven of a second)*.

She is perhaps somewhere between nineteen and twenty three years old, though it might just be the little cotton skirt that has her looking younger for there is a confidence in her poise suggesting she could equally be either side of twenty five.

A confusion of black curls roll on her shoulders, and her form is not tall yet toned, showing she is clearly no stranger to pushing pedals round.

When she turns to broadcast her smile to all the lads there, we are shocked to find eyes not dark or blue, as if her black hair were Mediterranean or of Ireland respectively, but somewhere between grey and yellow, and at first glance almost forbidding… like a wolf.

But the motley crew is more interested in her simply for being female, than in the colour of her eyes.

For her there is clearly nothing noteworthy in standing in a bar in a skirt that is an average length for London, but really pretty small for Cornwall.

Why has every glass of beer a beady eye across its rim observing?

What is in a leg?

Why get steamed up about a pair of legs… unless you're Joe?

Even legs that tell you they are really bare, all the way down, and all the way up, give or take a thin cotton skirt.

But Chris has got things well in hand now, and a complimentary glass of cider stands with bubbles rising now sits with his welcome on the bar.

The girl has climbed and settled on a wooden stool that everyone is jealous of.

It is in fact a sturdy wooden stool that in almost half a century's time a German girl who not yet born will venture from that post-war currently somewhat unpopular country on her motorbike; she will sit on this stool while she is introduced to drinking a Cornish beer that is not even sold here yet.

Old William leans surreptitiously toward Marlo and conspiringly enunciates;

"Don't you go sneaking off outside to sniff her saddle now Marlo!"

"Oh give it a rest William, what do you take me for? Or is it just that you want to get there first!"

"Well I reckon that's what I would have done a year or two back when I was your age Marlo!"

"My age a year or two back! You mean a score or two for starters; that's if we are prepared to believe that you ever were my age William."

This 'welcome girl' has settled quickly to the scene.
She appears to exchange comfortably across the bar with Chris; and he appears to be giving a run-down on his disreputable clientele, for as he feeds her chuckled phrases she grins sideways along the sequenced angles of his sight.
This very 'welcome' girl looks good on her barstool: If you sit on a stool in a bar that hardly ever sees a girl at lunchtime; or only now and then anything that qualifies properly as female of a night, then you look good on a barstool.
She looks good on her barstool because in contrast to when old William is on his stool and chuckles loudly, and stretching across to thumb-jab some poor sod's ribcage, he would then normally unleash a ripping cabbage'y fart.
She looks good on her barstool because unlike Joe, she has no bony kneecap peeking knobbly beneath the trousers of an over-short de-mob suit that he bought years ago in Camelford's Oxfam shop.
She does have a kneecap, but not that juts in angularity; her's is cushioned and golden, and makes you not want to be sitting two stools away.
She looks good on her barstool, tilting in conversation, or lifting the small of her spine while her golden legs decompress and miraculously alter shape, calling the eye as though they played a visual Chopin rhapsody that human eyes cannot resist.
For once, even the resentful fox looks fondly down with an aspiring gleam in his sad eye, so glad that Joe gave up his stool for her to look good on.
The unspoken, yet undoubtedly the opinion in here today, is that she looks rather good on her barstool.

Young Marlo sees that Chris has grabbed himself the 'lion's share' of chat-up time; he himself needs a space to grab his rightful chance, but it's a bugger that not only is Chris more easily able to hold her attention from his side of the bar, but he also has the authority of the licence, and the traditional role to offer words of friendship and attention to a stranger.

"The bastard knows I had a sort of prior claim... why can't he call me over to say who I am."
Old William who while watching sideways sees how Marlo winces at the landlord's son's advantage, whispers quietly:

"I know what you are thinking boyo; but it's not as if you've got your name stamped on her arse is it!"

"Sod off you old shit I'm pissed off!"
He hisses beneath his breath:

"You wait till the next time Chris tries to get his leg over with that randy but slightly reluctant farm girl from Polyphant again: I shall begin making overtures from across the bar; I reckon she has always had a bit of a preference for me the truth be known."

"Yeah, and what if he just gets his dad to ban you for the night: You won't look so clever making ovaries from out in the lane Marlo!"

"I'm not after her ovaries you dozy old twonk... though I could put up with getting a bit close to them now and then. I was referring to 'overtures'; you know, like when they play little bits of all the tunes you are about to hear in an opera or something, woven together to get you in the mood for the whole thing... Oh Christ almighty, why do I bother, it's like feeding caviar to pigs: one old pig in particular!"
William's face is pretty blank but there is still a certain amount of chin jut, suggesting that though his brain is still working to make sense of the previous text it also displays a dismissive angle that declares no subjugation to Marlo's metaphor, or to his insult.

The outlook still seems pretty bleak; Chris still holds the high ground, and looks fairly determined to hold on to it. Even if the girl would like to cast her eye around she is far too polite to do it with the landlords son making such an effort to entertain her.

Marlo plays a waiting game, though not as perhaps Clint Eastwood might have in 'A fist full of dollars', but rather more as might 'A cat on a hot tin roof'.

With thwarted indignation he repeatedly picks up his beer, takes a gulp, and returns it to the bar for a few seconds, huffs towards it and repeats the process.

Something seems to have griped this centre area of the bar. There is a disconsolate mood hovering around Marlo and Joe: Joe wishes he could 'hold forth' to Marlo, to reveal some truth or clever quip from the experience of his long life.

The problem for Joe is; that although his life has been averagely long, there really isn't all that much to draw on that relates to modern life or the pursuing of sex. There isn't to be honest anything very useful except perhaps: How to survive a humdrum domestic life with a woman who does not excite you at all; if he has ever known a sniff of real eroticism it has been blighted by a lifetimes gagged memories.

Joe starts to mutter a few collected reassurances aimed at smoothing Marlo's disappointment.

After only half listening to the first few phrases Marlo distractedly but glumly throws back:

"Oh, so I suppose you would have marched right up and demanded your right to an interview would you Joe?"

"Hey settle down Marlo, I only meant that just because it doesn't happen the first time, well your chance can easily come round again."

"Sorry Joe, it wasn't really meant to come out quite like. I was miles away and thought you were saying I hadn't made enough effort to get to her."

"No that's not what I was saying, but it doesn't matter, if I am honest I would admit to being a bit disgruntled myself today. Everything seems to hurt; not the stuff you were just saying, I mean that my back hurts, my arthritic feet feel really achy today: Today… even my memories hurt."

"Ah you poor old shit-bag, let's see if we can drag Chris away so I can buy you another beer shall we?"

"Well I like the sound of that except that it wasn't you who bought me the first one Marlo, so it isn't really 'another'!"

"Blimey Joe, do you want to drink this beer or wear it… Hey Chris, we're all dying of thirst down this end with the hoi-polloi; if you can tear yourself away from things up there at the posh end, old Joe who is fairly close to his final croak anyway, is starting to croak because he needs another beer."

"Yeah hold ya horses Marlo, I've been watching everyone's glasses, and I saw you two have only just swigged the dregs this second… is it the same again?"

"Yep the same again Chris; except you'd better pull Joe a pint and a half, he puts it away like a fish!"
This humorous dig at the old chap is pretty standard 'Sun-speak', but seems to lift the ear and light the eye of the 'welcome girl'.
Chuckling across at the barman, then sideways though without direct eye contact towards the 'gruesome two-some', she decreases her heading on the barstool by around forty-five degrees, to settle almost facing them.
In Marlo's fertile imagination her knees seem to be shouting at him, as to him it seems as if they have a megaphone; he imagines it is held softly between her thighs beneath the cotton skirt; or perhaps there is no audio call, it is simply a trick of the light.
The golden wood of the bar glows amber in her translucent eyes like he often sees colour refracted by the sun on some gushing peaty moorland stream.
True enough, almost any female could appear like a princess to the eyes of these Cornish yokels. There has never been a female that sidled in here of a lunchtime and was not given an admiring once over by nine out of ten of this motley crew. So this one with her hair and eyes and knees and all the rest unquestionably contained inside her little cotton dress was guaranteed to cause a stir.

Marlo has grinned at her, and been repaid with a careful yet confident smile. He feels flushed with triumph and prepares to relax and really enjoy this next pint of beer. At least he will he feels be able to chalk up a degree of progress today.

He swigs and gazes happily at the optics on the wall, then hears the hissed tones of Joe coming sideways at him.

"Her glass you tosser!"

"Blimey,"
thinks Marlo,

"Joe's not such a dozy old twonk as you might think; and why was he the one to think of it."
Marlo takes a couple of steps to get round Joe, then leans along the bar to look casual and informal. He speaks out, employing the Jimi Hendrix grin that he often practises in the mirror of the pub's bogs when he's had a few beers.

"Hey there little lady, can I get you a drink?"
Marlo is so impressed by his inspired delivery that he nearly snaps to attention to salute his own prowess. But the spirit of Jimi is there to steer him through, and he is able rather coolly to lace on:

"I should have asked you before Chris took our glasses up the other end."
Then as a sneaky addition embroiders his thought.

"But he's hardly going to mind taking a glass back up there for a lady like you!"

"Jesus,"
he thinks,

"I'm really on a roll with this one; everything I say sounds more and more like Jimi Hendrix. Perhaps I should have said 'Chris won't mind taking the glass back for a 'foxy lady' like you'."

She has smiled and acquiesced at each presented angle. This is spot on what you expect to get from a girl on her first visit to somewhere she has never been before, and who is having a drink bought for her.

If her acquiescence was being presented to Joe, he would probably think in his innocence, that it meant she was already falling in love with him. Fortunately Marlo is, though only by a whisker, a little more worldly than his old friend.

Chris is going off back down the bar for another pint of cider for 'The welcome girl', and Marlo is mentally chewing over the best order for pleasantries.

Just now he is displaying his amiability by saying what a nice guy Chris is, but at the same time trying to think if there is any girl Chris can be linked with to 'queer his pitch' a little. Nothing comes to mind so he carries on with the 'Mr nice-guy' stuff.

Then Joe's hissing comes again into his windward ear:

"Her name Marlo!"

Once again he wishes he had been on the ball enough to think of it himself; and how he asks himself might Jimi ask that: *'Hey little lady, I know it will be something really pretty… will you tell me your name?'*

Yes that would be perfect, but can he carry it off."

"Yeah, that would suit a treat, but what if I muck it up: Let's just go for it."

"Em… my name's Marlo; er… who, or what?"

"Oh Jesus-wept, how can I make such a bollocks of simply asking her name!"

"Hello Marlo, and thanks again for the cider; yes my name's Anita."

"It's a privilege to meet you little lady."

He is surprisingly fast to regain his composure and even pulls off some 'Jimi' drawl, though still uncertain just how much 'Jimi' to evoke; she appears to him to relax in the amount he uses.

He continues, and thinking also with his hero in mind that his wedding tackle has responded in prominence to the words and influence of Jimi.

"We don't get so many little ladies like you around here…"
As soon as he says it he wishes he had not; it makes him sound so cut off and rural. His hand moves up to check for any tufts of straw sticking out his ears, but snatches itself back to innocently scratch a cheek.

"I mean, of course there are lots of girls turn up evenings and weekends, but they all look exactly like their mothers, you know what I'm saying… Anita?"
Her name did not come instantly, bringing an internal *'bugger'*.

"Oh absolutely Marlo: Sometimes when I am out with my mum and my big sister, people assume that we're siblings."
Marlo isn't at all clear what siblings are, though remembers that they often suffer rivalry, and deduces from her use that it is not a word for mothers and daughters.
He knows that the diving board he has launched from was a little bit wobbly; he begins to suspect the sea he is plunging into may have a few sharks lurking. 'But a faint heart never won a fair maid.'

"Hey that's really nice Anita, and a real ego-trip for your mum. Yeah some of these mums are pretty cool, it's just that when you see the one half, you can't help thinking of the other."
He bangs shut on that point. Common sense tells him that he has done as much as he is likely to do in regaining dry land; further explanations would just sound apologetic.
Anita has grinned uncondemningly as she swigs her second free pint; though having said that, when is a drink ever really free?

She is tidy in her little cotton dress though not meagre. She is certainly blessed by adequate lushness. Where flesh sits it does not settle heavy or corpulent, nor hanging in the webbing of its wearer's clothes; as with some old scroat who has spread her flabby arse on too many barstools. If you allow your eye to explore Anita's curves, you rather have the impression that her clothes are supported by the pleasantly full body they contain.

Anita has grinned uncondemningly, and still swigs her cider; and is asking herself if there is something in here for her today. It seems to be a lot more fun than lunchtime with the vicar and his wife. An evening might be even better; though that will mean pedalling down in the dark, or home in the dark afterwards at any rate.

She explores in her thought whether she is really ready to bring herself here.

When you bring yourself as an unknown girl of mateable age to a place where girls are certainly at something of a premium; you are presenting them all with an available female; you are whether strategically or not, thrusting your female form beneath their collective nose.

Conversely, if you arrived and immediately began shouting at them not to come near you they would just say: 'so why have you come here?' Anyway, she wants to be a woman, and she wants to see men move and be moved to look toward her; and certainly wouldn't like it if on seeing her, 'to a man' they moved the other way.

Therefore she treads a careful path, polite, and yet not hiding what she is. A bit like fishing she supposes; not meaning here and fishing for a man, just that she wants to cast her net across the whole pool of life, and knows she could haul out just as much of life's frog-spawn as tasty wild trout in the process.

She lifts and turns her face, and coal black ringlets tilt and swing like a fragrant curl of freak black honey-suckle; and golden olive tinge's on her lifted cheek.

"So what of you Marlo… and while I think, your name doesn't sound very Cornish to me."

"Funny you ask me that; I only found out from Mum a couple of months ago why they called me that. She said that they were really into a film they had seen called 'A Streetcar Named Desire', and mum admitted that she really fancied the star Marlon Brando, as she couldn't use the whole name she made Marlo out of the two."

"Hey that's really cool, but in looks Marlo, are you the image of your dad? I see him dark as you, and swarthy as a moorland fiend."

"Christ no Anita, he's got ginger hair… and only half as tall as me; anyway, how many moorland fiends have you met since you've been living round here?"

"I suppose you're probably my first Marlo… So anyway, if your dad is small and fair skinned, I suppose your mother is the tall dark handsome one; though I find it a bit hard to imagine why any dark handsome woman would let herself get talked into marrying a small ginger man…! Yes I like to think that after what you said about mothers and daughters, you're like your mum."

"No hardly like my mum she's short and blonde!"

"Oh… then a different postman I presume?"

"Yes I reckon that's the most likely explanation Anita."
Her name came quite quickly that time, and he thinks he's back on level ground.
Marlo knows that Joe will see this all as a young man's game and not butt in; though glancing beyond Anita, Joe is nodding inclusively at the conversation of the next folks on, but seeming like he's not quite in it and wishing he was.
Joe seemed to distract himself from following Anita and Marlo's banter quite purposefully, though with no apparent stimulus. None of that is pondered over by Marlo, yet subconsciously a note has been made in the front of his currently 'parked' long-term memory.

The atmosphere in this lunchtime bar is quite unlike how it might usually feel. There is that tingle of men who have been stimulated by… well by a stimulus that is not usually there.
The greater part ceased years ago to pursue the rump of womankind. Despite that, being now in a room of men where a nubile female glows and emanates pheromones in their midst, has stirred something primeval in most of them.
There is scarcely one of them who has not in the back of his head estimated his place in any likely pecking order, even without any conscious thought of chancing his luck with her.

Nor has anyone here not found his eye repeatedly absorbed into her softly feminine warmth.

Most eyes have tried repeatedly not to tuck themselves up beneath the hem of that light cotton skirt.

Some eyes have made almost no effort not to tuck themselves where they shouldn't be: These sinful eyes will not be going to Heaven, except perhaps on earth!

But a room full of male eyes and egos has a collective consciousness; it asserts that when a succulent female like this turns up, someone in this room will end up being taken to Heaven: But which fortunate male will be picked for that ascent?

You can discount 'Old William'; sure he displays both adequate interest and enthusiasm to get to grips with her, or with any female who would be prepared to abandon herself to his tender loving touch. But he is far too long in the tooth and gnarled to be in the running.

There are several other 'end of the line wrinklies', who not wishing to be ageist, we can save time by crossing off the list.

Half a dozen thirty to forty something's might produce an outsider who could cause an upset by slipping past at the post, but the 'odds' on that are pretty slim.

In real contenders we count no more than four. There is Chris the Kiwi barman, very handsome, but at seventeen he is so young he may not be what she is looking for.

'Rocky', as was christened Ronald, or Ron Ockford, a tractor driver and stockman from Bolventor. He is by far the most statuesque and desirable male in the bar, but so shy that he rarely speaks many words, even to his best mates.

An amiable builder of around 'thirty' with a receding hairline but superb wit and a likeable personality called Cedric, though only known as Ric, and carrying a long track record of popularity and success with ladies, must be in the running.

Then Marlo: What can you say really; he's youngish, he's tall and not bad looking. Despite his self-belief that he is the Cornish embodiment of Jimi Hendrix, it is quite apparent that he lacks Ric's way with words, or his gift of making women feel they're in the right place at the right time.

It's Marlo who has put some thought and leg-work in. If someone has a claim it's him; except too many men know how much that counts for.

When female flesh is up for grabs, a heaven-sent contrary muse will anoint and pluck the least deserving from behind the throng of nice guys every time.

A ribald murmur lifts and travels round the bar.
We see come in, and almost never have we seen before the pub's entrance frame the Vicar of Davidstow… now we do.
The Vicar has the face of a late thirty year-old, but the hair of… well, someone who has no hair at all.
Smiling grey eyes are thrown towards these 'semi-sheep' of his wider flock. Most of this lot just do weddings and funerals and a modicum of Christmas stuff, or maybe the odd Harvest Festival; there is sadly for his kudos none to whom he can throw a smug yet jovial,
'Another good turn-out for Sunday prayers/harvest festival/remembrance day, did you not think Mr Blank.'
So he has to content himself with a few well meaning grins and sundry thoughtfully knowing nods to any here that his addled memory thinks may have had a recent bereavement, or wedding, or some other reason to be in his church which he ought to recall.
Of course all Vicars wear faces displaying aspiration; it is a part of their ecclesiastical college training, like perfecting the hooting voice of the wise old pulpit owl.
This one here mixes aspiration with a mellow fruitfulness, as he does his greetings with this room of men.
That bit all done justice to, now thrown sideways just in passing, like a man not over zealous, but who'd better not forget to do what he came in for:

"Ah Anita, I heard you might be down here; I needed to come back this way…*(which might be true)*, and knowing what a climb back up it is from down here, just stopped by to see if you preferred a lift up to the moor. There's plenty of space to get your bike in the boot."

As he speaks and smiles toward Anita you might be forgiven for thinking that each of his eyes now glows with as much aspiration as shortly before had been the sum total of the two.
For her he lifts his chin a little more, nor is a slouch allowed, or pot to bulge above his waistband.

"If God was really good he would give me hair again, for surely such a gift would cost him nothing to bestow?"
Did that dubious plea issue from the Vicar?
It wasn't really clear enough to say;
we heard it as his hand began its climb to fluff a 'Bobby Charlton' wisp to pose as head of hair, then veered away;
falling distractedly towards the button of his warm trousers.

Anita looks genuinely torn. Here is no sulky adolescent glum to spurn all grown-ups and to stick to what little bit of 'scene' she's found like glue.
She is visibly weighing up her desire to find what life there is around this little oasis, against the uncertainty of making that ascent to the moor before it gets dark.
Anita draws in her horns of thought and lifts one foot from the floor with both palms turned upward; and as in a Victorian oil painting of a flower fairy she inhales to describe her balance of options.
Mr Hennacy enjoys her cherubic pose; he even wonders whether if he had her posing beside him in the pulpit while he was giving his weekly sermon, and she was portraying his words like someone 'signing' for the deaf, would his congregation get larger week by week.

"A few of the men would certainly get larger…! holy saints above did I say that, or think it which is just as bad; it's lucky I don't believe in god any more or I would either have to wear a hair-shirt or flagellate myself."
A sweet voice filters through his guilt:

"So you see my predicament Mr Hennacy, without lights on the bike it will be pretty grim if I run out of daylight won't it."

"Yes that was what I was worried about Anita, hence my appearance in here *(which might be true)* this afternoon."

"Though on the other hand unless I hang around too long I should be across the airfield at least an hour before it gets too dark."

Then Joe 'pipes up',

"There is another choice you have of course Anita… young Marlo's Oxford has got a boot like a garden shed and he goes back up that way, and he would be pleased to be of service to a lady, and he's about to buy the lady and I another beer, and you as well I dare say Vicar!"

"Yes it's no trouble for me to run you home Anita… and yes… I s'pose I'll get another round."

Marlo knows there should normally be something to object to in most of that 'buying beer' bit, yet this time feels happy to go with the flow.
The Vicar declines a drink, *'has calls to make'*, so Marlo's round contracts to more comfortably affordable proportions.

"Okay Marlo, that's very kind of you if you can do it; and you seem a very sensible sort of chap, I'm sure I am not being negligent in entrusting Anita to your care."
Marlo has quickly and a tadge reluctantly to fight down an image of Anita supine across the capacious back seat of his Oxford with her little skirt up round her tummy, and one smooth brown leg hooked over the back of the front seats, as he assures Mr Hennacy:

"Oh she will be quite safe with me, and it's easy for me to… *'shit!, I almost said turn her on'* …run her home, on my way back Vicar; I reckon she'll be back in time for tea."
Then adds with a slight gleam in his hitherto steadfast eye:

"Well… in time for supper anyway."
An expression half of mild concern and half of perhaps wishing he was to enjoy her company in the warm interior of his own car, lights the Vicar's eye.

"Well earlier rather than later I suppose we ought to say Marlo… anyway, you all enjoy your beer, and yes Anita, you enjoy some time away from 'The Vicarage' and being stuck with your…*"nice soapy warm"* arms in the kitchen sink!"

"Oh thanks Mr Hennacy, I'll see you back there later on then."

So suddenly it all drops into place from Marlo's point of view; to him it feels as if the plumpest most succulent pigeon has finally fallen almost ready plucked into his lap: The only question left is how best to cook it.

It is old Joe who really deserves the credit Marlo supposes, for he has steered the boat and nudged the fates toward this happy departure.

What's actually in it for Joe, Marlo wonders: If he himself does get to grips with this girl in an unequivocal manner there's no obvious spin off for the old chap. He certainly won't be allowed to 'watch the match', and most certainly not to encourage or intervene from the touch-line like the frantic coach at village football.

It's quite probable that he just likes to see fair play, and to see that things come right for the right chap; and that thinks Marlo, is unquestionably me.

Then 'strike-a-light', it's that confounded Kiwi again:

Chris has leaned across the bar with a half of cider to top Anita's pint glass up with; and of course it comes accompanied with a smirk and a few words intended to engage her and coax her bow towards the open sea of his bar.

Marlo feels thwarted and frustrated. What he thinks if she spends the rest of her visit here chatting elsewhere, and only comes back to him when she wants her lift home. He can see it now: Having driven way up to the moor, and at the sort of time when he would otherwise have been getting round to asking her if she wants to go out with him some night she will come out with:

'Oh Chris is really kind isn't he Marlo, he has offered to borrow his dad's Zephyr on his evening off so he can take me to Tintagel for a fish dinner. He reckons there is a restaurant on the cliff tops that he thinks I would love to eat at.'

Or some other equally dispiriting fly will be flicked into the ointment of his horny thoughts.

If fate lures her elsewhere in the bar, he will feel like something has been taken away from him without him ever really having had it in the first place. Nor will never having had it make it seem any less odious, for unrequited desire is the most impassioned.

Outside and to the sun-faced slopes, we see a trickled dimming to a softer light; and linnets not their final, but their evening twitters tisk from larches with a tone that eases down, and do not sing like in the morning shouting what they might achieve.

We hear a pause in song… that holds one stave in suspension till… the next, as the listening bird sits head cocked though not for the territorial response of his rival; it is almost as if he believes that the softening air should return an echo of his own voice.

The hours nudge their way past languidly and imprecise, like ambling school kids heading for their morning bus.

From the climbing slope of the mellow green hillside, where marsh grass and bog-cotton nod urgent and chilly in a wind that sun has ducked the brow to hide from: where from our view of the pub below is distant and detached, the lives inside are lost to us for now.

Time elapses… although how much seems not clear?

Though buzzard has no clock-borne sense of time they know where they should be and when they should be there; and here seeing from so high there's nothing can avoid their downward stare.

From high up in the air we would see two match-stick figures issue from a darkened door.

You can hardly make out steps or strides but as they cross the expanse of the car park they move as if a divine hand is making them go at the same speed.

The tinnier form halts halfway then turns back, and the larger one waits facing sideways with head bowed as one foot swings back and forth relative to its earthbound neighbour.

The smaller form has gone out of sight past the end of pub, almost as quickly reappearing with a bicycle and moving in parallel as it re-converges with larger match-stick man.

They move once more across the space till in beneath trees that obscure them from our distant sight.

Far off and out to sea the sun sinks like a molten globe towards America, or so it looks! But still awhile before it sinks into the sea; then sunk below there climbs behind a burning wall that fades so soon to sombre glowing grey… and soon to night.

Again a buzzard rises darkly on the wind… its distant cries rain out like spears of yearning; and circling on the high-borne rise another also launches forth into spiralling ascent. They cruise towards the sliding dark.

Looking up, is it now and today we are looking at; are these two hawks that circle in evolutionary syncopation only there for our present eyes? They appear so remote that it seems as if they might be from the past or the future.

Looking once more down, a car is driving out and off along the lane like a child's escaping toy.

As these below,

And those above,

We too have left, and not just left the pub now we ascend the hills of peaty moss, so too also to slide through years and lives and hopes and dreams of if we could… and might have beens?

First over trees and farms and chapels where below the lane is hid from sight and deep in falling darkness, then as higher up to leave the valley farms and see the larger moorland fields expand in a moonlit glow which lifts the flaxen moor grass to be a dancing fairy carpet.

It seems that as we travel time too is shifting below us, though the moorland peaks up to our left are standing as they always have, uninterested and unmoved.

Now first sight of the old airfield shows not weathered aging concrete but clean dark tarmac?

The buildings roofed and functional some windows lighted?

Across the moor the sun has climbed with the day set fair again it seems, and Camelford is well awake as everyone there is getting on with life and work.

Sun curves across the town and time slides down.

At the town smithy it is now nearing end of work today and the blacksmith thinks he's done enough to knock it on the head quite soon, still not quite time to kill the furnace yet, as raucous metal clangs on metal and a tractor's red-hot lifting arm is clamped and soundly beaten till it's straight: Or as far from being still bent as makes no difference.

This raucous clap and ringing even makes a knob of moss roll bobbling off the botch-tiled roof.

The dinging hammer throws its instant chorus out, but does not have a song that sings of all that it can yet achieve; it more describes a weary arm that thinks it has seen quite enough cracked plough shares wanting welding, and baler arms that need re-riveting, for today.

The anvil bolted to its yard or so of new oak tree trunk recently planted in the old earth floor seems happy to be ringing like a bell; the forge is burning low now where the driven bellows have fallen silent.

He checks his dusty clock on the blackened wall, and scents of flux and tempered steel course slowly through his veins; in quiet longing dreams of what he feels his life should be slide past in flickered thought and growing hope.

It's getting near the time to scout below the bench to check where fallen glowing swarf may settle for a cosy night in bits of wood and dust and stuff.

Joe knows a smith in Truro, lost his 'smithy', cottage, and the only half-decent one of all his kids, that night when his forge went up; and it lit his stock of paraffin as well; the whole thing took at least a minute; closing down for the night is a serious business.

It's only a few years since Joe and his 'Old Man' unlocked one morning to find inexplicably… the anvil lying toppled to the floor, and the yard of tree-trunk that it was bolted down onto just blackened ash that had smouldered away to nothing through the night.

Ray said it was one of the strangest things he had seen in all his years as a farrier: not even the ceiling above was charred.

Joe's old-man only does the morning's now, and that is mostly just to check the jobs and talk about what's best to do with them.

Ray is keen to let his boy take the reins these days; it lets Joe see he's in the driving seat, and it gives Ray time to slope off in the afternoon. Joe's mum assumes he's out on some farm somewhere to sort repairs.

Ray is probably out on a farm somewhere, though not always just to sort repairs; all sorts of jobs come up that need attending to!

Today Joe rack's the hammer, throws the rivet drift into the box of 'sundry bits you have to hit'. He spots the centre-punch still with its end burred squiff and useless. Carrying it towards the bench grinder, he thinks he should put another point on it in case he needs it first thing, or his old man sees it and uses it as something to give him words of advice about.

Young Joe halts in the middle of the forge. Suddenly feels that he wants much more to act abandoned and irresponsible.

He has a strong desire not to do the right thing. Not to leave everything ship-shape for the morning, nor to scrub up with soap and towel, or comb his hair before making his expected appearance at Claire and her mother's house for a cup of tea on the way home.

In fact what he really wants is to do none of those things. He has a mind to march unwashed to the 'Masons Arms'…

(where except when out of a weekend evening with lads from the football team he would never think it right to go)

…and to have downed his first pint even before his cap is off. He wants to belch like a confident artisan before calling down the bar to Marilyn for a refill; and wink warmly at her when their fingers meet around the empty glass. He may hold onto it as she tries to take it from him, letting her feel the ease of his vice-like grip.

All of that feels more likely to occur if he doesn't re-grind the tip of the centre-punch ready for the morning.

Joe turns and looks askance around the smithy; his sideways glance is like that of a vicar who should be offering final nods and prayers towards the Altar before he locks and leaves, but cannot be fagged with nobody there to see him do it except the 'Almighty', and he's been pretty part-time for a couple of thousand years.

By some miracle, or other divine intervention, the snub-nosed punch clatters launched over-arm back into the tin box of 'things that need to be hit with a hammer', and there it can stay till tomorrow, or when Joe next needs it.

Then a small disturbance at the door puts time on hold.

"Hey Joe?"

And that would be a phrase evoking something all together different for Marlo and all Hendrix fans in '71', but we are still seeing 42.

"Yeah Joe, are you just closing up for the night?"

"In the next few minutes lads I will be."

A gaggle of Camelford boys have sought him out; they look like they have time to kill and mothers to avoid, and seeking simple boyish entertainment.

"Can you do your trick for us Joe... Morris and Peter here, are out of London from the bombing so never seen it."
Joe considers a no; but he sees the local boy's looks of eagerness to have their new comrades impressed and so capitulates.

"Okay then young Fred, show the littlest one of the new boys where the big hammer's kept, and he can bring it out."
Joe knows the little lad will struggle to carry it, and that will set the scene for his performance.
He puts a few more bits away for the night as they clatter about in the back room.

"Here you go Joe, he's done it."
The skinny little Londoner who looks no more than six years old, walks feet apart and pigeon steps with hammer head just off the ground and held by shaft.
Joe takes it from him and gives his ear a tweak. The little scrap stands back and glows.
Now the trick: a hiss of commentary replaces drum-roll; Joe grips the hammer by its three foot shaft, so the head is by his ankle.
With his back to the glowing embers of the forge to enhance the dramatic effect, he lifts it slowly up and outwards with his arm and the shaft straight. When his arm passes the horizontal it stops, but the head carries slowly on over the top and down to touch the tip of his nose. Then slowly up and back and down the other way.
Of course the trick only really comes true when all the boys take their turn to try themselves, and even the biggest ones cannot get it more than a foot from their ankle.
A chorus of 'thanks Joe' and 'see you at the match' etc. sees the little happy troop troop out and off to finish their day on the river bank, trying to knock out evening feeding trout with stones.

"Now straight to the 'Mason's Arms'... nor washed either, and give Claire and her mum a miss as well; I don't need a cup of tea, and I don't want a cup of tea; and I certainly don't want to be doing the same thing every day of my life... and at the same time each day."

The door bit's fairly easy, only half the wagon width is open today; but it drags along the yard a bit.

These are easy because he does all those bits every day: The walking out into the light needs no more thought, the dragging closed of the door is no harder than usual, the struggle with the key and the resolve to oil the padlock soon is thought every day. And walking down towards the river bridge is quite straight forward. It only starts to get a bit tricky when you don't turn right and cut through the ally to reach Claire's back street.

You are still out on the main street, though far beyond your normal operational limits.

He glances at his grubby paws as if they hold an answer; and sees in either palm the blackened hands of his grandfather as he remembers them from years ago.

In his memory Joe has stopped on the way home from school. Granddad, still a looker in his fifties, leans nonchalantly against the wagon wheel of some sort of cart. Forever in Joe's memory he will be twizzling a rusty horseshoe on the index finger of one hand while he jokes with the plump yet bonny girl from the big house, and she holds the horse.

Joe has never seen his own hands black in the high street. They would be black in the high street if he was driving their horse through to get rid of someone's repaired cart that was clogging up their yard, but then his black hands would have been working hands on the reins of their old mare.

Walking unarmed up Camelford high street, all seeing him might think that he has finished work, and some might wonder why he still wears his dirt at this time today. Nobody will guess why he has kept it on.

If he were hurrying, it would be assumed that he'd had word of a family crisis perhaps.

Ambling as nonchalantly as he can manage will set the eyes of the town upon him, then veering off into the 'Masons' will mean that the chances are Claire and her mother will know before he is halfway through his first pint.

Joe takes a breath and glances left into a shop window; his reflection looks like an Indian 'char-Wallah' and tilts his swarthy face askance at him, and he nearly jumps round to see who it is beside him.

"You dozzy twat... what do you expect to see!"
He lifts his grimy chin and his confidence expands. If Marilyn likes his rough unwashed look and treats him to a come-on wink, he thinks he might just go along with anything that emanates.

Then he curses god and mammon, and not viciously, but Claire's mother for telling her not to provide any sexual services till they're married, and not to talk of marriage until after the war.

Then he wonders if in fact it is just a characteristic of the Fig family women-folk, and it will always be kept to a bare minimum of hanky-panky.

Most people are subjected to rationing during war-time, and a life of plenty when it ends… will he have to suffer a great big 'bugger all' till it's over, and rationing from then on?

"I reckon some randy little bird like Marilyn could help to calm things down a bit. I shall buy her a drink so that she can see I've got my flag hoisted."

A shop door opens out of shot, Joe hears a voice he knows speak from his rear:

"Oh hello Joe, you must be working late. I found that I was getting low on tea so I left Claire and popped out."
He turns to face the unwelcome music,

"What time will you be round for your cup of tea tonight; I even managed to get some of your favourite ginger biscuits, but I had to swap some sugar for them, so you had better not just dunk them!"
Joe is still gripped by disconsolate shock at her appearance, and a more than mild irritation that she might try to control his decision whether to dunk his biscuit or not.

All the aspirations that he held of walking into somewhere alone and free have fallen like yesterdays wedding confetti round his feet.

He so wanted to drink a pint of beer, and taste the taste of honest toil on the greasy rim from sweat of his own cheek.

Halfway since he left the forge he's been swallowing gulps of air into his stomach so he can unleash a socking great belch midway through his pint. So why oh why today must she appear?

"Oh Christ, I wanted all that so much… if only for one night to be free of the two of them… well Claire without her mum might have been tolerable.

"It wouldn't have had to be terminal, I would have told Claire when she came to look for me tomorrow that I was called out late to sort a broken plough across the moor somewhere, then came back after dark and dying of thirst… or something similar."

Joe's mouth opens to vocalise abeyance to the seemingly inevitable; but something in him is not quite ready to lay down yet.

It seems the opening mouth has ideas of its own.

"Ah if only Mrs Fig, and ginger biscuits too, you spoil me. Yes as you see I'm working late, and shall be at it till who knows when tonight, so can you tell Claire I will see her soon… *(and that's it, 'see her'; all I will do is get to look at her)* probably tomorrow if I'm not called out again."

"Very well then Joe, and I'll save those special… 'non-dunking' biscuits till we see you shall I?"

"You can stick them between the cheeks of your fat arse and blow them up the stairs as long as I can get a night off Mrs Fig."

"That's really kind Mrs Fig; the prospect of tea with you both will help to get me through the day if it's a hard one."

"That's nice Joe… still I mustn't keep you from getting finished and off to bed.

"I suppose you're off to the ironmongers as you're heading up this way… if it isn't it must be the ladies hat shop!"

Mrs Fig chuckles at her own joke, and Joe tries desperately to decide where he should be going.

"Because if it's the ironmongers I shall come with you so you can tell me which brackets I need for those new bookshelves."

A stroke of genius arrives that mitigates against trouble if word of his whereabouts does get back.

"No not to the Ironmongers Mrs Fig, I was just popping out for a pasty to sustain me through the next few hours; the best ones you can get at this time of day are found in the 'Masons Arms'."

"Oh I see Joe… but do you like it in there; it always looks a bit rough when I see the people who go in and out: Do you not find it so?"

He pauses, searching for how best to angle his explanation. Then as if fired up by the bold account of his whereabouts he does not capitulate to this call to condemn the place.

Joe lacks much early evening knowledge of the pub, but.

"It's a working man's pub Mrs Fig. It's farmers, Shepherds, Aerodrome mechanics… and yes, I'm just a blacksmith, so it suits me fine."

He does feel rather a fraud, but defiant nevertheless.

Mrs Fig capitulates before his stand, as she clearly had not anticipated anything from him other than meek agreement.

Her tone is more soft and girlish as she says 'okay Joe', and reiterates that they will both wait to see him on a less busy day.

He says his farewell's, but still wants to see her heading up the street before he swings off into 'The Masons'.

Inside it's dark and woody and with leather benches lining the walls all looks much the same as on a Friday night with the boys from the football team, but the sound is different; the tonal pitch of sound is about an octave lower.

Joe hears the difference though does not register it consciously and it would not occur to him even if the difference had struck him, that the average age is twenty years in advance of the football team.

You spend these sundry reflective moments as your medieval eye checks the dark corners of the bar for cut-throats and highwaymen, but as none appear to lurk the eye clicks magnetically towards a most fabulous frontage of female flesh. You simply cannot not look. If you didn't look, they would be even more ample and alluring in your minds eye than in reality: So it's best to have a look and get it off your chest, so to speak.

Joe looks and then thinks beer, but the seed is planted:

"Holy pumpkins, that lass must have been sleeping in horse shit since I last saw her; I swear they've grown by around a third again in the last month or so."

So he has his look, then concentrates on who is in the bar he knows.

Unfortunately there are no distracting friends; of course there are lots of familiar faces, for every single face has been here all his life, but no one that he is going to rush towards, or his first pint will easily become a shout for four.

"Hello stranger, has Claire 'got wise to you' at last? Perhaps she caught you strolling up the town with her mum once too often!"

Joe jerks back to the here and now.

"Yes good evening Marilyn, and no, because I never stroll around the town with Claire's mum, nor ever would."

Marilyn eye's him with a smirk:

"Oh that sounds nice and simple Joe… except in explaining why you were walking past with her five minutes ago!"

"Hey that wasn't walking with her Marilyn, we just happened to be in the same place at the same time…"

"And also just happened to be putting one foot in front of the other perhaps, but relax Joe I am like the Priest in the 'confessional'… still, are you going to spend the night trying to play the innocent, or have you come here for a beer?"

"At last; I was beginning to think I was just here for your cruel entertainment… Yes, is the IPA on today; I'd best stay off the strong stuff in case some beautiful woman wants to have her wicked way with me later."

"I see Joe… you going to be out with Claire later then?"

She reaches for a glass from the shelf above the bar, like a comely sealion begging for a fish, and stroking his eyeballs as does still the happy youthful memory of one extremely succulent young teacher at his junior school.

Holding the glass beneath the nozzle, as a milkmaid might slide her pale under the cow she starts to pull. Halfway through she changes to holding with the right and pulling with the left: This causes a rewarding upheaval beneath her blouse, and Joe begins to think he is there to referee a wrestling match! Though not he thinks, a match between his conscience and his eyes: that tussle has already hit the canvass.

"There you are Joe, and I'm sure that a few of those won't give you brewers droop… will they sir?"

Her sudden change from 'Joe' to 'sir' evokes in his rather fertile and innocent mind a step from 'the girl from his old school', albeit a fair few years back now, to the 'dutiful serving wench', and the 'influential man of the town'.

He likes the feel of that, realising that it is a role that has so far been absent from his life. After all he muses, the town blacksmith is the lynch-pin of the functionality of the place; so the position therefore should earn him some grace and favour along the way.

"Yes thanks for coming down this end to serve me Marilyn… I'm sorry, I think something was distracting me, you said something that I didn't quite catch a few moments ago, didn't you?"

"No nothing really, I was just being cheeky, and probing your private life for a bit of fun."

"Oh well that doesn't matter, there's nothing in my private life that's… nothing that's, anything really. That doesn't mean it isn't sometimes good, or mostly good I really mean. I suppose I think you might find it rather dull and mundane if you probed too deeply."

"Oh 'tell me about it Joe".

"Tell you what Marilyn, I said it's fairly mundane? I can't think of anything really worth telling."

"No, 'tell me about it is modern lingo and means I'm in the same boat; you know, my own life is good at times but all very much of a much-ness."

"Yes okay I see now Marilyn… I suppose you picked that phrase up from some American's down from the airfield perhaps?"

"Yes I guess it could have been from some of them."

"And that as well!"

"What as well Joe?"

"I guess."

"Oh I see, well yes I gue… that's probably true I suppose. Oops there's Alfie drained his glass again, back in a second."

With two linguistic triumphs in as many phrases, Joe begins to feel that he's really starting to get to grips with how to master women.
He thinks: Not only is he an influential man about town, but potentially a womanising stud as well.
His ego begins to growl towards a nice piece of fillet steak that his leash is yet not long enough to reach.
Joe decides to enjoy this new departure by dint of the Buddhist mantra, 'Be still and know'.
Well he is still, and he's desperately keen to convince himself that he does 'know'; but sod this for a game of soldiers, he doesn't really want either to be knowing or still.
Joe would see himself if it were down to him on top of the naked Marilyn, struggling to contain a burgeoning bosom in each rough but skilful hand, and thrusting into her deep softness as if his life depended on it. Obviously she would be imploring him not to stop: Well what woman wouldn't he thinks naively.

From his mid teens Joe's had these sort of thoughts: Like that if he was given even half a chance to prove himself, his reputation as a stud would soon be round the town.

Strangely it has never occurred to Joe that all the other boys have similar self-belief, and similar equipment; certainly Joe would never countenance the thought that he could just be mister average.

"I suppose we've both seen a fair mix of times since we left school. I reckon that does put us sort of in the same boat."

Who spoke then can you say, for doubtless both were raking through the ashes of their time. We only heard the phrase as it was drifting out; not as it left whichever lips they were.

"You reckon Joe... I'd say its not been all that bad."

So it was Joe then; and I imagine the reiteration of the 'same boat' bit is to put the thought across that there's... not quite a bond between them, but certainly a tangible link.

"I wasn't really meaning bad *(though we know he would have angled it whichever way he thought would please her best)*, just all the different times that we've seen come and go round here."

What is he trying to say, he's talking crap: of course a town sees different times in twenty odd years, but it doesn't mean there is anything to bind you to anyone else, simply because they might have seen the same... but come on, Joe's a simple country chap; he hasn't even seen much of the sort of sophistication you might absorb in the bright lights of Launceston!

He cut his teeth on the banks of the river Camel, snaffling trout with stones and nets, and building dams to herd them through. It was a joyous and simple process. Here was your desire to catch a trout, and down there was a nice fat brown trout; what was needed to bring the two together was a process of basic cunning that was terminated by sudden frantic snatching and grabbing.

So need getting a girl be all that different to snaffling trout. True it could have a little more in common with tickling trout than swiping them as they try to shoot the gap in the dam.

Getting a half-decent girl can still require being prepared to snatch and jostle rather. If you don't, you just get left with one or two old pot-broilers: The un-sung lass who is still working in the Post Office when she reaches fifty. She will probably still be a virgin unless she years ago saw her fate coming, and in a fat-girlish way let it be locally known she was sort of available for the young lads to cut their teeth on.

Thinking back to their youth, Joe's thoughts arrive at a group of older than school age lads who seemed such a part of the town scene.

"Can you remember when we were kids just how many injured blokes… scarcely more than boys I suppose they were, but hanging round the town with legs or arms missing, or even in some cases one of each."

"Yes I do remember all that Joe. I can picture around a dozen, though all living in different streets of course.

"Yes then wasn't it about every week that they all met up in the park on those seats near the toilets if the sun was out; or the housebound ones who couldn't walk were wheeled to the park to meet up with their old comrades."
Joe can hear his dad's voice now,

"My dad said that they always chewed over who went where in what attack, and where the captain should have led them through if he had half a brain."

"But they must have been so young Joe? Probably only a little over half the age that we are now… where did they go? I haven't seen one since about nineteen twenty-five."

"Oh they're all long dead now Marilyn. My uncle who was out in France as well, said that you can't live long, not with leg stumps anyway, perhaps a bit longer if it's arms."

"So did he say why it made a difference Joe… oh just a mo, there's someone needs a refill."
Marilyn goes off along the bar. 'Go' is hardly really simply what she does; that sounds like to arrive up the other end is the only purpose. She goes, but as she moves there is a wheeze of welcome as

she passes: men brighten like bees that have found a sudden open flower in their path, and they smile as they prepare to inhale her waft of pheromones, and feed on the living dream that like a feast of fruitfulness that Marilyn presents.

Joe watches as she walks away, and whimpers slightly with trembling loins. He referees and scores her neat alternate tuck above each hip, now left, then right, now left, then right.

Her tight skirt ensures you get as many steps as possible as you go from one end to the other, and each step is a delight to all present. Though that excludes the landlady who is perched on a stool and bitterly spitting the blood of competitive resentment into her metaphoric handkerchief.

The old scrote knows that fate has got her by the 'short and curly's' now. Twenty years ago the eyes were all on her; and she wouldn't welcome another woman in the bar; but *time is a thief*; it has robbed her of the eyes of men; and of men who back then could smile genuinely as they complimented both her beauty and her beer.

These days men do not mention even her beer, in case it gets mistaken as for her beauty, which is gone. They nod hello, and then pretend she isn't there.

Ten years ago she decided to try a year without a barmaid: a slightly crippled moorland shepherd with a war-wound from the trenches seemed just the job; he was good and he could throw barrels around in the cellar too.

It would all have worked really well, she had a new haircut and gave away two hours of free beer on the first Friday evening of each month.

Those Fridays were a big success; most of the other thirty odd days each month 'The Darlington' was pretty full: was it the pretty full-breasted barmaid called Marilyn that lured them across.

So there it is: get used to being invisible.

Joe's cap is off and his glass bereft of beer. It is not hard to catch the eye of the barmaid. Although most eyes are at least intermittently tracking her movements as she goes back and forth, if she looks at them they quickly swing away; so any that remain she knows must want her.

It only needs his tilt of glass, his manly wink is thrown in just to let her know she's dealing with a 'smooth operator'

The referee watches her approach, though which will he score most highly, her recession or her approach? In either case it's a dead heat: when her rump recedes your trousers smoke; when she heads your way it is like witnessing a dead heat in a Zeppelin race.

Now she is here to fill his glass.

"Hey Joe, what do you fancy, same again?"

If only she could have said, *Hey Joe, where are you going with that empty glass in your hand*. It might have been close enough to the words one of Jimi's famous songs to have evoked the spirit of Hendrix, and number one fan Marlo would if he were born yet have been happy to think it was all going on down in groovy Camelford.

But neither him nor he is in the world yet: and only one of the two is anything more than a twinkle in his old-man's eye.

So Marilyn's 'Hey Joe, what do you fancy', does not raise a humming in the cosmos, though trousers do smoke a little; the reply comes across almost like an admission that very little is ever going to change:

"Another pint of IPA please Marilyn" *"Oh give me strength, is that really all I can think of to ask for, or find to say to her in response; she must see me as a contestant for Camelford's 'Live Wire' of the year award."*

She is not so short of thoughts.

As she pulls his pint from the adjacent pump she glances diagonally at him with a questioning eye:

"So 'stumps' Joe... you were going to tell me why you can't live long with leg stumps, as against arms."

"Oh Christ yes Marilyn, I forgot about all that... yes Uncle Ben was saying that if you try to get about and do things for yourself, the leg stump wears sore, and you can get septicaemia and blood poisoning etc. Then if you take to your bed to fight the illness, you may get thrombosis or a urinary infection; or if you can't move for a long time your lungs fill with fluid and you die of pneumonia."

"So I was just thinking about when we were at school Joe... can you remember that we were learning about the Great War and the trenches... do you remember Mrs Hassenein the history teacher sometimes read lines from that poem by some poet or other, about the young lad who had joined up then lost most of all his limbs: Can you remember any of that Joe?"

"Well yes… though only now as we speak; I hadn't thought of Mrs Hassenein… well, since we left school."

"Anyway Joe, there was a line that always stuck in my mind: *'Now he will spend a few sick years in institutes'*.
"I was sure it was saying that after spending a few years being sorted out in institutes, he would be able to have a sort of proper life again.
"Only today and the stuff you have been saying, has it now struck me, that most likely the 'few sick years' means that those were probably all he was going to have left!"

Joe isn't sure quite what to say. Marilyn looks quite down in the mouth about the thought.
He wonders should he confirm her depressing realisation, or should he try to extrapolate another outcome from the words.
He remembers their schooldays: his eyes stare into his memory, and he sits once more in the little echo'y classroom. It has a green lockable book cupboard beside the door, and yes, Joe can now remember their history teacher.
Summer's breeze of flies and pollen slides in below sash windows all along one wall.
Mrs Hassenein said she loved to let as much of the world outside come in to do the teaching for her.
Joe can hear a distant cuckoo, and remembers how sudden gulfs of warm air would take off from the flat rough playground with the scent of pressed cinders and the juice of new mown grass beyond the fence.
He enjoys a few long swigs of beer while she goes away again to do her job. It suddenly occurs to him from where Marilyn's haunted questions are probably rising.
Though her blonde hair these days has the look of being helped a little by bottle now, he can remember seeing it shining ash blonde in class, with eager upward tilt of her little face one day; she was keenly holding up her hand to answer a question. 'Miss' had been asking round if anyone had got family who went to fight in France.

Marilyn had been called on to respond to the class's question, and was insisting that her big brother was still out there; she said her mum would say nothing about it except that John was lost in France, and no trace of him was ever found. Young Marilyn says she thinks perhaps he met a girl, or got a job out there.

She tells Mrs Hassenein that when she leaves school and can save enough money, she will go across to France, and find out for herself where he lives.

Everyone looks down at their awkward fingers worming distractedly into desk cavities.

The cuckoo calls again from across the fields on the edge of town.

The tall poplar tree beside the playground lifts in the breath of a warm waft, and whirls its aspen fingers.

Everyone is quiet in the classroom.

No ink-well covers slide or click, nor is there nervous scrape of chair.

Again a waft of scented breeze arrives to bless them.

Mrs Hassenein has not spoken for several minutes; her mouse-brown hair is fluffed around her young face and her head has downward tilt.

By the returning wash of scented air, her hair lifts a moment from her face.

Remembering, Joe forgets what face she wore; but can see both eyes are fogged by brimming tears.

Having never in their long youth remembered that day, or found other reason to speak of John, what should Joe now do?

It seemed logical to Joe that in later years Marilyn would have realised that 'Lost in France' meant John was dead; though the process of realisation may not have been so logical for Marilyn.

Though 'what should Joe now do' cuts two ways: Joe feels that he now faces a dichotomy.

When he arrived here tonight it was with the mad yet invigorating thought that if time and the tide washed him toward some sexual union with Marilyn he was going to go with the flow.

Joe is thinking now that if he pursues a line that is angled to help his old classmate clear her thoughts, or to reveal and understand her feelings about her lost brother, it will just set a sombre tone that may dampen any likelihood of his getting to grips with her tonight.

If there is even the smallest chance of grappling with those jugs in the immediate future, nothing but nothing must be allowed to get in the way.

Joe decides to stiffen his resolve and say nothing more about the war, or John… or anything.

His glass of beer is way beyond the point where it can really still be called a glass of beer.

Marilyn like a dutiful angel sees the proportion of transparency; she comes along the bar but does not speak on arrival.

When you stand in front of someone like Joe, the epitome of probably any mans waking dream, and the accomplice of many a sleepy moan, there are certain likely outcomes.

When you stand head slightly to one side and quietly smiling without your lips slightly ajar, a chap like Joe will not stay easily remote.

He will be secretly aroused as he looks at you.

He will not find it easy to not focus on how if it all comes right he will coax all those buttons to reverse back through their slots. Then how sweetly he will kiss those sexily parted lips while he slides his spare arm through and round to de-catch and reveal the main course.

What sweet release and climbing warmth, and what delights will be unleashed: We would see one happy Joe.

So he is resolved not to say anything about the Great War, or John or anything that might come between him and such a well deserved feast.

Marilyn has hold of Joe's glass, but still she is not using words. She shakes her head minutely left and right as though playing out mild exasperation, though not that damps her sexy wayward smile.

She moves as if to take his glass from him. Remembering, Joe forgets the war and does not release, doing instead as he thought he might if chance arose.

"Oh don't if you don't want one Joe, I'll not wrestle you for it!"
Joe had hoped she might make reference to his strong grip. It would have been handy if she had come out with something like:

'Of blimey Joe, it's as if your glass is held in a vice... remind me not to get on the wrong side of you just before we all head home. There again Joe, if you were walking me home I would have no need to feel scared would I.'

And Joe might throw calmly back;

'I promise you love that you wouldn't have to be scared of me; and if there was anyone else who wanted to give you trouble they would have to get past me first.'

He likes the sound of *'get past me first'*; he sees it as a universally safe statement. It has the romance of stating that you will if the need arises lay down your life for the lady. In reality, unless you were blessed with the lack of shame to be able to run away and leave her to her fate; then it's only what you would have to do anyway.

It's one of the lines that his randy uncle Ben told him always to throw in for good measure: It sounds good, and costs nothing.

Joe must for now content himself in engaging her with the instructions for his next drink.

"Yes Marilyn, except this time can I have a Brandy as well... and have whatever you fancy yourself...*'please god, make her say something*

like, I fancy a night out in Bodmin with you some time Joe... it needn't just be a half for you girl."

"Whatever I fancy? That would have to be getting sent home early for a mug of cocoa with my feet up in front of my fire. *'And perhaps to take a blacksmith back as well and put his big strong hands to work'*. Oh a pint of cider would be really kind Joe."

"Why are you calling me kind Marilyn, I said nothing about paying for it; just to help yourself to a drink of some sort... Anyway, 'whatever you fancy' may not even be a drink, unless you count your mug of cocoa I suppose. *Oh bugger; why couldn't she have said something along the lines of, 'what do I fancy Joe, well that would be telling wouldn't it now, I'm sure there must be some use for those strong rough hands of yours'. Yes, why couldn't she have come out with something like that!"*

A sudden grinding rumble overhead the town sees faces lift like believers receiving communion. A not uncommon sound round here, yet one that still jerks the attention back to acknowledge that we are in a war that half the time you have no inkling of.

Vmmvmm,mmm,mmm,mm it goes away. It could be a new Liberator recently delivered from the States; and bound for some squadron at an airfield on 'The Wash'.

Or Coastal Command, sliding out to hunt for subs and incoming FW190's; the pilots fed and fortified by nothing but copious portions of raw carrots, to help them see in the dark; well that's what our phoney radio broadcasts are kidding 'Fritz'.

Either way it is a sound we get to know in 1942. Down here it seems a million miles from where it is all really going on; but even tucked away in Cornwall it somehow fills your life: as does the occasional rumble of big military lorries through the town, then gunning their motors out across the river bridge and up the hill to the airfield.

You cannot even start to imagine the kind of things these passing trucks have all turned out to do; always something seems to drag them through the town.

Joe sups his ale, and squints a laconic eye outside through the gathering gloom towards the hardware store across the road. In his thought he threads the question through as he ponders rather huffily:

"I fix people's garden forks with my furnace when they snap a prong. I put shoes back on the hooves of wealthy lady's horses who come waltzing in. Why am I just a 'hanger-on' and an 'also-ran' when it comes to having any command of the most desirable women, or any say-so in the going's-on of this town?"

His thoughts are drifting who knows where. Certainly in the ensuing moments they have moved on again from why he doesn't get the credit and kudos that he thinks his standing in the town should yield.

With his thoughts drawn windward to the blowy cliffs, where fulmars plunge to sail the rocky fall across; and common-gulls cry plaintive like the deep and distant souls of the drowned, his distracted eye sees unusual movement.

The movement is that of a stepladder carried in, now with legs bared provocatively wide and stood broadside to a wall that climbs the fireplace above.

Joe's attention is drawn back to his beer, then irrevocably on to the succulent ebb and flow of Marilyn along the bar.

When he looks towards the end wall and the stepladder once more, there is a figure putting a screw into the oak boarding at middle height.

He thinks perhaps that 'madam' has purchased a particularly splendid china plate that she wants to impress everyone with.

There is not very long to wait, though time ticks languidly and imprecise. And all who haunt the curl of Woodbine smoke assume much the same; that it be a hook for some new gaudy bric-a-brac.

'Screw putting man' re-enters stage left. This time he carries a medium sized cardboard box, but rather in the way that an Inca priest might have carried his eagerly torn and still pulsating heart from its cruelly opened donor breast to his grateful Altar, and muttering incantations beneath his breath.

Our man only renders one incantation, when blinkered by the carried box he drives his thigh onto the corner of a table.

His box begins to attract attention; others in the bar have seen that it is not a recycled soap or tinned bean box from the village store, but virgin crisp and stapled fast; announcing it has something new inside.

Now one or two have even ambled round the bar to wait like punters at the finish line, and though no hooves thunder you might think you hear a roll of drums as all wait pensive for the final show.

Sideways mutters of what it might be are proffered here and there, but the many who watch it seems are all agreed to let it wait to the great unveiling.

Seeing he's got an audience our man plays to the crowd, and even climbs with the holy grail still within, and the box just one end open.

Reaching in he holds the holy grail and lets the box fall clear away. Unluckily it takes a china vase off the fireplace mantelpiece and reduces it to kit form on the tiles of the hearth and there's a cheer, or is it for the brand new clock that he's left holding to the wall?

And a fine clock it is indeed. A small station clock is what it looks like, though big for a pub, with face at least a foot across. The imperial and forlorn roman numerals track round inside a ring of brass, and the white face staring through a dark tyre of wood.

"That's just so you lot know when it's time to go home!"
Announces Marilyn. Then ducks her head and scuttles as best an hourglass might scuttle off along the bar.
Our man is key in hand and winding, will at last it be a flop… but tick tock, tick tock. The tick sounds like a chef's splicer tapping the pan to get a piece of mushroom off; and the tock more like the noise when a piano tuner donks the point of his tuning fork on the wooden piano lid to get the pitch.

A call goes out for anyone who put their time-piece to Big Ben that morning.

"Are you sure someone tall can reach just standing on a chair so we can wind it each week without needing a ladder?"
The landlady calls from her stool beyond the bar.

Now our man is safely down so Joe moves forward. What he is going to see is just a rather nice clock. What he is going to think about what he will see is little more than he is thinking now. What he will do as he looks at it is… just look at it really: But step forward and look at it he must; after all it wasn't there before.
It will still be there when he's long gone! But how's he to know that?
Craning up it seems his effort was not wasted. There's a group of words and figures printed on the face to be read.
He mutters it like the incantation of the Inca priest:

"Smiths English Clocks Ltd…London…1942
"… ah bugger me, it's absolutely brand spanking new. It may even be the newest clock in the world!"

Someone at madam's request has brought a chair to check its windability. He's not the tallest chap in the pub nor the shortest either. The point is that he cannot quite reach.
The landlady is rapidly on the case:

"Then that's no use really. I must be sure that the average person can get up and wind it from a chair."

So out the step ladder comes again. From a chair it would be too low to fix another screw in the wall, because though the key winding gear which will need to be reached is at the bottom, it hangs from a lug at the top of the clock: Hence the ladder.

The 'clock man' looks a little as if he was eager to get done and off to somewhere.

Joe sees this and says:

"Hey, don't worry mate she's a fussy old bird with lots of things *'except with her men!'* he hisses under his breath *'she's pretty desperate these days'*. I'll get up there with the clock and a pencil, and you tell me how far down to bring it."

The man knows he could do all of this himself, but appreciates the input of a local; it makes her less likely to say it's wrong a second time.

This time it ends up on the plaster, so they need to put a plug in the wall to screw into.

Ten minutes sees it all secure, and Joe tells Marilyn to go and tell madam that Joe the farrier says it's perfect now, and so she does.

The clock man throws his tools into a box with final relish. Then winks at Joe and thanks him for the bit of help he gave.

Joe flips his hand dismissively to the side and throws across,

"I presume you have time for a pint my friend, I was just about to refill my own."

"Thanks, but I should be getting that really, you could have stood and just watched."

"And where would have been the fun in that? No I much prefer to muck in with the troops than just sit in the stands. So will it be a pint of mild or bitter?"

"Well if you twist my arm I'll have a pint of mild thank you guv."

The clock man is a year or so older than Joe, so the idea that Joe could be the guv figure, seems the wrong way round. Perhaps, thinks the ever aspiring Joe,

"maybe my rightful standing in this town is more apparent than I thought… but where's that Marilyn when I need her."

Soon enough he has two beers and brings one to clock-man.

"Ah thanks that's really kind of you er…"

"it's Joe my friend."

"Right thanks then Joe; and I'm Simon, or mostly Si if you'd prefer. And to save you the trouble of trying to remember all the old nursery rhyme, no I haven't seen the pie-man lately, and I'm not simple!"

"The verse hadn't even crossed my mind Si *(he lies politely)*, but it sounds like you feel you get ribbed about it too often Si?"

"No, it's no big deal, there's a lot worse things can be thrown at you than a few harmless words I reckon."

The two chat on, and beer slides smoothly down. And all around the tones of voices lift then slip, or verbally shuffle round to voice their thought some other way.

A barmaid simply does her job, and absorbs the eyes of many who are here tonight. One down this end who hasn't breasted her visual onslaught before, leans toward his new found comrade and intones with care:

"Holy saints above Joe, just how many hand-full's of what I could do with is that barmaid carrying up and down behind the bar?"

Then as if suddenly brought up short adds

"Oh shit, I haven't said something have I Joe: I saw you seemed to know her pretty well when we had hung the clock. She's not your woman is she?"

"God if only Si… I don't think any of us here have ever seen bones hung with such a sweet abundance of loin tingling flesh: *And certainly never known!* Actually Si, Marilyn and myself were at school together, and in the same class too. I suppose I've known her for upwards of twenty-five years all told."

"So assuming you've got one, is your woman one of these in here this evening… mind you that's a silly question really, there's scarcely another woman in the place, unless you count the landlady!"

"We don't count the land lady Si: The only woman she makes grudgingly welcome in the place is our barmaid; and only because she brings the boys in!
"But yes I have got a woman, she's called Claire; she lives with her mum further up but a few roads off the high-street. Mind you Si, if you ever meet them, I wasn't here this late tonight alright".

"But this isn't late Joe!"

"Well I usually go round there on my way home each evening for a sort of early tea, then I knock up a bit of grub not long before I go to bed at nine."

"Bed at nine Joe! And I was just thinking if I should see whether you fancied a trip up with me to the airfield… oh yes and I will be driving back down this way afterwards.
"I've got a kitchen clock that I'm taking back for the cookhouse wall, and there are some really nice girls who work up there. There are two Americans, or at least one might be Canadian or something, and a
couple of girls who have come down from Bude and St. Austell to work. And they'll all start sorting supper within the next hour so we may even scrounge a bit of grub.

"Mind you I'm forgetting Joe, I mean about your woman."

"What's that then Si…? Oh I see, you mean I might not want to come because of seeing Claire, or her not wanting me to be out and about. She will be comfortable by the fire with her mum by now, and they think I'm going to a late job out on a farm across the moor this evening, so therefore as I've engineered a night off I might as well use it Si… actually, I can't think for certain what I did tell Claire's mum I was going to be doing, I should have made a note."

"Then when we've supped these beers we'll head on up the way Joe shall we?"

It's hardly even mid evening, but Joe feels such a bounder to be making plans to head further away from home when he would usually soon be making moves towards his bed.

It's all rather exciting truth be told: At last he feels alive, like a man with jurisdiction over his life. He may see no one, and do nothing tonight, but the feeling he is going off to something uncertain yet with possibilities feels fascinating when compared to his normal evening. Joe drinks deeply from this well of prospect.

As they sloosh down the last dregs of their beer, Si smiles at the arrival of another evening doing things he loves to be doing, and this time with a new found friend for company.

Joe on the other hand feels more like he is Guy Fawkes swallowing his final gulp of ale to stiffen his resolve before he sets off to light the fuse that will blow up parliament.

The unlit streets return a hollow slap slap slap sl sl slap as their clattered feet go in and out of sink; the echoes die, and all noise is very close where they turn into a side street to find Simon's Van.

Joe is in a state of nervous rapture at this deadly cunning task that they perform. He wants to slink, then dart from door to door, or to run ahead and press himself against a wall and call Si quickly on.

"There's my van beside that lorry over there Joe."

They've made it against all the odds and without even having to fire a shot; and most importantly without being detected or observed.

"I think that door is unlocked Joe, hop in while I stick my tools in the back."

"Thanks Si… there's nothing delicate like a clock or something that I can trample on the floor is there; it's so dark with them not allowed to use the street lights."

"Something on the floor! no chance Joe, it's absolutely rotten as a pear and paper thin, I wouldn't dare put anything valuable down there!"
Then he laughs to show that at least half of that was all in jest. But Joe plays along to keep it going:

"But you would have me ride in there, and I was just starting to think you were all right Si."

"No you should be safe enough, but I would put most of your weight round the edges; and don't sit down too heavy in that seat either!"

The motor hacks and lumbers into life, though joy of rebirth seems absent from its voice… that it intones its presence and preparedness to move is all that is asked.
Creeping from this side-street Joe feels as vulnerable as Arch Duke Ferdinand driving through Sarajevo and awaiting the assassins bullet just a few years back, and thinks this escapade might just as easily trigger yet another world war.
When they begin to leave the town behind Joe senses less that there are gun barrels trained on him from every dingy back alley, or Gestapo informers scribbling notes to take to Mrs Fig.
He feels himself relax as hedges open onto fields; breathes out tense watchfulness where at last these fields breed bog grass and granite chunks along their lifted edge.

Summer night swaps darkness for a sort of dingy glow as town recedes. And once your pupils re-expose themselves it's really not so dark.
As the headlights only shine downwards through a sort of louvered grill they do not spoil your night vision; and off to each side you soon see moorland ponies that doze like lifeless statues in the dark.

The 'gloworm' headlights speak of little that is coming; potholes bring a sudden stunning thwack that makes the van hop sideways across the road to span the centre lines, or lunge at bank.
It is then with a gunning roar the tyres shout they've crossed the cattle grid onto the open moor and so to the airfield.
Si brings them up the slope across a taxiway that intersects the road. The taxiway sails greyly away into either distance bathed in moonlight like a dim lit river. It only falls dark where the huge grim birds have held on brakes to warm their engines, dropping oil and leaving tyre rubber as they swing to head away.
Up to a junction the van swerves to the left and Si's head starts to oscillate both ways. It's a runway they are reaching, but as all seems clear they sail across.

"Do you often have to stop there Si?"

"I don't that often come up here Joe; but of the half a dozen or so times I reckon I've stopped perhaps… twice?"

"I suppose you see them pretty well even at night with their lights and stuff."

Yes… in fact I'd say it is easiest at night; even ten miles out you see their landing lights."
They swing round past some big old sheds. One has got its huge doors open and an airforce fire-engine waits inside.
Even if all doors were closed, that they are vehicle sheds is easy to discern, their massive hinges high above the floor.
An airfield mechanic steps quickly away from the huge fuel tank with a length of hosepipe in one hand and a two gallon tin in the other. Peering out into the dark he cannot make out if it's friend or foe, so the shadows to a rear door seem the way to go: But he thinks he got

enough to take him to Launceston to see Angela and back at the very least.

Si parks where he has not been in the way before, just beyond all the big vehicle doors, but before the main track to the living quarters.

"We'll leave it here Joe and go and see what's what."

As they both get out Si leans across the van's roof to Joe and snuffs the air:

"Hey Joe, can you smell that?"
Joe wonders if it's some risqué reference to the presence of women in the offing, but still uncertain he returns a 'not really' sort of thing.

"Don't you think that's stew and dumplings on the air tonight mate. I reckon that we've got our timing on the nose."

"But we can't walk in with me unknown to the cooks and so on, and expect them to serve up a dinner can we Si?"

"Christ no of course not Joe. But once I get the ladder out to hang the clock, then find oh blast, the old wall screw is coming out; lucky I brought my mate to pass me tools and hold the ladder still while I climb up and drill to put a plug in the wall. Yes once we've puffed and cursed around a bit, and say the boss said we'd be home for grub by nine at the latest…!"

"You cunning weasel Si; I wouldn't have the nerve to try that."

"So it's lucky that I have mate or we'd both go hungry tonight wouldn't we? Anyway Joe, we won't just be walking in demanding food as they're serving up; I can keep an eye on proceedings from up the ladder. When I see they are about to clear things up we make our move on whatever's left!"

All this ducking and diving on Si's part makes Joe feel like some yokel with tufts of straw sticking out of his ears, when he wants to be seen as some slick operator himself; perhaps one that women throw admiring sideways glances towards as he flicks back the collar of his Burberry raincoat *(which he doesn't posses).*

But he doesn't really feel up to all this scull-duggery, and a bit of him yearns for the safety of Marilyn and 'The Masons Arms', though not quite for the arms of Miss and Mrs Fig.

Conversely though, another bit of him rumbles from a day in the forge and nothing since his cheese sarny at twelve except a few beers early evening. Beers early evening sink down a treat and fill you up; but the effect doesn't last: Soon enough you need to fill your gut with something solid.

So they walk past huts with hard cold sides, and their feet echo back and go flap flap fl, fl, flap; in and out, and out in out of sinc: Though not for long and they reach a hut with chimneys tall and steam belched also.

"Here's where the clock has got to go Joe: Go Joe, hey I like that, I'm more of a poet than I thought!"

Joe feels even more straw eared in being slow to pick up on the fact that 'go' and 'Joe' are being presented as a rhyme. A perfect rhyme in Si's opinion, except that that is about as far as this burst of creativity goes. Joe still feels as dim as one of the dumplings that they hope are stewing in the cauldron.

A blast of light as door throws wide: Two blokes in pilot's uniforms come out, and laughing how they thought they should take another run along the coast to try and get a better look at this reported submarine. It transpires that the coastguard then called to see if they had seen a capsized fishing boat that night, or anything not in the normal run of things.

Their laughs tail off in darkness as they tramp away to who knows where. Much might follow what they saw, but they are for early beds it seems.

"Now you carry our stuff and go and show your face in there first Joe."

They are entering the side door into a kitchen area where a cook and two of her girls who clear and help are hard at work.

Sudden steam whooshes from a pressure cooker full of spud, and a pan down the end demands immediate removal from heat or there'll be trouble.

They sight Joe with assorted friendly smiles and he grins back for all he's worth like a Chinaman at someone else's tea ceremony.

"Hello my love, what have you got for us today?"
Then behind him they spot Si and they know what's arrived.

"Ah, at last thank Christ. We've been burning the bread, and singeing the meat; and what's worse, working way past our time for the last week."

"Yes alright ladies, but the workshop only got it out to me this morning, and I had one to pick up in Padstow, then a new clock to hang in The Masons Arms in Camelford. This was the earliest I could get back up here wasn't it; and I bet there's one of you who has a watch to time things with!"

"And I bet the job in The Masons took the longest to get right didn't it? And funny it saw you back up here at feeding time Si!"
Cook is certainly no fool. Joe's tongue fair tingles with the aroma of the thick Irish stew, and his ears twitch like a fox in a chicken run who smells his meal but finds the door to the hen-house is shut; he thinks too, that Cook will take a lot of chivvying up if she's to spill some beans and bread in their direction.

Si left a ladder lying out the back when he took the clock away to be fixed. He gives Joe a wink and a nudge towards the rear door, and says that if they take an end each there is less chance of wiping out a stack of plates or something.
As they re enter the scent of stew assaults Joe's nose a second time, and increasingly he is possessed with the conviction that there is nothing more vital in this life than to get his hands on and mouth around some of that stew and dumplings.
Then a girl who had been sorting stuff for the next day, out in the storehouse when they both arrived comes back.
All Joe sees, because he is making sure he knocks nothing over with his end of the ladder, is Si change posture.

Si straightens up to achieve his full height as he takes a big breath and braces his shoulders to try and look broad-shouldered.

As they get to where the clock has got to go back on the wall Si tells Joe to let go so he can put the ladder in place himself.

Joe wants to know what suddenly made Si puff himself up just then; and turning back to look thinks it will not be that he was fronting up to some cocky corporal.

And scanning as he turns there's nothing but the kitchen bench and cupboards, rack of plates and garbage bin. Then a movement pulls his eye towards the gap between the bench and stack of boxes.

A female rump bent rummaging through a bushel of potatoes smiles; then its mistress stands and turns with an armful gripped and tangled with her pleasant frontage.

"Oh look at this lot Susan… and there's one or two others are only just going to be ok."

Her pleasantly rounded 'R's' *(in her accent!)* tell Joe she's from America; Her ebony curls and heart shaped face make it obvious he is dealing with an angel here.

As she sees they have a newcomer in the camp she smiles, and rather apologetically lifts her armful of potatoes and 'things' up and down as if forming some explanation in her thought that cannot yet find words.

Joe wants to be a potato.

He wants to be gathered in those sort of arms, and smiled at by those sort of eyes. If only he could be one of those potatoes for the rest of his happy life: for such he is convinced it would be!

"Hello"
She drawls,

"Would you like a potato?"

"I'd rather change places with one of them"
he intones silently, but responds with:

"I could eat the parson's horse if it was tethered to a gate!"
And is rewarded with a chuckle and a toss of what Joe might think were her night bathed jungle jasmine curls.

He wonders whether to attempt a film-star drawl like he hears in the movies himself, to make her feel at home. By some miracle he chickens out, and only states:

"I don't want to try and look terribly clever; but you my love are undoubtedly from America, I'd hazard a guess at Texas?"

He is probably thinking of Cowboys and Indians. And he harbours a strange belief that anyone at all American sounding will as like as not have some connection with Texas.

"Then you don't need to worry about looking terribly clever, I'm from Canada!"

"Oh fu…!"

He nearly curses internally; the outward response is more genteel, but still makes a rather extravagant attempt to look like he was generally on the right track, rather than just stabbing in the dark.

"Well I knew it was somewhere over there, trust me to pick the wrong bit."

"But my 'bit' is about as far from Texas as you are from Russia."
But that's a completely different country!"
All part of Europe though; and anyway, so are we a different country!"

"Well yes, to some extent perhaps."

Joe had never thought of Russia as being anywhere even remotely close to Britain; whereas America and Canada he thought were the same place really.

Yes, in his mind Russia was a million miles away and it had revolutions where it killed its monarchs. Not that they were really proper Kings and stuff: Without a doubt he thinks that if you killed an English King or Queen the whole world would be in uproar until you were caught and grilled on a spit! Even tribes in the darkest deepest jungle would somehow know and join the hunt.

Russian monarchs on the other hand were little more than names in books, and even in Russia people probably wouldn't notice that much if one disappeared.

The young Canadian could see from Joe's rather localised sense of world geography that his horizons have perhaps not spread much beyond the Tamar: the river that separates Cornwall from Devon. She can see also that his smile is warm, his young eyes bright, and his shoulders broad.

Anyway, she was told to expect that lots of the locals might seem a bit like the Cajuns in the Mississippi swamplands.

The USA is still a land she hasn't seen either, but all her family's examples of people who are thieves, or thick, or fat, or anything except handsome or intelligent, all can be found typified in some particular state in America.

She muses:

"I shall peel these few in case 'Cook' decides that we should get some in the pan to use as fried potatoes for breakfast… blast it, I've dropped the biggest one in the bowl and caused a tidal wave that's drenched my apron… oh never mind.

"Hmm hmm hm hm over, the white cliffs of Dover, daa daa daa da da..! I wish I could get all these crummy English songs out of my head; it's those mechanics' fault, whenever I pass the hangars they sing out at me like serenading Venetians.

"After weeks of all that the tunes get into your head. I hope that the next planes to be delivered from the states will be loaded with some decent gramophone records!"

She gets on and is well engrossed in her task of spud bashing.

The other girls are happy to be cleaning and clearing, and the open mess-room is a clatter of cutlery fencing its way through the wave of chat and laughter.

One table is dominated by the confident displays of pilots who know their lives are always on the line so therefore might as well blow their own trumpet while they still can.

Another table is mostly of mechanics. They would like to enjoy the kudos of being in flight-crew, for it often brings easy access to the more beautiful girls; or more specifically: access to easy girls, and occasional access to beautiful girls.

They are however quite happy not to be up there when the FW190's come ripping through the clouds emitting eager streams of lead. True enough one will now and then lob its relatively meagre bomb like a somewhat unloved baby at a parked Liberator as it arrives. But before it has another run to squirt its hail of venom around, the mechanics are all well out and into the relative safety of the blast shelters.

So mechanics are quite happy with their lot it seems.

Another table is completely southern Irishmen. They are weathered and tough, and the skin on the palms of their hands is like the skin on the soles of an African bushman's feet… or the hands of a blacksmith!

Their job here is to dig holes and to fill holes. They dig one if a new drain is needed, or for a cable to be laid. They fill holes if an FW190 has had a particularly lucky hit when Hans lobbed his bomb; or conversely if one of our boys has a particularly bad landing.

But none of the other tables have such a distinct grouping or function; they include laundry girls, radio operators, fuel tanker drivers, and an incongruous mixture of one or two rather nervous, and others surprisingly phlegmatic characters from the ammunition and bomb store.

The lass who had a clutch of big King Edward potatoes jockeying for position with her breasts, is still scraping and musing, and snatching an occasional glance at the progress of the ladder'd pair; not ladder'd pair of stockings, but our boys with the clock.

Si is up there, and loudly stage moaning that the original screw is crumbling out of the wall: This means they will need to work on late to drill and plug it.

He lets it be known that he doubts they'll be away till after ten!

She has noted that the sturdy lad holding the ladder is often just looking away as she glances up from her labours!

She does not feel, yet it is so, that her primeval eye is making connections unbeknownst.

"I am not certain why this comes to me now: A lake and pine trees on what could be Vancouver Island; and up above the shore a little cabin on the grassy slope.

"It might I suppose be a sort of home for me… and him perhaps; I can feel tones of a beginning… it's not just tones I feel, it's tingles; tingles inside and deep ones as well. These are the sort of things that I would usually only get when I think about Darren and our eventual marriage when he and I get home again.

"There really should be none of this, I mean these sort of thoughts; not with Darren fighting somewhere with all the boys from our home town.

"He needs to know that his girl is waiting for him. It would destroy him if he believed his girl might seek comfort in even just thinking about another.

"So if he needs to believe, then I must certainly do nothing that might stop him believing!"

Throwing her final spud across the bowl into the pan she rinses off the peeler and her slicing knife.

It's the sort of time when one or other of the girls makes tea. She tonight will make tea. She somehow feels though does not consciously identify, that she is moved to show her natural feminine tendency to be a vehicle of fertile preparation.

'Spud girl' checks the urn is full and steaming, sniffs the milk to confirm it is nor sour, then calls like an Angel to the shepherds:

"Hey are you guys up for a cup of tea then?"

A brace of heads veer through ninety degrees, with smiles alighting on both faces.

"We thought you'd never ask!"

There's no need to say which one that was: One of them says that sort of thing all the time; the other would probably never say it in a lifetime.

"That's really kind of you, yes thanks."

This one's eyes smile like a hungry happy child seeing the prepared spread for his birthday tea. He grins at his increasingly desired feast, and the fact that Joe's tummy is so empty does much to heighten the effect.

Then he starts to think. Not though to think about what he is there for, or about having a cup of tea made for him by this gracious little woman: His mind has drifted askew. It has slid sideways though not to a perfect parallel, and found its way into a sort of jumping off point.

Undoubtedly it is the girl who has provided this mental springboard, but it is not completely her image that has made the leap with him.

Joe floats in some form of semi trance. There are in his drifting mind, *'queer blots of colour, purple, scarlet, green'*, and his inner ear seems filled with song and sound from somewhere that his mind has not the sight to see. But it's the warmth that keeps him standing where he is. The heat is much like when he returns to his furnace from fitting a wheel to someone's cart in his yard on a winter's morning.

There are dissimilarities: Joe feels this particular heat grow in the pit of his stomach, though true indeed his eyes feel bathed by warmth as well. But his attention has slid sideways to wind its way through modes of other being; as if his rather leather booted spirit is desperately trying to find the right sort of connection that it should make with this angelic little female.

Joe watches as she busies herself at the tea urn. She shuffles cups as deftly and instinctively as someone who had previously been a juggler in a circus.

Joe visualises elegant young Indian girls walking to fetch their mother's water pot-headed, as with poise and balance this small Canadian alternates between the urn and crockery.

Like a church bell tilting to clang its call and summon the flock, Joe watches her pelvis go over-centre and lock one way, as under her discreet white pinafore she braces herself to lift the heavy metal gallon teapot.

Joe tingles as his eye is barged by the sudden bulge of buttock to the north; and marvels how rewardingly a woman's body swells around inside her clothes. He sees this all as somebody else's thing that he is sneaking a look at. Perhaps like he is watching a private boxing match.

Still it appears in his mind's eye to be somebody else's very pleasant thing that he surveys. And the match would fight on, or the film proceed, had she not suddenly rounded on him with two cups of tea and,

"You can take that one to your boss if you like"
and Joe or the incarnation of his pride come straight back with:

"He's not my boss… well anyway, this evening I'm just helping him to sort things and get finished."

"Oh I assumed you worked for Si; where are you from then… er?"

"Oh me, I have the Smithy in Camelford? I don't know what that would be called in Canadian!"

"In Canada that would mean you were probably a blacksmith!" Spud-Girl says with a cheeky smirk; then lifts her face and adds;

"I suppose in the most un-Anglicized parts of the Quebec sector of Canada you would have a different name."

"Why, are they all Eskimos who live in that part of Canada?"

"They're French!"

"What are you talking about: why have you suddenly got lots of French people in Canada; they can't all have come there because of the war surely!"

"It's not like that at all… there's a huge bit of Canada that is French, where they all speak French; they're called French Canadians. I also live in Quebec, but where there are a lot of English speaking people too.
 " Look all this would be a lot easier if I knew your name!"

"Yes I can cope with introductions more easily than I can get my head round the idea of some of Canada being French… it's Joe, and I'm really pleased to have met you, and feel that I am learning a lot tonight… about Canada!"
 He feels pleased that she wants to know who he is; for Joe it is such a big thing that a woman has asked for his name that even with nothing else happening he should go home happy (*'last night I met this girl, and she even asked me my name!'*).
 Some sort of nudge from the gods puts him back on track.

"I suppose you will be a Mary-Sue or something?"

"Ha ha Joe… no I reckon that even you will be able to get your head round this one: I'm Anne… nothing more, nothing less."

"That's really nice… yes I reckon I will be able to cope with that; I'll certainly have no excuse for forgetting it: It's my gran's name… *'And I would also say you appear to have pretty much everything that any man could ask for in his life, and his house, and his bed!'*… What brings you so far from home Anne?"

She smiles her girlish cheeky smile again, then says:

"I suppose down here you don't get reminded of it at every street corner, but you still cannot have overlooked that that there is a war on!"

"Well of course I've noticed there's a war on."

"And Canada is in the war, and so I am over here to play my part in all of that like my…?"

She halts her text to turn off a gas. Anne steers clear of a verbal return, as if she were avoiding a dancing partner who had just revealed possession of an unpleasant bodily odour; or that the 'my' thing, had been superseded by other events in her life that made her past less relevant now.

Anne turns back to her task, and muses as she pours the next few cups of tea.
At the other end of the canteen there is it appears to her a plethora of lives being juxtaposed and traded: Someone with 'this', is comparing it with someone who has 'that'; it doesn't follow to say that there will be any fusion of the two, but the trade of comparison rolls on.
She wishes she had not been made to reveal that she has got a 'my' of any sort. It is rather tiresome not quite being part of social possibility.
It would also be nice to include herself in stories when she is alone at night.
At night when she is not tired enough to fall quickly away, her mind plays games of life, a sort of future happy-families with houses and schools.

It does not work using Darren and herself, because she can only connect their eventual union to their return to Canada, and so to the sort of life and scenery that is likely to emanate from that.

Anne plays out many of these love and family woven tales; a typically recurring scene is where a young mother with many children is organising the girls to collect as many wild species of flower in the river meadow, as well as supervising her boys to net them a few trout for their tea that evening. Then usually the father turns up to smother them all with kisses and they all set off home together.

A good one is where a young Canadian girl, even prettier than herself, though remarkably similar in almost every way joins the 'Royal Army Service Corps' to serve as a nurse. She gets posted to France.

Because Anne knows little that is actually happening out there now, her mental sequence uses France in the first war.

Obviously it is necessary to brave all manner of privations in the field hospital behind the front line. She sticks to her task and is well loved by the men she looks after; at guarded moments she may reward some favourite with a soft kiss on the lips if he is doing well in some way.

The Canadian girl's unsurprising popularity with her patients leads to her being noticed and admired by the doctors. A handsome young army doctor falls in love with her and woos her with flowers and Greek poetry that she assumes to be about love and wine, and cool arbours.

With their combined help the war is won and they return to one of those nice big houses where the river Camel winds its way out of the town. This girl is still slim and young and beautiful in the story when their large sloping lawn is a tangle of children, some dark, some fair, but all of course perfect.

In not using herself in her little self directed films Anne is not unfaithful to Darren. If she played the heroine she might expect to feel the astral hand of her distant future husband tugging at the shoulder of her conscience. But she keeps herself a step away: Albeit a very small step.

Si is down the ladder now; he swaggers over as might one who steps forward to receive a prize; like a nodding boxer with one arm lifted, and relieved to have made it to the end of a long hard fight. Si's winded look is all a feint of course.

Turning with his own mug of tea in one hand, Joe sees him come straight past two other kitchen girls and right up alongside where he himself is positioned ready and eager to exploit any further contact with Anne.

Joe wishes Si was not there. He really likes Si and is enjoying the evening out with him; but it's like he has just found the most wonderful pearl in the ocean, and wants to keep it safe from prying eyes.

Joe so wishes Si wasn't there. Any other solution would be preferable; but if it were absolutely necessary it would be better at this spoiled moment if Si were not even alive.

Si on the other hand seems utterly alive, and eager to exploit the advantages of being so. He fixes Anne with the desiring smile of a lion that has spotted a small gazelle cornered in a thicket, and having not eaten for many a day almost purrs at this presented meal.

All things being equal he might have 'clocked' Joe's aspirations and left the field clear for his comrade.

Si however knows Joe has Claire? A woman who he has not met, but can imagine is quite likely more than everything Joe aspires too in a woman.

Being fair to Simon, this is not the first time he has met Anne so is not really butting in. He chats them all up, and though he reckons Anne is probably the best looker, had only spent less time on her because he knows she has a boy in the Canadian army, and doesn't know how big or how far away he is.

All things taken into account, and with Joe clearly only making polite conversation... he is probably Si assumes, telling Anne where his girlfriend lives in Camelford or goes to work etc... well, all that means that with regard to Anne, it's open season for him.

He does his best, though it doesn't butter many parsnips with the girl, who remains polite and friendly, but a little distracted even though it is certainly his best foot getting shoved forward on the dance-floor... soon enough the end of task and time for home invades his hopes and chances and so they go.

You see a long damp night of moorland tors and turf as at the first cold rays sheep bleat to greet the dawn, and on through dingled valley down to sea the cliffs of waking fulmars and kittiwakes crouch, and gulls glance seaward and spot returning fishing boats still a mile out from the keyside and sorting the un sellable fish to be thrown overboard… as the gulls sail out to meet and feed they cry and cry like the souls of generations of drowned sailors.

Back inland away from the sea the sun asserts itself above the hills and the day feels to be growing warm, though a lifting breeze across the moor will be enough to make you keep your shirt on.

It hardly seems worth the wind's trouble.

Soft white woolly heads of bog-cotton dance so readily sideways in the moorish waft that you think they would move almost as easily without its tilting breath.

Still it does take the trouble… and it tugs and sings across the expansive slope of the moor.

So huge the inverted bowl of the morning sky that our eye sails up into.

How long has it looked down onto this dumb process of peat and rain and sunlight.

You are looking back at five thousand years BC, and forward at five thousand years AD simultaneously; and there's scarcely room to slide a fag-paper between the two if you are looking for differences.

Two buzzards sail out from a ledge just down below the nearest peak; they have no chicks yet, so the pressure to find food is not intense.

In these modern times they can enjoy the luxury of rabbits hopping dimly around the lower slopes; hot and tasty like generous mobile dinners, or 'meals on paws'; and if you sight one in the open and it makes a run for it, to be certain you don't veer off in the wrong direction it employs a furry white homing beacon called its tail that it flashes from its arse.

It was different before the Romans came, they kindly brought the first rabbits and before that a buzzard had to search out moorland mice among the rocks and scrub oak. Mice are not bright, but they're nippy little buggers, and they like nothing more than to fire in under a rock and hear you rap your beak against something good and hard.

The feathered moorland wraiths rise on a bulge of air and light, which flows in as if a hump of the Earth's chemistry had become dislodged somewhere out in the Atlantic, and is pushing in between Cornwall and anything that is not nailed to the surface.

The sailing sentinels of the grey wind ascend in circles of evolutionary syncopation. Rising level with the peak one breaks in mid orbit to slide away along the ridge and only now she really starts to look around and down, and her amber eyes burns so brightly that they almost throw a beam.

In her ascent she certainly had her eyes open yet her attention seemed dormant, or at the very least enthralled by the benign horizon.

Cruising east she heads away
And does not haunt or lurk the inky coombes,
Where black oak and dull hawthorn clamber down.
Or curve the tip of wing to search where mossy granite echoes with the aqueous flush of tumbled stream.
Instead she curves in high clean air,
To climb where marbled nitrogen hisses in cloud.

Her eye is pin-sharp, almost to infinity. If something is there she can see it. If we are there she can see us. If she is not in line of sight, another of her kind almost certainly is.

Anyone out on this moor between 5,000 BC and 5,000 AD is almost certainly being watched by a buzzard.

When are we? I'm sorry, but I really haven't got a clue. Nor is there any way to know. Are we in 1942, or back in '71' again; you cannot tell by buzzards or the moor.

The moor is millions of years old. Those who live here have been here since the dawn of human time. If you are questioning a pause of thirty years don't bother. The gap you seek is not snatch of breath, or even less the blinking of an eye!

Those years you quest might as well be happening at one and the same time: Your 'astral' pint is on the bar; you lift to drink but it is gone.

It doesn't matter 'when we are', our bird has seen the night slide in and go back out; one rabbit down she settled on a windy ledge to rest and let it sink awhile. Many hours creep away, she has sailed out and back when she felt moved.

Eager hissing round the rocks where wind has lifted also lifted feathers wasting heat. She shuffled round to face the cold black wash and saw, *'the quiet no-mans-land of daybreak'* chafe the dagger'd frozen sky, as out to sea reluctant fluorescence swells the dark.

Buzzard sails east across the moor.

It is not long before its eye is caught by movement. Far across the grassy slope a figure alternately strides and breaks to scuttle from dry tussock to the next. His quickest way is through this soggy piece of swampland which this early in summer is still drying out.

Three months on, across here will be dry and arid like the Serengeti plain, and silvered marsh grass will turn dry and yellow. but for the moment you must still accept damp socks.

He is not too fussed about his feet; the main thing is to get round the moor and be done.

Beyond Roughtor is a small rocky gorge where a stream cuts through, though its cutting was done a million or so years ago. Today however, sheep like to use it as something to fall into in the night.

Marlo climbs between the mushroom rock and the peak, *(Yes of course, that name Marlo means that 'when we are' is 71 again)* then ambles down the eastern flank enjoying the weak though life confirming caress of the pallid sun on his face.

There is a point you get to where you have a fairly good view of the shallow gorge. If it was beginning to spot with rain which it often does as time ticks by and the land warms up, he might be tempted to send his dogs for a sniff around, then call it done and veer across the moor towards the further slopes where another crowd of his flock prefer to be.

This day is dry perhaps set fine, though cloud is building further on the moor. It did this yesterday and the day that came from it in fact was not that bad. Therefore he gives the gorge a thorough search, he even gets a chance to bomb a fair sized trout with a handy boulder; a foot nearer may have been close enough to concuss it with the shock wave, and through years of bombing is pretty nimble getting down stream to snatch it safe as it washes past. You move quite fast when breakfast is heading down-stream.

Sadly today there will be no tender mouth-watering treat for his breakfast in a few hours time.

The trout stays still beneath an overhanging rock it shot in under, and does not rush to get back to the sun. It is aware that something rocked its world as never before in its living memory;

though how long is that, five or ten minutes. If a goldfish has a three minute memory, a trout can't have much more?

An hour and a half later, Marlo has been right to the furthest slopes of Roughtor. His gaggle of would-be mountain goats are halfway up the nearest shoulder of the next rocky lump; but there's little point sending the dogs up, though they would like nothing better.
If he brought the sheep down, he knows in half a day they would be back; at least, he thinks, being up there makes them easy to count. It's as easy as charting the freckles on a woman's bum: unless of course she is heavily tattooed… sadly Marlo has not in his wild but nevertheless sheltered moorland life, had access to a tattooed bum.

Marlo is often drawn to end up on a particular rock. It is flat and somehow attractive to his weary herdsman's eye, and rump! It gives a particularly good view of your live-stock as you sit. He always seems drawn to it when he is over this way.
Now and then he imagines he is not here in '71'; he thinks he can feel another life, or another time sitting with him.
This day he heads over to it as he has before, and being a dry day it will not give him a damp bum, just cold.
He likes to sit at around this time because it forms a sort of unofficial breakfast-time. He doesn't even have a flask of tea; but he has got some of his mum's flap-jack wrapped in foil and stuffed in a pocket.
The oats and brown sugar crunch and heat up as they slide down into his rumbling belly; and the oil of melted lard smoothes around inside making good conduction for all the calories of heat that are released.

There are bits of the slope that always catch his tracking eye: That small outcrop before you get down to the grassy slope, it has the appearance of some sort of flightless bird; a cassowary, or perhaps a scraggy chicken with its tail missing.
Then the greening expanse decaying longitudinally to the left: A strange patch, not bald of vegetation but the greenness absent and re-grown by flat leafed sedgy looking

plants that can show little pink and purple flowers very early in the spring. And this peculiar un-grassed area is large and formed in the shape of a cross.

These items that his thought regularly plays with have no absolutes or finality in his knowledge. The bird looks like a bird to him as he sits here, but Marlo has never bothered to seek it from another angle.

The area of un-grassed vegetation in the shape of a cross he thinks is something to do with Joe, and some aeroplane during the war. He has never asked about it, it just comes from something in his youth that he had once heard: A crash or something. Perhaps Joe built a sort of medieval catapult in his forge and managed to bring down a German Focke Wolf 190 one lucky day.

He knows that was not really what it was, but he never gives it a thought except when he is up here. Now it is one of those things, like having left it too long to ask Joe why he likes to sit on the airfield in his red car on frequent mornings. It will always be in the back of his mind unless something happens to bring it forward.

Who wants to ponder stone birds and singed hillsides when there is the possible return of Anita to look forward to.

She said she would be back as soon as she had a few pounds saved. Marlo's insistence that she should not worry about that, he would keep her glass filled seemed not to sway her. Said she would not be known as a free-loader, the local scrounger of drinks, did not wish to abuse the kind welcome she received that first night.

When Marlo had given her a lift back up to the moor and to The Vicarage; all the way he was in a quandary: was anything she was saying any sort of a come on. was he ignoring vital signals that she was flashing at him; for it would be terrible if he blew everything by grabbing at her uninvited; but very nearly as bad if he sent her home thinking he was a dumpling for not picking up on her randy signals if they came.

Several times he had asked himself what Jimi would have done, or at least would have said to her to draw forth the lady's aspirations. He ran a few lines like a verbal film in his head with a Hendrix drawl:

'Hey little lady... they generally seem to start with that... *it's such a lovely night, are you in a hurry to get to your bed or would a little night air please you.'*

He also played around with *'would a little night air turn you on'* but thought it was trying too hard to sound groovy. He was very keen not to fall at the first fence with this girl.

His worry was that even if she wanted a bit of kissing and fumbling, faced with the risk of being alone on the moor with a guy she had never seen before might lead to her playing safe and opting for a ride straight home.

All the time he was driving he was monitoring the position of her legs with his peripheral vision. He was sure that if she slid down in her seat and allowed them to extend at all from her dress, it would be a sure sign she was liking the ride and feeling comfortable with him. If either golden knee lifted independently of the other, or if she unclasped her hands from her lap and cupped them both on that lifted knee lifting it even higher: that to Marlo must surely mean she was hoping for some serious intervention.

So what in comparison does it mean when the hands unclasp, one goes down to scratch her ankle, *(probably a sheepdog flea)* then returns and folds with the other arm before breaking and forming a cup around her mouth to go: *'Ahhhyiyiyiooooh dear, excuse me Marlo, it's been a long day'*.

Of course she could be trying to float the idea that she's a tired little girl who needs to be helped into bed and soothed to sleep by a pair of willing hands.

She may just be tired of course?

So the drive home passed with his thoughts a tangle of indecision, but a frenzy of desire and fantasy towards this edible girl.

On arrival at The Vicarage Marlo swung onto the verge outside beneath a fragrant leafy overhang of flowering shrubs. Their garden was deep with trees and glowing bushes, but up the drive you could just make out the yellow light from several windows downstairs, and one above.

"I can see that someone is reading in bed tonight… I should think it's Mrs Hennacy. As the Vicar left me in your care I expect he feels obliged to stay downstairs and see me safe home."

Marlo nods and smiles past her into the leafy dark shrubs along her drive. His window glass is an inch open and the first scent of the garden night slides through.

The tail end of some striking natural music trails off outside the car. Quickly spinning his window winder brings the thrum of crickets nearer, and flowering azalea bushes draw the scent of leaf mould from the wormy ground. Their flowers glow like dull pink lanterns hanging sadly on the deck of some deserted or stricken ship that might not carry life again. A deck that tilts toward a watery grave where the deck moths must learn to fly an ellipse around the leaning lights.

"It's so quiet here Anita… down in Camelford, there would have been maybe two or three vehicles go past since we've sat here. How many…"

Something sudden scores the air; words and thoughts are shredded or held dumbly fast.

"What in heavens name was that?"

"That was a bird singing Marlo."

"Yes of course Anita but what… and that fantastic voice, it must be a nightingale?"

There could be no mistaking the nightingale, even if heard for the first time. A super musician of a heavenly state: Every bird note thrilled the air, and notes that seemed could not come from earthly living creature. I stopped abruptly at the first note heard.

Marlo abruptly stops thinking his randy thoughts at the first note heard; though probably not for very long.

Anita likes his sudden distraction and absorption by that wondrous sound. She liked as well being the object of his attention, and felt a tingle each time out of the corner of her eye she saw his head tilt toward her to visually stroke her legs as they drove up across the moor.

If it could simply just be done without significance; she would like to do something warm and sexy for Marlo, as a thank you for the night and being who he has been.

"I expect they saw the lights pull up, and now with the engine off they may begin to wonder."
Glancing away from the house she continues:

"It's been such a lovely night Marlo, can I buy you a beer sometime soon?"

With her bag clasped in her right hand, but held away across her left arm towards the door she smiles sweetly at Marlo in the dark car, her she-wolf eyes glowing like Egon Schiele's Madonna.
He grins back at her with his left hand on his gear-stick, and his other elbow on the lower edge of the steering wheel allowing his thumb to support and enhance his heroically *(he would think)*' craggy profile.
Lips part to tell her that he will look forward to his pint with her. Before the words have left the hangar, eyes descend. They fall into the open neck of a soft loose cotton dress that in his mind has opened like a parachute.
Her forward slant with arm across her front presents a valley of sweetness; and the flesh of right arm lifts her breast up and across in a swelling ascent of dark golden warmth.

Marlo can only just about cope with this unprovoked visual attack. His astral lips and tongue are already down there licking and nibbling and sucking like a boy who spends too much time chasing sheep around a god forsaken moor.
But his earthly frame is still erect. That one's soon to be his next problem: What size were those last pairs of underpants his mum bought him?

He has the visual thing nailed down by tearing his eyes away, and muttering about another good pub in Camelford... then the cavalry attack: Anita must have flipped or smoothed her dress, or fluffed her hair or something. A pungent sweet and hormonally intoxicating waft lifts his face, as if he were imbibing juices from the air; or kissing where magnolia petals part to render the hot internal darkness open to light. He draws one breath, then dares not move: *'There could be no mistaking the nightingale'* and equally, there can be no mistaking the breath of heaven, or the sweet juices of love that vaporise into this mouth-watering night air.

He nearly groans, he nearly goes silently mad in the dark. His trousers smoke and scream objection, and his desperate cock throbs and struggles with its captors.

He can complement himself on having not actually ejaculated. Though he may as well have done because his pants are absolutely wrecked.

Anita hovers almost uncertainly in front of him, but smiling kindly and attentively in the dark.

She still has it in her mind that she should do something sweet and sexy for him; but what is appropriate for a pint of cider and a lift home.

She can feel a buzz in the air so is aware that he is fairly on the boil. She seems rather surprisingly, or because of his languid poise with chin on fist and elbow on wheel, not to have grasped just how steamed up he really is.

Anita knows that women often slate a man's desire by blowing him. She knows it can be carried out in a confined space and carries no risk of pregnancy. Though instinct suggests it might be a bridge too far this time, and just after a first meeting.

She's never done it, but is fascinated by the thought of controlling a strong man, as if he was a dog upon a lead; she has often mentally rehearsed how she would coax him with her lips and tongue until he cried out and exploded in her mouth.

Anita learned that that's what passionate romantic women do when she was fairly young. A friend's sex obsessed older sister read them some bits from DH Lawrence and they all giggled like fairies at this hilarious though profoundly fascinating thought.

A year on when there was a crowd of small boys and girls all being naughty and silly in a summer meadow, Anita sneaked off with a young boy and another girl. When they settled some way off and began the customary looking down or up clothes to compare equipment, the boy seemed nervous but still quite eager to play the game, and be played with.

Now in Marlo's car, and with the warm night air outside, Anita can feel again the sultry heat of that day. That summery buzzing of flies and bees, and the coloured waft of butterflies beneath the spreading boughs of trees, like beech and hornbeam at the edge of field; while a husky cuckoo confirms that *'summer's lease, hath all too short a date'*.

As the three became more daring, Anita and her friend undid his shorts, and took turns to hold him in their nervous hands and giggle. Neither really knew, though one or other may have vaguely thought, how to work their hand up and down, nor were they entirely certain what they would see if they did.

When Anita became more adventurous he was uncertain and just became scared at it all.

"Oh blimey Jonathan, boys are supposed to really love that!"

He then made a split-second, though unfortunate decision not to reveal that he had never had it done before; though at his age who ever would have?

"Well I just don't really like all that Anita."

Jonathan blurted ignorantly and idiotically… and no doubt started biting his stupid lip straightway.

I dare say he cursed himself for years to come. If only he had admitted being new to it, as she was anyway, she would have been straight back on and probably taken him to a happy ending.

Today and here in Marlo's car.

Anita still hovers with her kind attentive smile… the velvet glove of darkness holds the car with the fingers of another world: in it on the bank outside a minute shrew darts sizzling from tasty worm to worm and on.

The almost forgotten driveway finds a house now curtain twitched and waiting. The sombre tone disconsolate, of pallid light falls flatly on the lawn, illuminates that were the dwelling's keeper in the running for sweet fair flesh, or aged to stake a claim he would be there.

"Well I hope the vicar won't think I've kept you out too late Anita?"

Marlo should have kept his mouth shut a moment more: she was tilting slightly forward as he spoke, and may have further stooped to span the silence: nor needing hand on back of neck.

"Yes I suppose so Marlo. That is I don't think it's been that long yet, but time I s'pose is shifting on."
He sees her lifting back from stoop; unwelcome veil is drawn on golden orbs disclosed in moonlight; he spots too late that buzzard may have been about to dive and choke the blind mole from its velvet dingle.

"Was she… oh flip me I don't believe it… I think she was you know; but what now? Well I can hardly say 'if my guess was right, you were about to get down and give me a nosh just then, so let's just wind back a bit and carry on from there for a minute'. Nor is a hand on the back of her neck necessarily going to be that well received!"
With laboured resolve Marlo knows he must unless she makes another move be steadfast in his role of a safe hand home; it wouldn't do to grab her like a hungry hound… in daylight he might try the spaniel eyes, but here in dark and growing late there wouldn't be much point.

"It's been really… nice seeing you tonight Anita."
Was all the words that would form for him just then.
Is it really nice to have your underpants entirely wrecked? Marlo refers only to the easy 'seeing you' bit first, as you can hardly make reference to the state of your undergarments, or to the rapturous throbbing abandon of your wedding tackle that has howled at the moon like a love-sick coyote, or a tall man left holding up a pole-less tent for the past twenty minutes.

Yet here ensconced on his favourite slab and with most of the flock accounted for, as day renews its routine lease it's not that bad. You will last night have hauled off somewhere along the road and sorted the aching balls no doubt.
Now in the morning sun she feels no longer like the only thing you need in life; though not to be passed over that's for sure.
And scrunching flap-jack isn't quite like mouthing women's flesh but fills a different sort of need.

Marsh-grass makes a suddenly realised hiss in lifted breeze and seems as if it's set to walk away, relents and dips in recognition of its roots.

An hour on, a young woman is on the bus on her way to her work-place in Wadebridge. The bus snakes through a long and wooded valley and she thinks about her man and what their life will be when they are wed.

Ginny knows her man will want to be married soon because whatever they do, like with kissing and cuddling and everything, he always wants to do more. If they were married he could do it all as often as his heart desired, so it's bound to go that way quite soon.

The man she calls 'her man' is called Marlo, and his face slides across her thoughts as the bus slows for an S-bend threading across a narrow river bridge. He is tall and dark, and wants no one in the world but her: he said as much one night when she was fondling his balls, and looking set to take him all the way, yet somehow didn't!

Yes she is so lucky to have Marlo for her future man. Yes indeed there's little that won't be good in their life when they are wed.

"Oh flippin' eck, just imagine if I could have slipped Anita a length last night; blimey, that would have given them something to chew on at 'The Sun'. It would have put that cocky sod Chris in his place for a while I reckon… not that I would have gone around boasting about it of course, but somehow they would be bound to have worked it out."

A curlew calls to something in the stratosphere; its rising tloo tloo tloo roo roo peels like some extravagant claim of height and air; Marlo hears and thinks the time is soon to go.

We set off down and see no red car where huts and runways fuse the green, so the eye traverses dislocated from the details of this view, yet with the mind still drawn to seek it seems.

"Come on then you mangy curs, let's get you home for some breakfast shall we?"

The answer such as it is, comes in the form of two streaks of black fired lengthwise down the slope.

Marlo rises weary on his questioning legs, with one last look across the rocky slope he launches forth to join two tongue lolled faces *'lagging loath'* a short way down.

And they perhaps do not know, yet on arrival it will seem as always; that there's still a little bit more work to do in the meadows back along the lane to home, but that won't take too long, and so they go… though unlike them, a kink in time will slide us through the worm-hole to the war again as on Davidstow Airfield the clock ticks languidly on the cookhouse wall.

Cookie and Anne are the only kitchen staff in this morning, and even they're just meant to be on light duties today.

They sort a few bits on the shelves at the back and Cookie says.

"Bring that note-pad to the shed will you Anne, let's make a count of cooking oil and tins and stuff."

Outside, day is growing bright and cloud scud blue; and little blue 'forget-me-not's' like azure buttons popped from Air force corsets seethe between the stems of green.

Anywhere you go today might feel like this.

People are easy in their way and do not seek for absolutes nor look askance towards the sky.

Joe's granny, Anne, fusses in her kitchen; each Sunday morning unless there is something that Joe has to do with the football team, she looks forward to the arrival of her treasured grandson. He fixes window catches, chops wood for her sitting-room fire, as also now her wrists are so arthritic he can wring a chicken's neck instead of her having to struggle with it and wincing at their shared discomfort.

Yes Sunday seems generally almost a day off from the war.

The Germans are a pretty Churchy lot and like to do a bit of God to get them through the coming week of nastiness. The chances are there won't be too much in the sky today.

At first they thought we'd be to a man in church on Sunday, so sent a few unholy shocks. They soon learned that our anti-aircraft gunners were a bunch of Saturday Sabbath'ed Jewish refugees, and keen as mustard.
Now if they turn up it is all a bit half-hearted. They like to get their bomb lobbed off and out the way, so they can head back with enough juice to give it a handful in the event of being intercepted and chased back across the wet bit.

If there seems to be a sort of *'Sunday morning peace'* today, it's not alas for all: A Vickers Wellington bomber with half the cockpit shot away, one wing root nastily gashed, and one engine running at half the lick and spitting oil over the red-hot exhaust manifold, comes pushing against hope and fuel, and wind and dreams; and thoughts of younger sisters many miles away, and girlfriends and their mothers scratching out potatoes from the earth in soggy Eastern European fields.
The hazy tilting sea glows glumly far below, and surely soon there must be land on this heading.
If the radio were not just a raided biscuit tin of ragged and torn wires they would call to try and find their position. Even with the radio that would be something of a challenge; Jan their captain is getting pretty good, but the spoken English of this Polish bomber crew is still a struggle.

British weather is almost in reverse today; the wind is flowing in from the North-Sea as a saturated dull grey mass: a bit like Cornwall often is from the other way, but it is bathed ironically in sun.
All the south coast is cloaked in grey; it's only when you get to Devon that you start to find the sun is burning through.

Jan thinks he sees a strand of harder line twenty-five nautical miles off, and on a relative bearing of about three one zero degrees. He nurses her a bit to port and blinks through his frozen eyelids like an emperor penguin in Antarctica anticipating the springtime return of its mate.

All intercoms are dead in this rattling stricken bird, and with the grumble of its engines, and all that sea beneath, it may end up having to fly like a penguin yet. But all men feel the nudge to port and wonder what the skipper's seen ahead.

Even the lonely frozen rear gunner suspends his dream of warm girls and cool summer beer to note the tilt.

He sees a ship so far below that he had been watching recede beyond his ratty gun, now tip and slide to the right of its barrel. Are we banking to avoid weather or other aircraft? When the next few moments bring no return to the old heading he knows it must mean that Jan has seen something… or thinks he has seen something.

Petr will always be the last to know of any changes, even when there is an intercom that works.

He light-heartedly accuses his comrades of passing a flask of coffee around and forgetting him tucked away in the tail.

They in return remind him that he has got the cushiest job because he will always be the last of them to crash.

The old bird grumbles on and minutes slide; and Petr can feel through his seat that Jan is trying out the first few degrees of travel of various controls and levers: The flaps are moved a tiny bit and his seat ascends, then quickly back. He hears the slack in the rudder cables over head take up, his seat yaws slightly to the left and soon returns.

For several minutes there is nothing more to note, until the grumbling rumble of the engines starts to fall. The sick one seems content to struggle on as it is, so isn't meddled with. The good one is pulled back to join it and Petr feels his seat tilt somewhat back like a dentist's chair as the nose goes down.

When the nose falls you always get that here we go type of feeling. Even when it only means you've made it home and you're up for a beer. It still tells you that you are leaving a stable mode, and entering other possibilities.

As the rear gunner you are drawn backwards towards everything. Everything you can see has just happened. You might feel you are immune from facing reality, like a fairy prince reliving his favourite dream; but when that sudden unwelcome

Messerschmitt pokes his nose up your arse and spits lead at it: Everything gets very real very fast!

"I wonder what we're going down towards in the way of weather?"

Petr twists round to get a look forward through the fuselage, but there is too much in the way to really see that much out the front. At least it looks nice and light; if it were dark they could be plunging into a forest, or the ocean.

"I suppose it's half an hour since Jakov staggered back to tell me that half of England and the English Channel is all fogged in; we must be getting near America by now!"

They are in fact now converging with and tracking down the clearing coast. Jan and his injured co-pilot are struggling to control and read the flapping map in this semi open cockpit. The deafening scream of the wind means that they cannot exchange thoughts other than by pointing and gesturing.

Suddenly the co-pilot jabs rapidly between the map and the ground, and nods his head like mad. Jan looks out and back, and out and back… then sticks his thumb up with a nodding grin.

Finally they know where they are and Jan turns to grin reassurance at any he can see behind.

Now quickly back to work on the map he sights the nearest airfield, and it's little more than twenty miles inland on Davidstow moor.

He begins to relax, and even wonders what the entertainment is likely to be like in the evening.

The sun is shining and they slip down through a few thin cumulous across the southern fringes of the moor. A big old fire behind a farmyard shows that there is very little surface wind down there.

From five miles out he spots the flattened plane of green with its criss-cross of runways.

"I should fly over and alert them that we have a problem, but as there are no electric's how can I flash my lights. And if I then do a circuit and pull too much 'g', the wings on this poor old thing might 'clap hands' above its head.

"

Joe is not long arrived at his Granny's cottage on the edge of the moor.

Today he is out the back splitting logs for her evening fire. Five minutes back she brought him out a cup of tea as she always does.

He stops to drink and gazes up the flat and rising slope toward the peak. Thinks as well how much he loves her little cottage; it occurs to him that one day far off it will probably be his.

Joe hears a rumbling buzz away to his right. It is not of course unknown, but is unusual at this time and on this day.

The growing spec reveals it's not a Liberator, having just one engine on each wing, and one of those is belching out black smoke and grumbling resentfully.

Jan who has decided to come straight in to land, is already lined up on a runway. His flaps are eased gently down and he clears the switch to drop the wheels:

"Oh holy mother Mary, I had forgotten for a minute that we can't put down the wheels without *the electric's. A belly landing on concrete will probably light us like a torch."*

At that moment the sick engine growls and misfires, belches even more black smoke and shrieks briefly as it seizes solid. Without a live wire in the whole thing Jan cannot even feather the blades to cut their drag.

Three miles on he sees a plane of rising flattened green about a mile before the runway starts.

"This I think is going to be my only chance, if I don't take it there will be no going once round the airfield and back for another try."

Jan can just find time to nudge his comrades arm and to gesture that he is going down, and then he hauls back what's left of their engines. The nose falls and he gestures desperately at Jakov to wind down the remaining degrees of flap.

So many things fly wildly through his head in the next seven frantic seconds: Should he keep the only engine going or kill it now to reduce the risk of fire when they dump it down, and it won't be long because the moor is rising to welcome them and…

"Hedges coming, they're not a problem, stone walls converging from the left, Jesus no… turn her up the slope a bit… and miss that cottage, Christ, and it's still all green and smooth ahead, we could still live!"

Joe's open mouth is nearly to his knees as the stricken Wellington avoids their cottage, and almost balletically belly lands across the slope of Roughtor, and skidding sideways till it stops.

"Fuuu… oh blimey what now?…finish this couple of logs first? God what am I talking about. Just get up there and see what's needed, I'll soon be there.
"Get rid of this axe first, no point carrying it up the slope… unless I take it just in case!"
He's over the wall and off and up the slope axe in hand; and short sighted Granny shouting from her window…

"What was that Joe love?"

He's a fit young man, plays football, and wiry as hell. Halfway up he rips his pullover off and then he's flying.
Just three or four football pitches to go he sees a bulge of orange growing from the broken wing, and also sees a flailing group of airmen round the plane who should be giving it a wide berth by now.

"What in heaven's name are they all hanging around outside the plane for; have they never seen a petrol tank go up?"
Though neither has Joe, but he has heard stuff and can imagine it, and as he runs up he can see that smithy in Truro where the paraffin dispenser went up and took the farrier's cottage with it, and a child too.

"What the hell are they all hanging around for?"
And now he's nearly there and he can shout at them, and there's scarcely one looks over twenty-five years old.

"Get away you twats, it might go up any minute, you can't save the plane!"

"Not the plane mate! Our friend in there. Back turret, and we can't turn it to get him out"

Only as he's bounding up the final yards can Joe see that they are all grey faced and desperate, and breaking down in tears as well; the only ways out of the rear turret are through the fuselage which is starting to flame, or rotate it with its now dead electric motor. Petr however, is still inside.
Joe turns in horror to the plane.
Petr from inside looks out and gasps and chokes out smoke inhaled inaudible words which are if you lip-read Polish,

"Holy mother forgive me please, there's nothing can save me now…"
The heat of flame is burning across the wing and into the body, and soon could find a tank and that will fry them all.
The crew are helpless, each one going quickly mad at the plight of Petr who they are about to watch burn in front of their eyes, or turn screaming to run away from.
It's at least ten seconds since Joe arrived; and it's taken him that long to work out why he brought his axe. He drags away the co-pilot who is screaming at the turret window in his own personal hell:

"Just give me room a second mate."
Joe goes utterly berserk you could say: In one minute he delivers as many strokes, and with three times the force of all the log splitting he has done in the last two years.
Aluminium sprays and fabric peels before his cleaving axe, and hardly has one blow fallen before it's up and raining down again.
The crew almost have to physically stop Joe when the hole is plenty big enough to get their comrade out; for it seemed like Joe would have had the whole tail off if left to him.

So Petr struggles coughing and half cooked into the daylight, and tearing the side of his face on a sharp corner of aluminium; but that which he cannot feel. Jan shouts the command to withdraw. They all run down the hill though none too soon before the whole ship goes up like a firework and some of them get burned by little splashes where you cannot whack them all out fast enough and at the same time.

But those little scars will be their pride and joy for many years to come.

Joe stares aghast as he tries to fit the last five minutes into his life. He can remember drinking half his cup of tea, then the burning Wellington coming into focus as he was running up the hill to get to it. Then it became a tangle of horrified faces, and the feeling he was hurling himself against an unbeatable foe, but with a desperate fury to win or if need be to die in the attempt.

A hundred safe yards down the slope and still panting, half of him still thinks there could be more to do; Joe is as tense as an over wound spring because nothing in his life has asked so much of him in so short a time.

He is leaning back up the slope almost like he is ready to run back to the Wellington as it burns; in his trance has not felt a gentle but persistent tugging at his trembling over stressed right arm. Then Jan the pilot helps to wake him up from the front and turns him towards the arm tugger.

Petr stands below him on the slope and almost speechless… just,

"thanks comrade…"
then;

"God bless you."
Joe reaches out his hand as if he were going to pull Petr from some churning sea. Petr grips it then falls to his knees and kisses it. Joe's hand has never been kissed, except probably quite often when he was a baby.

He is well aware that times like these are not like after a friendly match against Padstow; where you magnanimously pat the disconsolate backs of the blokes in the team whose arses you have just whipped, and gracing them with a sideways nodding wink of, "well it could have gone either way".

These are times when someone with a thousand things he wants to say can think of nothing, even in his own language.

You know you have achieved something unusual in a day when somebody kneels in front of you to kiss your hand, and says God bless you.

A grumbling whine of gears ascends the slope and they all turn away from what's left of the safely flaming plane and see a lorry and a fire truck and a couple of jeeps coming up the green expanse.

This will jump them back to reality, will wake their gaping trance of disbelief.

The lorry and jeeps come straight to park beside them, but the fire-truck just halts, and the very senior looking sergeant major shouts out:

"Was there anything special to be saved in there like equipment or documents?"

Adding with a wry smile,

"or crew members I suppose!"

Jan salutes, and responds with a grin and,

"Only Petr, but this chap came and got him out for us."

"Ah nice one lads, we'll let it burn and save our water then."

But Joe suddenly comes to and spins on his heel as if searching for something, which he is!

"Hang on now boys, where did I put my axe. My Granny down there in that cottage you just managed to miss, she'll be at me with a rolling pin if I don't finish splitting her logs today. I reckon you lot should by rights be giving me a hand to get it done."

Amid the laughs someone says they saw him throw it by the plane as they scarpered down the hill. The fire-crew have parked up, and the sergeant good-humouredly details two of them to *'take a butcher's up there for the axe'*; but first turns again to the captain to ask was there any live stuff left on board, or fuel tanks that haven't blown yet.

"Every bomb dropped, and every machine gun belt exhausted sir."

"Off you go then boys."
The sergeant offers Jan a cigarette and produces a notebook to get a few details down.
While they chat and jot, he looks up at the smoking frame where it hasn't melted in the heat, and back along the way it landed at the hardly scuffed slope.

"I'd say it's a bit of a shame that you got lit by something; it looks to me like it could have been repairable otherwise."

"Yes it settle on nicely, but one engine had seized as we heading in, and I suppose it was red hot but the wing around it keep cool until we stop moving. Then how do you say it in England; all the shit is in the fire!"

"That's it er… Jan, then the shit really hit the fan!"

"Of course, the fan."

The two firemen are coming back holding a pair of big fire tongs that have a red-hot axe head dangling from them. You might think they had just made it in a forge and were about to plunge it into water to temper it.
Joe sees it and attacks them with,

"So why didn't you bring the shaft as well. How am I going to chop Granny's logs with that!"

Then the sergeant major brings things to order and says it's time to get the crew back to the airfield to get cleaned up and debriefed.

"Jan tells me that only one of you got a bit knocked around up there and our medic has already sorted him a bit, and your rear gunner's face will need a few stitches. But any other burns and stuff just let the orderly know at the airfield and have it looked at. Okay then, everyone on the lorry I think they're doing dumplings and cold lamb for Sunday lunch."

The crew and Joe clamber into the back of the lorry, and various medics and firemen head for the other vehicles.
As they lumber and lurch back down the slope towards the lane back to the airfield Joe suddenly shouts to the driver:

"Hey, can you just swing along this track to the cottage, my Granny's eyes are so bad that she won't know what happened or if I'm dead or alive."

They swing off and soon they're stopping by her wall, and Granny comes toddling out to get the low-down on what's been going on up there.
Joe clutches her still hot axe head in a piece of sack, and motions them all to follow him out. They meet her at the wall.

"Hello Granny, you probably couldn't make out what happened up there. These blokes had their plane catch fire, and I had to help one of them out of it with the axe. I'm afraid it's only got a head now, so I won't be able to finish your logs today. I will give it a new shaft in the morning."

"Well don't worry love, as long as you finished your tea."

Joe turns and sees the cup standing on the wall where he stood it before he vaulted over. He steps along and has a sip: Surprisingly it's not quite completely cold, but the idea of some food at the airfield calls him and he shoots the rest into the grass.

"We'll be off then Granny."

"Okay love, and you boys too… and be more careful not to let your plane catch fire next time!"
Granny fixes them with a wicked grin and throws them a wave as they go back to the lorry.

All in and off and rumbling down the rutted way, as firs and larches either side along the track applaud the wild heroics of the day.

In the back of a canvass sided lorry Joe is remembering years ago once setting off with the '1st Camelford Scout Troop'.

What days those were, so warm so light. Back when it all seemed new and possible; when nearly everything that could happen did happen, and even that which didn't happen looked as if it might.

Times when village boys from poor families who'd often not even seen Padstow would get to camp on Dartmoor in a real Great War army tent, and be cuddled up against by boys who were suspiciously of an age to have left Scouts at least a year or so ago, but seemed still keen to serve God and the King a while longer… and sleep in tents beside younger boys.

The canvass sides smell of kindness to Joe. He can see their Troop leader Mr Stokes, yet only ever known as Skip by generations of the boys; he never married, which of course raised eyebrows amongst the parents in Camelford, and he clearly loved his boys with a passion, devoting his life to helping and serving them… perhaps a few rumours went around but nothing too severe.

Here bumping along the moorland track Joe is straight back in that first war army lorry stacked with surplus first war army tents and poles and pans, and bulging with the sons of young men some gone, but some who were lucky to have survived the first war.

Now is not then. This is modern times beyond the first world war now with metal aeroplanes that you can sit inside; and there is no skulking and being pounded in trenches now; today you zoom around in tanks that travel faster than a man can run: this modern warfare.

Though you don't see much in Camelford that would count as modern.

A squeal from the brakes brings them square to a road crossing; from which they grind forward so painfully slow, and with a gnashing of gear teeth and a rumble on the metalled road of non-pneumatic tyres.

The jeeps and the fire-truck are already back at base and making ready for the crew's arrival.

Joe can see why it is so reminiscent of their old scout lorry: Cornwall has had all the remaining first war stock dumped on it.

Even if it was a bumpy ride on its hard tyres, it was fun to be with this gung-ho devil-may-care band of Polish airmen; with their stories that would often start in struggling English for Joe's benefit, but break into Polish when they ran out of the right words; only struggling back into English if Jan prompted them.

Joe is suddenly aware that these canvass flapped jolting moments, inhaling the fragrance of sweat from a Polish bomber crew whom he has in the previous hour fought to help, are as memorable and precious as any moments he has lived through or been part of in his life. Joe feels that something of this is now who he will be as he inhales the smoke of new possibilities.

In fact Joe is increasingly aware as he looks along the grateful to be alive faces of his new comrades in the lorry; that his life from this point on will be forever subtly changed.

Because the fire truck had radio, the airfield has been briefed about general details of crew etc. and a bit about some local chap who saved the rear gunner's life with an axe.

Someone from the fire warden's office has been down to the canteen to tell them to get some bacon in the pan.

Cornwall has never had a young Polish bomber crew before, and though it believes it has had many young men who became knights of the Round Table to serve King Arthur at Tintagel, never in the history of its people has a Cornishman ever saved the life of a rear-gunner.

This is all new ground, and because of all they are hearing about, of their man and his axe, the local airfield workers all start to feel less like walk-on extras in the performance of the war.

"Well Vera, we thought we were going to have a really nice quiet day today; all of a sudden people seem to be dashing madly around as if there's a war on!"

"You've got it Anne, though at least it may liven this place up a bit... Sundays often seem to drag to me... there may even be a nice young man arriving here for somebody!"

Anne knows the phrase was angled at her, she is quick to flip it back towards Vera with:

"I thought you had someone Vera?"

"So I have Anne, but you have to spend a lot of lonely evenings don't you."

"But all by choice, remember I have Darren out there somewhere with the Canadian army, fighting and waiting patiently till we can be together after the war."

Anne as yet has no clue that it is Joe who may soon *around the angled doorway thrust his nose*, and her internal flutter that occurred the other night when he was there with Si, has left her rather fast to play the 'Darren card'.

Vera continues:

"My experience of boys is that they have a different way of waiting than girls. If we waited as patiently as them, we'd each have a family of five before the war is through."

"Yeah sure Vera, that's true enough for most boys, but Darren is even more keen on kids and settling down than I am!"

"Yes and you're the first girl ever to think that, so it must be true!"

"Oh give over: You know, for only thirty something years you have become a real old cynic haven't you!"

"Oy mind your cheek young 'Anne of Green Gables', or I'll have you on spud bashing for the next two weeks!"

Anne smiles sheepishly back in mock apology. The big pans are ready on the stove, with onions chopped and potatoes ready to be fried. There is an overlarge stack of plates warming ready because they were not told the exact number to expect.

Vera has dug deep into the furthest reaches of the cold store, producing a black pudding sausage that they can fry slices of, and one or two other bits that she thinks a Polish aircrew may fancy for breakfast. It's all stuff that would usually only be produced for visiting top brass.

Today she even finds some decent un-chipped plates for their Nazi hating comrades.

A Big lorry rumbles up and stops outside some sheds nearby, and the girls know this must be the crew and crank up the heat under the pans.

Anne is busily cracking eggs while Vera leans over to a side window, studies the descending group and relays:

"They look a nice group of lads Anne, two are certainly pretty dishy; and their pilot officer, well it looks as if that's who he is, is a real looker; you know Anne, with your looks and youth you should be setting your sights on a chap like him. Don't you want to come and see Anne…? And yes… there's a chap as well who I think you saw the other night Anne. Does that mean he…"

"Which night Vera, who do you mean?"

"You'll remember him when you see him Anne… mind those eggs don't cook too hard now."

The mess-room door pulls open and is held back by an orderly or the fire sergeant major perhaps who we do not see that stays outside.

The crew and others usher shyly in but with nostrils flaring they accelerate toward the servery hatch and peer longingly at the array of eggs bacon tomatoes etc. that would tempt a saint, but actually can be theirs.

She ticks thing off inwardly:

"OK the eggs are keeping warm, I've got all my serving bits and bobs… 'Hmm hmm over the white cliffs of'… hang around; so that's the other one that Vera said I had talked to the other night, Joe the farrier.

Well he wasn't slow in wangling his way back for some more food. I wonder how he stumbled across this lot today.

"Hmm hmm da da da daaa the white!'... Hold on now? Was it then Joe that was involved in saving their rear gunner; there's certainly no shepherd or farmer to be seen with them. But surely he would have been down in Camelford?"

Cookie steps to the fore:

"Okay, let's be having you boys, what can we do you for?"
And spoken in her broad St. Austell drawl.

A couple of lads just stand dumbly, while two more return "I am sorry". Their captain is a year ahead of them with English and interjects on their behalf;

"Today they are just glad to be alive, so will eat anything that gets put in front of them madam... and that includes you two attractive ladies!"

Vera blushes slightly, but enjoys being madam, and even more the thought of being hungrily set upon and munched by an entire bomber crew.

The effect is only marginally diluted by her supposition that at least three quarters of his desire will have been inspired by Anne.

"Well sir, we have tried to serve as many things for you to choose from as possible. You are our first Polish crew down here so we have no previous knowledge of the sort of things you will eat."

"Yes well even in Poland people still eat a combination of protein and carbohydrate, these are the words I think? much as they do here you know!"

But Cookie is no slouch either; she can fight her verbal corner well enough.

"Well that's quite a relief Sir; we were worried that you might come in and insist you can eat nothing but sauerkraut and pickled gherkins for breakfast!"

"Okay fair enough madam, I think you say the French word 'touche' perhaps; either way it was impolite of me madam to make a joke when you were offering us hospitality. So I will say for my crew: A plate of whatever you have cooked will suit everyone I think."

Then with scrape and clink of crockery the file of hungry faces makes its sideways shuffle along the counter.

Joe had a fair breakfast scarcely more than a couple of hours back; so though he's peckish it's not like someone who has spent hours in a wounded bomber with wind whistling past the broken edges of cockpit glasswork. Or while the feeling in the pit of your empty stomach is that you might at any time be picked off like a lame duck by some eager '109' before its pilot scoots home for a coffee at an occupied airfield in France.

Joe noticed also that Anne is on duty. However hungry he is he would still have slid to the back of the queue where there will be more time and a greater chance of engaging her in further comparisons of life.

The crew of course have already sighted Anne. It happens before they even feel their eyes alight on her, and they were just now milling around inside the doorway, and really wanting nothing more than the breakfast that had been promised to them, nor aspiring to anything else except to sit with a cup of tea while breakfast is sizzled and sorted for them.

But believe this: There will not be one who did not find his eye subconsciously drawn to the dark almost oriental complexion of Anne's face and eyes; or had not their eye lured up and over her ample though pertly contoured rump.

Each has only made silent and guarded mental adjustments of her attire, and certainly without nudged reference to the other boys.

As they shuffle sideways along the servery to reach a spot directly in front of her like in a dancehall cloakroom mirror, it is only their own eyes that stroke down the sides of the hourglass. They will stand before her as a simple male primate in a primeval wilderness, holding out a posy of options for her to sniff inquisitively.

Petr the rear gunner with face taped up till after breakfast, answers her kind enquiry with a few words of Joe and his axe.

Petr thinks how kind her eyes, and how sad that he will never see her after this day.

"So Joe the farrier, what brings you back here to the airfield so soon?"

His first thought is that perhaps he has been naughty and came back to see her, for such it feels. While he is thinking how best not to confess to it, and in his quaint modesty blushing awkwardly and wondering what sort of an excuse he can use…

"I'm not interrogating you Joe; I'm asking because I gather you were very much connected with helping these Polish chaps… so no need to look so panicked my friend!"

'My friend'; those last two words kissed his heart as rich gravy being poured over a Sunday roast.

He hears that there is somewhere in her where his image is not a foreign thing.

Joe does not too easily articulate thoughts to himself; but his instincts tell him that between the first time Anne saw him and now, he has in her minds eye made at least one other appearance. And revulsion or abhorrence would not have seeded 'friend'.

"It was quite a lucky thing Anne; I just happened to be at my Granny's cottage splitting her some logs for her open fire and having a cup of tea on the garden wall."

"Ah… so now I see why you would have been over there. The word came back that the Wellington went down on the slopes of the peak Joe."

"Yes and almost took Granny's chimney-pot off as it turned to belly-land up the hill."

"So when you ran off up there Joe, I reckon it was sharp of you to know that you were going to need your Axe."

"I must be a bit dim really Anne: If I had had my way I would've left the axe in the garden."

"So it was your granny told you to carry it then?"

"No Anne, just something made it seem a good idea; you can do all sorts of stuff with an axe... when without it, just a pair of hands are almost useless."

Joe looks at Anne's curves as he says 'useless' then adds silently as an aside:

"Useless perhaps... but given half a chance, very busy!"

Anne is still pushing mushrooms about in the pan so she will have time to finish her question. She is worried that Joe may be ravenous and not wish to be chewing the fat about his escapade on the moor when he could be chewing sausages and black pudding with the bomber crew.

"Sorry these are being a bit slow Joe, maybe the gas bottle is getting low... do you want me to hurry things up?"

And it is asked as she looks up from the mushrooms with a sideways smile, and her lower lip extends and curls like an opening summer tulip, or a calligrapher's ornate question-mark.

Joe can hardly say *'I want you to make them take the rest of the day'*; nor is he the niftiest wordsmith on the block. As many, he would probably be kept awake for hours that night going through various combinations of words and phrases that refused to form at the time.

Though Cupid is no slouch today it seems, and if it is too much to expect him with his arrow to significantly sharpen Joe's wit, he at least keeps Joe on target for her heart.

"That's kind Anne, but I am quite happy to stand here talking to you while I unwind and relax after all the dashing around up there."

Strange that isn't it: He wants he says to stand there to help him to unwind and relax after all his excitement. I suppose it would be difficult for him to reveal that he wants to stand there to increase the likelihood of him one day lying down with her. What is this fear that men all have of even allowing it to be thought that they are there because they want the other person.

Either way, Cupid's unleashed arrow sails forth and settles in her soft interior. Nor herewith does the haunting spectre of her future life tap at the pane.

She feels a rising tingle in soft tissue where her spine meets her pelvic girdle, and it resonates like a minor chord drawn from the mahogany of a piano, while a suspended fourth is stroked two octaves below.

Somewhere far off in the moorland night that is not here yet, a star calls kindly down saying that Anne is a young woman whose life is in the world, nor months nor years away, but now.

Other stars wake up and wink, and smile in confirmation that this day when a life was destined to be put to the cruel sword of fate and burned, yet then was saved; is one where she should share this oxygen of life and hold it in her.

"If you are happy standing there Joe, I am happy pushing these mushrooms about."

Then she giggles like an imp again, with her face lifted to the light and Joe can see that she is beaming like a baby.

Anne piles a plate with much of what is left in her pans, then she nods her head towards the eating hall, comes round from behind the servery and sets off with Joe's breakfast.

Joe feels like he has just tagged onto a religious procession. Anne holds an offering that they are about to make like eager Druids to their gods.

If they were approaching an Altar Joe's eyes would be lifted heavenward, and the corners of his mouth be tweaked by an aspiring pious smile.

Here is not. Here he walks as owl clock eyes go left and right where oscillating bum cheeks nudge alternate flap of pinafore.

He walks straight into back of her. Anne has 'anchored up', and looking up and backwards over shoulder spoken,

"I'll go back and get you a tea in a moment Joe if that's alright?"

As he nods a thank-you, she grins up with,

"It's alright Joe, I wasn't falling over!"

He finds that he is holding her waist like in a waltz, or being from behind, like in a tango. He is not in a hurry to let go. Joe's fingers lie softly bedded in her warm flanks, and he is tempted to thus pick her up and carry her, plate and all to the table to demonstrate his farrier-strength; but the awfulness of dropping the lot is too much to comprehend; he would lose his breakfast… and might even put a few blemishes on Anne.

"I'm sorry Anne, I didn't realise I had grabbed you like that."

"I wasn't complaining Joe…! will that corner table suit you Okay sir?"

"Yes madam it will be perfect."

"Jolly good sir, I'll just fetch you a mug of tea then."

Joe quickly sits faced out so he can watch her walk away. He swallows the shock of someone who suddenly sees why he is alive; and that everything he's done thus far is as nothing. He blinks into the light of this awakening day.

But, Joe conjectures… is someone here her boyfriend; any minute now will they come striding up to stake their claim and set him straight.

No one marches up, nor even any glare at him; but how could such a succulent little woman not have a man; or at the very least a gaggle of aggressive admirers. Then maybe she's a lesbian, and has a big butch woman with a strapadictomy!

He would have spotted the male admirers by now, a resentful group eyeing him sullenly. Or if she had a mouth full of the most hideous rotten black teeth he would have seen it when she smiled. Joe sees a soft lipped cave of perfect pearls, and in his dreams a mermaid's sensuous tongue licks kisses at the landlorn sailor.

So that's not it.

It would all be far more urgent to make sense of, were there not this plate of fried beans and mushrooms and bacon to devour. Joe finds a sudden appetite arrive and attacks like a man who will take no prisoners.

He is roused to glance right by the 'heyup' and 'yowboy' from the Polish table across the canteen. They have tea cups raised and grin at Joe who feels like a regular hero.

Pilot officer Jan winks at Joe, and tilts his head big-eyed towards the kitchen girl who is fussing round her tea-urn; and juts a fertile luck-confirming thumb behind his mug.

Maybe some deity has sent her to him for saving the rear gunner's life?

Maybe not, but undoubtedly he was saved,
> and she and Joe are here.
> So who's to say?

There is none to say nor need it be said, and that spark of chance will either fade and die or glow and grow; though in her heart it plants the seed of seeing that this man ran towards risk and saved a life and did not stay crouched behind his granny's garden wall.

There is much is going to grow from this and Joe will not when he walks through town be ever just Joe the farrier again.

When boys after school loiter at the smithy door you won't so often hear, "can you show us the heavy hammer trick again Joe?" it going now to be, "could the plane have blown at any moment Joe… was the rear-gunner close to being toast?"

Then sometimes not just boys but mums and dads will call to see the farrier who saved the Polish crewman, and if his comrades had refused to desert him as the plane blew up, then by running to help he saved the whole crew as well… yes Joe is as close to being a civic hero as anyone Camelford can lay claim to… if you don't count King Arthur.

Dreams and legends weave around ahead, we leave this wave of time and space and wartime lives, as far beyond the moor the main A30 from Exeter brings a steady stream of life in cars and caravans and families proud to be at last heading west in their new Commer Highwayman camper here zooming past, then here again a Standard Atlas rocks and rattles by and after another twenty or so cars is a colourful hippy VW campervan with a family inside who we hardly know of yet, though soon we will.

Soon enough we are going to be used to hearing stuff like:

'Yeah dig this high sweet air man'.

How much air, how high and how sweet does it need to be? It needs no answer even in the hippy lingo that we will inevitably be hearing plenty more of at the magic mushroom festival on the moor.

However much the actual quantity of this high sweet air is, it is not even a small waft of the whole gulf air stream that ascends the big-toe of England, all then lifting over as a mother draws and smoothes the covers up the shoulder of her sleeping child.

The hippy family are still a fair way off.

This sweet air does not rush today, though it flows in blind from Lands End and the Lizard. A molecule that rises clutching its snatch of H2O from the ocean waves then scaling cliffs, will scale the moorland peaks two hours on, and doubtless dump its aqueous cargo on the peaks if there's any left.

Nor will the bleating scarce grown woolly lambkin's shiver be shown mercy.

Fluffy bunny lollops tastily through the moist net curtain; every paddle leaf of clover or proffered palm of alpine herb is a cup of moorland wine for her, so her thereby steaming bunny-jobs will issue prolifically into the light.

Today there is no marbled nitrogen hissing in the cloud; all static has been seeded to the ground by moisture droplets so all clouds hang; the cloud sags heavy, darkly not though; they are infused by sun from high above, which striking top is fluorescing through.

So that all said of cloud, the air across the moor is bright and high and sweet; and breathed in pin-prick droplets cool the tongue, for each breath holds a fairy's thimble-full of the tumbled north Atlantic ocean.

Beyond this moor to the east the sun is almost through; roads hiss and rip like wet tar might where tyres pass, then waft with steam.

The A30 wakes from winter when the swallow returns. People who have thought of little except beer sex and weekends off work since Christmas, now realise they should be out on the sand with the kids along the Camel estuary; or exploring caves and raiding rock-pools at Boscastle and Trebarwith Strand.

So the westward drone of rubber climbs as day by day more trippers swoop to bridge and cross the River Tamar.

Here *'as time ticks blank and busy'* vehicles pass sporadically, not constant stream but now and then, and all with polished gleam to the happier times they travel toward.

The earlier sighted camper van with a mauve roof and a fair few flowers painted on it, and perhaps rather too neatly done to have 'the look' comes whooshing by, but the woosh is only 'cos it flies down hill: getting up the other side is a rather longer story.

They have travelled from the flat east of England to the land where every up is like climbing to the clouds, and every down like falling to the sea; where feet are yards, and yards are miles, and miles take in horizons and the sky.

The male and female in the van do not sing like they would have to if they were driving along in a Hollywood film; an Irish band called Skid Row is blasting out, and as Phil Lynott rants against the injustice of being left by yet another cheating woman, our driver nods like he was beating some invisible drum with his forehead.

The woman has a look that says she might be happy just to talk and give their ears a rest for once; but accepts that if you do this sort of hippy thing you have to do it properly.

In the back of the van there is loads of stuff like *'tins, boxes, bottles, shapes too vague to know'* and a little dark haired boy of about three years playing drowsily with a kitten.

Mum turns in her seat to watch him for a while; she smiles that smile of pride and love that only blossoms when a mother sees her child.

After a minute or so, and when a sudden pause between the final two tracks arrives,

"Are you happy back there Maxikins?"

"Oh don't call him that, it's just not cool 'Annabel Patricia', you'll make him grow up hating his name. You of all people should know what it's like to have an un-cool name shouldn't you!"

"All right it was just our little joke… It would really be easier if you two blokes had completely different names really."

"That's why I said we could call him Maxwell; at least till he gets a bit bigger; perhaps when he goes up to senior school it can change to Max: there you go Bel, that's the answer."

The final track on the tape is quite a short one, and as it belts its way to a close Bel takes the chance to turn quickly back to her little boy:

"Hey what shall we do Maxi, shall we sing a song?"
(Oh my giddy aunt they're not going to do the Hollywood thing are they? I knew it was on the cards!)

"What about 'the wheels on the bus'?"
Little Maxi smiles amiably but shakes his head from side to side. Then a sudden thought comes into his mind,

"Are we there yet?"

"Well if we were already there, would we still be going along Maxwell?"

"No don't be mean Max; it's a long time to have to sit still when you are that age, so we are lucky he's been so good, and I bet you would have made much more fuss than this when it was you!"

"The furthest we were ever taken for our holiday was for a week in a caravan at Camber sands. We reckoned Dad took us halfway round Kent and had a lunch-stop at his favourite pub on the downs so we all thought we were being taken on a proper holiday, rather than twenty miles down the road."
Even young Max seems to get the gist of what is implied in this hard-done-by story; at least something in it has him smiling. Then,

"Was it just as far going home Dad?"
Bel looks impressed at the logic in his young thought.

"Yeah well done Maxi, 'cos if it was quicker going home Max when your dad assumed you were all tired or asleep, that would show for certain wouldn't it?"

"Yeah I guess… but that's just it, we were all asleep on the way back. And for a couple of hours while him and Mum had another beer on the downs again I expect."

All this talk of family holidays has broken the cool-hippie spell rather; but even Max senior (23) feels a funny warm, if rather un-cool tingle of knowing he is part of a family of his own, and more than being part of a wider family of cool hippie dudes.

Most of the time that he thinks about where his life is, he sees things as a sort of hippie fashion statement. The arrival of a child was the cool result of free love; it gave him more respect and kudos with the other guys, and proved he wasn't firing blanks. It also gave him a chance to think up some meaningful names.

Max wanted Hurricane or Windboy, but Bel thought they both sounded flatulent.

Bel fancied Kirk, because… well because she fancied Kirk Douglas.

Max's mum pointed out that her husband and his dad and his dad's dad had all been Maxwells; saying you can always have a silly second name.

Bel thought that Maxwell was rather a silly name anyway, but didn't say so because she wanted her man to feel properly involved in being the father. It seemed from then that the die was cast, so he was Max. Anyway, Max thought that having a son with the same name as yourself was a really cool earthy sort of thing.

Max's dad said it was really just to save her indoors having to learn another name.

Now looking back, by which we mean, now looking back in the rear view mirror, Max smiles at little Max and realises: that this now is his family, and for the foreseeable future their three lives are going to be inextricably linked, or at least two of them. There will be no sloping off to something else more cool in another year or so. That little chap in the back of his van will demand attention for… well, with him only being twenty-three… and Max only three…

"It could be for an un-cool long time… shit!"
Those passing thoughts belie a deeper glow of something that he knows will stay with him that does not quite engender fear.

He looks back at little Max playing slumped with his kitten, and shouts above the camper's air-cooled rattle as he looks forward again and swerves to avoid the bank,

"There should be lots of other kids at the Davidstow festival Max; Mum and me haven't been here before but Mitch and Sandra said there were always lots of kids about… and there's a great big hill or a little mountain or something that you can go up, with funny mushrooms made of rock at the top.

"Sounds fun you reckon Maxi?"

The lack of a response, and a mirror check shows that Max is in the land of nod, if not as hoped in Cornwall.

Sandra and Bel had conspired about shopping while the men were talking about foraging for nuts and berries; Sandra said she had on the previous visit found a shop in the old airfield buildings called Andy-Store; remembered being told Andy started the shop in the war and although quite old had kept is going till now.

Frank the kitten does not care for shopping and dozes happily, too young to have his whiskers twitch with dreams of rustling mice in hedgerows yet.

The camper van steams on in blank determination. It always sounds like it is flat out at this speed… or at any speed. But it always somehow gets there… though excluding the times when some stupid niggly thing goes wrong and it stops and they get stranded, or limp for home, but that doesn't count.

Some way further on they leave the A30, and soon the road is climbing. The light and space around them lifts and opens where all walled fields cease; and sheep include the road as transit route from hill to pastures new.

A little flock heads down a slope converging now, and some are shouting to some more who went across some minutes past.

Max senses conflict of aspiration, if you can consider that sheep aspire, but he has anchored up as three on left decide to cross then veer away again. A dead sheep would have taken a lot of explaining to junior; and a tall young dark haired shepherd watching with his heart in his mouth from some way off is likely to have yelled a bit too.

That little crisis over, Max starts to wonder if they're in the right neck of the woods? It is certainly what you think of as moorland every way you look now.

"What do you think Bel? Should we expect to start seeing other camper-vans yet? Have a look at that little sketch Sandra did for us."

Bel has a quick rummage in the front glove compartment.

"Here we are Max."
Then after studying it for a few minutes:

"… hmm, it's a bit strange really,"

"Can't you make sense of it Bel?"

"If you try and match it against the road atlas we would have turned left to get onto the moor. I think perhaps Sandra has drawn it with south up and north down… hmm, yes if you turn it over, then it does match up a little better. Though I still can't see that it's going to be that much help really Max."

"Of course it will help Bel: We follow the right road and we end up at the camp."

"Yes, but most of the roads aren't joined to each other. I think she kept forgetting or changing her mind where things went, so just left off one road and started again with another."

"Oh my giddy aunt, that's so bloody typical; I should've sat down and done a map with Mitch then there would have been none of this ponsing around."

"But we're not lost yet really Max; anyway you and Mitch would have had to sit up not sit down, you were both stoned out of your heads on the floor: It was only me and Sandra that weren't quite seeing double that night."

Max grunts begrudgingly but has run out of responses so the wagon clatters on.

Little Max pipes up.

"You went to sleep, and I was still awake dad."

Bel smiles back, and makes up something about dad being really tired that night.

As it all seems to be moorland they stay on the mainer road and further along it they drop down into a small town.

There is a steeply sloped car-park before the river passes under the high street. Various food items will be worth getting. Big Max is a bit new to this hippie camp sort of thing, and wonders if other people will just be scouting the hedges for blackberries and hazel nuts. They may look really out of place with proper food; then again after a day or so on blackberries it will turn their guts blue and see them dashing into the forest every ten minutes.

Bel favours tinned stuff like beans with little sausages. In the big town store she sees the tinned ravioli that little Maxi is mad on so she grabs five tins of it. They have a stove in the camper but if push comes to shove the wee chappy is just about as happy with it cold.

She re-emerges armed also with two loaves of bread and two bottles of cheap red wine.

The Max's are on the river bridge pointing at trout. It's the first real river that little Max can remember. He is totally absorbed by the whole idea of it. What is there up beyond that next bend: However much water comes flooding beneath the bridge, the river further up does not go empty; then how does it keep coming?

He asks his dad:

"Does it run at night as well Dad?"

"Yes Maxi, there's always water for the fish to swim around in."

"When it's night Dad, is it going back the other way?"

"No Max, it only goes this way."

"What the same water... so how does it get back to come past again?"
Max feels he may have been bowled a question he cannot take a swing at. Then he remembers how simple the process really is.

"Ah... well you see Maxi; when the water has gone under the bridge it goes on out to the big blue sea, and out there it gets sucked up into the air and turned into clouds. The wind blows the clouds back in across the moor... you know, with the big mushroom rocks I told you about? Then the clouds turn to rain and that keeps the river running down into the town here."

"When it rains on the big Mushroom rocks... do they grow bigger Dad."

"Ah I see what you're thinking. The mushrooms are not like the ones Mum buys that you like eating before she has cooked them. Mitch told me that the ones up on the mountain are as big as a house!"

"So can you bite them Dad?"

"No Max, they're made of stone... but we will be looking for magic mushrooms growing on the moor."

"What magic do they do Dad... and when they've done it can we eat them?"

"No I'm sorry Maxi, you won't be able to eat them."
Max is suddenly aware that he has brought a son with him who is wild about eating raw mushrooms, but will not be allowed to eat the mushrooms they are looking for. It will be like Ulysses

tied to the mast and still able to hear the sirens singing but not able to get his hands on them.

Little Max thinks also in his curious three-year-old logic: That he, a known raw mushroom fanatic has been brought to a land with stone mushrooms growing on the mountains, and magic mushrooms growing on the moors; and none of which is he allowed to eat. It almost feels like he's been brought here to be punished for something.

Bel arrives with two carrier-bags of stuff.

"Mum… what magic do mushrooms do?"

"What magic Maxi? Oh well yes I see; the magic is what happens when you eat them. I have never eaten them so we will have to ask Mitch and Sandra when we've managed to find their little bus. But children can't eat wild mushrooms Max."

"Why?"

"Because they can make you fall over."

"I like falling over."

They drive back out of town then take the first turn that climbs towards higher ground. Stone walls sprout on left and right, and mossy dingle valleys gutter streams.

Through scrubby oaks with lichen bark and wispy rye grass waving round the rotting arms of fallen branches. So the road ascends to reach the open moor.

Little Max has left his kitten snoozing, and clambered onto the bench-seat at Bel's shoulder. Kneeling wide eyed he has one hand on the back of dad's seat and one on the side of Bel's neck, as if rousing her. It rouses her attention and she takes his little hand in hers and kisses it.

He smiles a smile at her turning gaze then big eyed out the front again.

As they come to the top of a hill with a panoramic view Max pulls onto the verge saying that they must be able to pick out vans from up here.

All three climb onto a large chunk of granite just off the verge. Well, big Max climbs, little is passed, then Bel is pulled by both: Onto the rock that is!

Two crouch and gaze while Max employs his height to get an even better view, and the moorland wind is like liberated breath of peat and grass and turf sunk granite.

Bel feels like a she-wolf with her cub, and holds him closer to her heart in the wind.

Max feels like a distant life is waking in him: Which Max felt that, can you say; for doubtless both had eyes that drawn to distance were away from them. And primeval instinct is as close to a three-year-old as anyone, or even closer.

The three are on a chunk of rock that has not moved for twenty million years. When Max has been dead for a thousand years, it will still be here for twenty million more.

"Is all these hills, and all this far away; is it all Cormbill?"

"Yes it's all Cornwall Maxi."

"And why is the sky much bigger than at our house?"
'When feet are yards, and yards are miles, and miles take in horizons and the sky'...

"It's because there are no churches and trees, or shops and factories; and I suppose because there's lots of air coming over you from the big ocean. It sort of blows everything up big like a balloon Maxi."

Rocky scrub meadows now tumble-walled, amble each side of the lane to the moor. Greenness edged and cut by darkened grey recedes, and where it climbs again toward the peaks is fused with speckled pips of stone like the flanks of a distant giant green lizard.

It feels as if the wind god has thrown open his lofty window to see how things are getting along. He thinks it needs a bit more oomph and waves an inclusive encouraging hand at his minions in the stratosphere to crank it up some. And suddenly one by one, disjointed fracto-stratus feel a shove from behind and lift their brow as pace increases.

Little Max hears and feels a murmur in the rocks, and up in the wizened oak tree poised with its gnarled arms spread possessively over him.

It seems there might be voices. The wind makes him shiver and he shuffles closer into Bel's side. She turns and lifts him to sit in her lap so only the soles of his little boots touch the cold granite.

'The wind comes posting by in gusts', and big Max has hunkered down with the other two. He was muttering something about picking out some distant car roofs near that forest at the edge of the moor, but is now silent.

Little Max holds quickly away from his mother's warmth as if roused from sleep, or jerked back from a distant thought:

"Where's that voice coming from Mum?"

"Dad was saying about some cars…"

"No Mum, not that… a man said something to me, from over there."

At first he is pointing down along the hillside where the lane slips and descends to a little bridge across a stream. And where far beyond the climbing moor is laced and cut by rows and rectangles of arranged boulders, like the remains of some ancient village.

"There it is Mum!"

Now little Max is listening up and into the wind with his bright eyes scanning left and right. It is as though he knows someone is on their way, but not the exact direction they will appear from.

Bel wants to hold and remember this moment and being here with her son in this energised light, and this wind. She believes that he will see things that she may never see. She listens intently with her face against his.

"Yes Maxi… I can hear the voice of the wind now. It's telling us about coming over thousands of miles of the Atlantic Ocean to speak to us."

"Does it talk in your words Mum?"

"Well, yes… but it's sort of pictures too."

"Mum…?"

"Yes my little Maxi"

"I want a poo Mum."
The spell is broke, the granite boulder's time is done, and it must wait another thousand years for their return; though ten years or ten thousand years is just a blink of granite's eye.

As Max vaults down and helps them from the rock he says untypically,

"would you like me to do him Bel?"

"No I'd like to Max; we were in the middle of a really intimate moment up on the rock so I'll do him."
Bel takes Max round behind the lump and de-trousers him to squat him down. The other Max bounds to the van for the bog-roll and the spade he brought. He thinks about little Max with the wind whistling round his little goolies; then he realises that this is going to have to be him as well very soon.

Bel wipes his chilly bum and pulls his things back up again. Max who was hovering with his spade moves in to dig the turf and turn it into itself. He is determined that nobody will label them dirty hippies; if they do it will be unjustified.
Next time, he thinks:

"Next time I will dig a lump of turf out first that can go back, then none will ever know that we were here."
Big Max is in the mood to move now. Bel looks a little sad to loose the thread of where she was with Maxi; but knowing too the moment came and went, and another day may bring it back, though here not now.

"Let's carry on along this lane towards the moor Bel. There's that little bridge down there beyond those fields that looks fun for Max to throw sticks over and run to the other side to see them come out."

"That's called playing 'Poo sticks' Max"

"Is we bringing the poo with us Mum?"
Piling back inside Frank lifts a weary eye, though not for long; then stretches out as if he's only just seen how to get really comfortable. But he jerks up momentarily as Max bangs the two side doors closed.

He is able to bump-start the van and save some battery on the hill as they roll away.

Around the first curve and up a small rise Maxi squeals between their ear-holes that he sees the sea. It retreats grey below the ceiling of cloud, and looks as pallid, stretched, and flattened as the inverted sea of stratus cloud that it converges with.

The road dives and twists into a small wood of scrub oak, so the bridge below is lost from view for a little way. Rounding a bend it reappears, and looks narrow for a van but undoubtedly wide enough; but there to its left is a water-splash!

Max has anchored up before Bel has even noticed what he's seen. Maxi senses intrigue and his eyes dart left and right between his mum and dad so as not to miss the slightest hint of what has caused the sudden stop and atmosphere.

"What do you reckon Maxi… over the bridge or through the stream, I can't decide!"

"Through the stream Dad, will we make a big splash."

"You bet Maxi, it will almost make the water go back the other way up the river I reckon."

"Go on then Dad, make it go fast."
Bel asks if it's really a good idea, and is met by a perplexed face from both big and little Max that says: What's that got to do with anything?

Then brakes released they gather speed, and it feels too fast but if you do these things you have to do them properly. Just thirty yards now and they'll go shooting through and out the other side.

At ten yards the stream suddenly looks more like an estuary, then Whoosh, as the camper ploughs in and pushes up a mini tidal-wave of its own creation.

Maxi is halfway through his 'cooee' as his world feels to go into reverse and the back of Mum's seat flies backwards under him and his feet swing above him. He winds up nose against the glass having completed a forward roll. The screen is a fountain of sheet water forcing up and through the overhanging air-vents at the top, and blasting out through cab vents in the ceiling as other jets shoot through the clutch and brake holes in the floor.

Bel is bathed in enough water for a complete shower were she at home, but here delivered in two point seven three seconds, and almost likewise Max. Little Max in the middle has stayed the driest, but being disorientated by the tumble, and knowing he is never allowed to ride in the front thinks for a second he's being naughty there.

Now all is silence. All the throb and rush has gone. Water green slides down the screen to carry on towards the sea, and overhead cab-vent goes from tap to dripping roof of cave.

"Ah Dad that was really cool… can we go back up and do it again?"

He's right you know: They are indeed pretty cool.

Max turns and blinks astounded at his boy.

"It wasn't meant to really be like that Maxi, I only thought…"

Then looking up he catches sight of Bel's helplessly shaking head; and if anyone ever looked despairingly at someone else then this was it.

Maxi looks out through the clearing windows and sees they are in the middle of the stream.

"Why did you stop in the middle Dad?"

"Yes that's a good point Max, I thought we were just going to make a big splash and go shooting up the other side!"

"Alright Bel, it didn't happen quite as I imagined it would, though you can see how much Maxi enjoyed it."

"Well glory be that's put my mind at rest then Max; just as long as I wasn't buried under a ton of freezing water for no purpose… you complete tosser!"

But as she divides and brushes back her head of dripping hair she is smiling. And Maxi sees and takes it from her and passes it to Dad who dare not smile quite yet; they are after all still in the middle of a river with a stalled engine: And on his head it be.

"And what's more Max you're half as wet as me!"

"It's this air-vent Bel, remember that it only opens a little way on my side; so most of the water had to go out your way; though come on, there was a fair bit of water shot up my legs from the foot-pedal holes."

"Then let's change seats and do it again."

"Ah cool, and can I stay sitting here this time?"

"It was just a joke Maxi."

Max is finding neutral and getting ready to fire it up again. There's a red ignition light, but cranking bring brings no comforting throb. German engineering fails to save the day.

"I reckon the leads are all wet"
he announces confidently and knowledgeably;

"I shall have to get my feet wet and go and dry them off."
Max fumbles for a nice clean cloth under the dashboard.

"Here we go Guys… and can you keep Maxi away from the starter button Bel!"

Like a man with little concern for wet feet he winks laddishly at Bel and Maxi, and throws open his door, then swinging nonchalantly out he closes it.

He does not wade straight to the rear of the van. He seems to throw a sudden flurry of involuntary Morris dancing steps using his nice dry cloth for the traditional waving handkerchief and then just disappears; and a caboosh of freezing moorland wash flies up like any harbour wall in a winter gale with a high tide.

Maxi is first across to the window, and Bel not far behind. Little Max at first is scared for Dad and starts to cry, until he hears Bel's helpless mirth behind.

Max had stepped on the edge of the built-up concrete submerged road and feet flown out flailed wildly off into deeper water; and now he flounders to reach the edge.

Bel opens the window as Max scrabbles and slips out over boulders and she calls,

"That was poetry Max… can you go back into the deep bit for a photograph?"

"Hey man… no I can't."

He sits down coughing and cursing on the bank. Bel shifts Maxi away from the window and settles chuckling in the driver's seat.

"I may as well have another try Max."

The cranking winds, and then alternate beats join in, until that rattling roar and Maxi whoops. German engineering finally saves the day and all is well. Then coaxed and gentle they ascend the slip.

Bel pulls it round onto the verge beyond the ford. When push comes to shove she can probably drive it at least as well as Max can: he wouldn't agree mind you.

They clamber out onto dry land. Bel reaches into her bag and this time the photo opportunity is not missed. Whether the lens can capture Max's rising steam is probably doubtful, but the sour expression on his face speaks volumes.

"Best get out of your things Max."

"But I'll make the inside of the van wet Bel."

"So do it out here, it will be easier to get dry as well."

"I can't take all my clothes off out here Bel, someone may come along!"

"Blimey Max, can you call yourself a hippie when you don't like being naked outside!"

"It's not so much that Bel, but it might scare Max, he's always been asleep when I have a bath."

"But lots of times when he comes through in the mornings you've been getting dressed. It won't bother you will it Maxi?"

"Daddy's got a willie just like me hasn't he Mum… when he's asleep… why does it look like a banana?"

"It's because when he's asleep he dreams about bananas… yes it's just the same as yours Maxi, although when he's awake it's not as big as yours!"

XXXX

"Right that's it: the gloves are off!"

Max is peeling off his boots and trousers and all the rest, and doing a silly dance to entertain Maxi. Bel applauds and hoots with laughter and snaps one or two more for the album as Maxi squeals delighted.

The dance becomes a hollering Indian war dance as his whoops alternate from the road to the sky and back to the road as he rotates on the spot.

The whine and groan of perished brake blocks on a push-bike that has just come round the bend lifts him in mid warble and makes his mouth an even bigger O, and other hand dives to cover tackle.

The bike just stops, and with front and back wheel brakes both braying like a donkey. Max is dumbfounded, and the only thing he can find to say to the rider is,

"Sounds like your brake-blocks are made of wood."

And the rider splutters nervously back while translucent eyes flick from face to tackle and back to face,

"Oh thanks yes, I'll ask them to change them next time I'm in the Camelford cycle shop."

One or two seconds later Bel and Maxi emerge from behind the van and Bel is almost incontinent with mirth.

Seeing the red-skin has got his own squaw the cyclist relaxes and even flashes a smile at little Maxi. She says a quick hello to Bel: yes our cyclist is female, and throws another smile with a friendly question towards Maxi, relieved to be able to look away from Max! He reanimates and bounds off into the van to find clothes.

"Hey man, that was proper hippie stuff I reckon. And even better it was her and not some big old local matron coming home from church."

As he's dragging on dry pants and trousers he glances out to Bel and the girl as they smile and chat on the lane.

"Yeah, and as chicks go, pretty as a picture too I'd say. Wouldn't say no to a bit of that if there was any going. That little cotton dress shows what it contains better than if it wasn't there at all I reckon."

(Yes it is Anita.)

Anita has stood her bike against a rock and sat beside it to talk to little Maxi. As Max re-emerges she's done the little boy's name and is asking him why his dad had no trousers on just now, and Bel is still laughing about it because Maxi's account is so different to what she would have described herself:

Apparently Dad got out of the van in the river to do a Red Indian dance and wave a hanky, and just threw himself into the river for fun and because Mum had got more wet than he had when they tried to drive through the ford.

Bel thinks that Maxi's account is probably the one she is going to remember the longest.

Max sits down amongst them and Bel announces Anita's name and tells her 'Max', and Anita notes the name is shared and says she likes that sort of thing.

Bel jumps up in the sudden realisation that this is a perfect time for hippie dudes to put their kettle on.

Max tells Anita they are looking for the hippie camp for the Davidstow festival. Anita says she has never heard of it or knows what it might be celebrating, though has seen a couple of vans around. Max admits it is their first time down here but tells her that everyone comes here to eat mushrooms. Anita grins impishly, telling Max that they sell really nice locally grown ones in the greengrocers' down in Camelford.
He makes a plausible explanation regarding the fact that you wouldn't be able to buy this sort of mushroom in Camelford; then as he begins to warm up from his dip, and having this comely lass gently teasing about his mushrooms, Max finds that like mushrooms sprouting in the night, his new trousers are displaying something of an organic growth.

"They make you fall over."
Says little Max,

"What does Maxi,"
The girl asks glancing away from Max's expanding cod-piece, smiling yet obviously thinking that the wee chap has gone off completely at a tangent.

"You eat the mushrooms so you can fall over. But I won't need to eat them because I fall over anyway."

"Ah I see now Maxi, do magic mushrooms grow round here that people eat?"

"You can't eat the ones on the mountain, they're too hard."
Big Max explains that Maxi means the mushroom rocks up on the tor.

"Ah yes, the amazing flat piled up rocks on Roughtor, I've climbed up to see them, they're fantastic; when you get up to them they are so huge that you feel really small and alone. Not lonely though, just a small part of this huge net of time and distance. I promise you will love it up there Maxi… I wish I could come up there with you when you go."

"And you can Anita, *'provided that you climb in front of me in that cute little cotton skirt… cor shit!!!'*"

The settling bulge in Max's trousers becomes reinvigorated. He decides not to worry too much: He is after all a hippie, and she may just think he's got a particularly big 'package' and it will make her envious of Bel, which he thinks is always a healthy way for another girl to be.

"Well yes Max, that would be really nice to climb up it with you lot sometime soon."

Bel calls out from the van with a question for Anita about milk etc. and anticipation moves towards the arrival of tea.

Now they sit comfortable in the sun. Max brings Bel up to date with Anita's wishing she could climb Roughtor with the rest of them. Bel is keen on having another girl in their camp and says she would love to have Anita along. Max says how it will be good for Bel if the numbers of males to females gets evened up a bit; not of course because he enjoyed the impromptu bulge that was forced on him and his trousers just now.

The women-folk chew over how soon they should plan to make their attempt on the summit.

Max says he believes that really cool hippie dudes would never make a date to do something in the future *(he's got that image of a little cotton skirt up ahead of him!)*. They don't he says, drive around with appointment diaries in the glove compartment.

Things should happen in life that are 'of the moment'; that are distilled from the spirit of the world today, and should be done here and now or not at all.

He is making a fair speech along these lines to his little audience and all nod and smile acquiescent to the dictum of its philosophy. Anita finishes her nodding and smiling then adds an afterthought:

"I go along with everything you have just said Max; but I am still glad you made the plan to drive down to Cornwall today."

"Yes Anita, but that wasn't really a plan, we were sort of driven by an impulse to come here; I suppose it's a sort of collective consciousness with other hippies that brought us down here: More like a migration of birds perhaps."

"But I thought you were meeting a couple of your friends down here Max?"

"Well, there's a pretty good chance they might turn up some time I reckon if the vibes are right."
But Bel pipes up:

"They had better turn up Max, their van has got a fridge, and Sandra said there would space for me to keep my milk and stuff in it."

"Won't having milk in a fridge spoil it for you Max, I imagined you would want to be out there milking a sheep each morning!"
Max may not always be the brightest candle in the church, but is realising that this chick has singled him out to have a dig at. This is all the proof he needs that she fancies him.
Bel makes a mental note that Anita has incisively spotted Max's rather pompous tendency to display high ideals, and pretend there are ethereal reasons for doing things that other people might just get on and do.

A decision is arrived at, though strictly not a plan: They should drive the van to a car-park that Anita knows of. From there, if they walk out across the moor they go near where Anita had seen vans up a track beyond a stream that morning and they can check they are not just work or forestry vans of some kind.
They load Maxi, Anita, and her bike into the camper and fire it up. The engine still coughs a bit but clears its throat and settles down. It grumbles up away from the ford but makes more cheerful noises as it finds the level run towards the moor.

"You don't sound all that Cornish Anita?"

"No Bel, I'm only here for the job I have… except that I suppose I went for this job because I wanted to live in Cornwall."

"So what is your job then?

"I'm a nanny-cum-home help for the Vicar and his wife."

"So is this your day off Anita?"

"Yes, though I do get plenty of other time off as well. They're really nice people to work for."

"So today you were just out for a quiet ride on your bike when a naked Red Indian jumped out of a river and ran after you."

"Yeah, well I suppose so… you know, for a second I had forgotten why I had come this way today. I was actually out to see if I could find a young shepherd called Marlo. I wanted to know if he was heading for the 'Rising Sun' tonight. He gave me a lift home from the pub in his big old car with my bicycle in the boot, so I wouldn't have to pedal up miles of hill to get back to The Vicarage. I wanted to find him so I could be there to buy him a beer to say thank you."

"It's really nice that you are looking for him to see when you can buy him a beer Anita. I think if it had been me… before I was with Max of course; I would have given him a quick kiss and let him have a fumble and called it quits."

"Well yes Bel, that was what I was thinking of doing really, but Marlo seems a really quiet sort of guy; like at one point he quickly wound down the car's window to listen to a bird singing outside… I think it might have freaked him out if I had tried to… to do anything to him that night"

Do the heavens rumble with consternation at the injustice of life; or Marlo's spirit wraith cry plaintively across the moor?

A sudden curlew's rising tloo tloo, roo roo, roo roo… throws searching word across the wind, it seems to sing that that which time and chance had brought perhaps to be, was never quite.

Bel who sitting side-saddle on the bench-seat to talk back to Anita, smiles as she looks also at little Maxi's rather distant dreamy look.

"You know Anita, there's someone in here who won't need rocking to sleep tonight. I think I won't try to make him climb the peak today; I shall just amble out across the moor a way with him and look at flowers and rocks and stuff. You two can go up though if you like." Big Max's ears prick up and he is about to say that yes it will be a shame not to see the top today. Though what he would like to see the top of is another matter! He does make a feeble attempt to suppress images of Anita's healthy toned form ahead of him.

But Anita in sudden consternation:

"Oh Bel no, it's not that important to see the top today, and half the point was to show Maxi those big rocks. It will be just as much fun to go some way across the moor and look at things.

"Yes and thinking about it Bel, I know where we can go: There's a ring of stones not far beyond the peak, with a flat Altar stone in the middle for ancient sacrifice or something. And there are ponies and lambs to look at too."

Max is relieved to have stayed silent, and not to have said how keen he was to see the top today; he might have ended up having to tramp all the way up there with no little cotton skirt in front of his nose for a donkey-carrot.

Anita directs them to turn right at a little cross-roads and the car-park then is not so far away.

Parked in a corner they all have a biscuit and a swig of water before they head across the grassy slope. Maxi wakes up a bit and tries half-heartedly to catch the lambs that gamble from rock to tussock.

It is so clear across the moor. The sun now strikes down through a sky devoid of dust to dull its rays, and though you feel cool in the breeze you need to keep young or fair skin under cover.

After ten minutes or so they arrive at a small moorland tor. Its rise is perhaps just fifty feet above its surroundings but it still has a commanding view of everything, especially the ring of stones.

"Rather than let Maxi get too tired I think I will climb and sit up there with him while you two go on and look at the stone circle and the Altar stone."

This time Max makes no attempt at all to suppress his fantasies: Anita is lying naked in the middle of the stone circle on her back with her hands tied behind her, and her ankles also trussed tightly with rope. Or maybe she has a little meagrely thatched grass skirt and a string of beads round her neck, something like that.

He is Great Maximus the high priest; it is in his hands to decide whether to slice open her exquisitely upholstered chest, and tear out her still beating heart as a sacrificial offering to the gods. Or whether to let the gods sort themselves out for once, and keep Anita all intact for later on. What a tricky decision for a guy to have to make.

Surprisingly he settles for the latter. He cuts the ropes from her aching wrists and ankles, and she is so grateful at being sparred that she insists on giving herself to him for the privilege of keeping her life.

Max thinks about it, and makes a sudden change to his plot. He rewinds the tape to re-record some of it: Not so that this time he can cut out her still beating heart, but instead of untying her he commands that she turn over and kneel; then he rips his cloak asunder revealing his stupendous manhood and lets her have it doggy fashion. He's always liked it that way so he can pull silly faces at whichever girl it was without her knowing.

"I'll be happy to sit and talk to you Bel. It looks like it's the two Max's are flagging rather as well."

And true indeed the girls had opened up something of a lead on the boys; it seems however that they are all naturally drawn to this little tor, and they ascend.

Max has pointed out the standing stones to Maxi who peers quizzically across the moor at them with his sharp little eyes.

"Why does there be a ring of stones Dad?"

"I presume they were put there by some ancient people a long time before we got here Maxi"

"What does ancient say Dad?"

"It just means very old Maxi."

"Why didn't they have any children Dad?"

"Oh I see what you're thinking now… no, I meant ancient, meaning from a long time ago Maxi, not that they were all old people like Granny and Granddad."

"I see… and the circle of stones Dad, did they be to drive their cars round like a roundabout?"

"No Maxi, there were no cars in those days, hey, just look at that great big bird flying across the sky there!"

Will the big bird distract little Maxi from his train of thought for long; Max has never been very good at fielding questions that just lead to more questions.

"Yes Dad it's a black one… but if they lived high on these hills, how did they get to the shops without cars?"

"Ah, now if you want to know about the shops you should be asking your Mum or Anita; between them they will know how to get to every shop in the world!"

"Did they go to every shop together Dad?"

"Well obviously not Maxi, they only met each other a couple of hours ago!"

"So how did they know all the shops Dad?"

"I don't flipping know Maxi… they're women, it's a genetic thing, it comes from their mothers!"

"What's a 'gentic thing' Dad?"

"I don't know that either Max, I've run completely out of things I know… I feel as if I will probably never know anything thing again in my entire life!"

"Why won't you Dad?"

"Oh my giddy aunt Maxi…!"

The girls had lagged back from walking ahead, and so caught the tale-end of the male conversation.

"Hey Max, it sounds like you're being mean to our little boy. Don't be nasty or impatient with him just because you're older than he is."

Anita draws a breath and glances away to the furthest peaks on hearing Bel say 'our little boy'. The words and the thought tingle inside her.

She can see herself up on a high point: A high point both on the moor, and in her life.

Anita can visualise herself holding her own little Maxi in the high clean wind, and cuddled up together for warmth with their backs to some large boulder while he asks about everything that they can from there see. And she of course is never lost for an answer or irritated by his questions.

Even better if there were a father figure there too, who adored them both like a regular dad in an American film would.

It occurs to Anita that Max is a pretty good average in respect of fathers. Her own had been way out of sight by the time she was Maxi's age.

Yes, looking at this little family group, she feels she would happily change places with Bel right now: Though she can of course see the contentment in Bel's face, and has no serious expectations of a life swap. She is just a girl with a strong love of sensuous life and all its tactile roles.

Bel has gone and sat with her boy, and is asking him all he was wondering about; Anita sits down on a rock nearby.

Max has climbed to a little outcrop to clear his mind and have a look across the moor; Anita has space to muse distractedly.

She leans back, then looks down at her foot which rests on a chunk of granite.

This chunk is vaguely triangular, in some ways like a crudely cut crystal. She thinks it is around the size that a very strong man could lift. But is the short tough moorland grass grown up around its seated base, or could it be just the protruding tip of a lump as big as Cornwall!

Whichever, it in unarguably grey. This colour Anita had always assumed, was the intrinsic colour of the rock. Perhaps that is true, but what you are really looking at on the surface are a patchwork camouflage of several lichens, not rock.

First there is a flat rough grey one, as if an old tin of congealed matt emulsion paint had been slooshed here and there on the rock.

There is also a black growth almost with leaves, though in lots of ways more fungal in appearance. It strikes Anita that it is half between something grown on land and a miniature dried shrivelled seaweed.

Leaning forward towards her foot Anita can see that the first one has got what appear like numerous crustacious growths on its wizened surface, as if it were the barnacles on a break-water.

The third and prettiest lichen is also grey, but grows into a tangle of tiny dry scratchy arms, like diminutive wind-tugged thorn bushes on the Sussex downs.

Anita taps her toe on its rock as if she were preparing to break into song to entertain her new friends; or to sing something to summon the elves and spirits of the moor to attend her: yet nothing comes, either in the form of song or elves.

Looking beyond her little lump *(or tip of subterranean Cornwall!)* her eye falls clumsily onto a veritable operatic stage, or equally could be a transported corner-stone from the Statue of Liberty. Whether attached to the rest of Cornwall or not it must weigh hundreds or even thousands of tons.

There is a mystifying little valley weaving across this flat rock's generally level surface from where all forests of lichen are absent. But if you get close enough you will see that it's not bare rock but a river of that old emulsion paint lichen. Anita wonders, for how many millions of years this particular lichen has held this valley over the otherwise level surface of the slab.

Her thought also plays with images of little Maxi; or some child of his type and likeness, and all these things today are interwoven.

Anita is absorbed by her terrestrial investigations, and as she leans forward over her folded arms and ponders life nature and the child of her future, her thumbs travel up and down across her nipples until a warm glow tingles in her spine.

In her mind's eye she has just found a little Maxi, a year or more younger than this one, and seemingly abandoned on the moor. He is crying for a breast and she is there like a miracle.

Of course her little mental mothering play does not include such complications as the need to ascertain how the baby came to be out there alone on the moor, or how he was then disposed of, so to speak. The dream just sails on with Anita, as if chosen by the gods being deemed the natural choice to be the boy's mother.

Seeing the valley of lichen managing to search out its meagre life on the hard stone, confirms in her mind that it will be less hard for her than for many to find a continuance of life and growth in her time.

This slightly tingling, quietly smiling female sends her eyes beyond the slab stage granite that footlights her feet.

Greenness of sharp vertical and bunched upwards with tassel growth near top tilt leeward.

The tussock'd moor-grass silver leaf winds sharply round where sudden whistling whirlwind cork-screws past.

What little dry unattached debris it has raised, is swept along and swirled around with spiralled haste.

The vortex recedes, sweeping and circling across the moor.

She feels its passing, hears its haunted moan; it breathes like suspended resonant wires of a telephone, across forsaken tumbleweed blown railroad station.

Her eyes sight the horizon. Green to powder grey dissolves, till distant silver must she would suppose be sea beyond St. Austell.

In the seven minutes since she sat she has been where? Perusing lichen, feeding infants, dodging whirlwinds, dreaming over miles of green: Searching through her future world for where she wants her life to be?

Max is back from his wander up across the rocks behind them.

"Hey Maxi, do you want to come across the moor with me to have a closer look at that stone circle? I can give you a piggy-back if your little legs are tired."

"Yes please Dad… and can we gallop?"

"Blimey mate you don't want much do you. It all looks pretty rough going across there but we'll see if we can get a bit of a trot now and then."

"Hey Max, do you want us to come too?"

"I think we'll leave the women behind shall we Maxi, we can travel much faster on our own."

"Yeah come on Dad."
Mum wears a face of hurt at being left out, though she likes to see them going off together. Anita feels a bit left out too; though that's a more general desire to have some of this tactile life of children for herself at some point in the not too distant future.

Maxi is already mounted up and they are off down the bank.
He loves the feel of jolting up and down on his dad's back, and being so high above the swishing moor grass as they stride and sometimes canter for a few steps; though never quite gallop.
There are boggy bits where Max has to jump as best he can from tussock to tussock, and the water in the grass between comes over your boots.
Sometimes they get too ambitious considering the weight on his back and fall splashing short with oaths and curses… and wet socks.

A little over five minutes sees their arrival at the stones of this nearest side of the circle. Maxi shoots to the floor like a fireman down his pole and is straight off on his little legs zig-zagging between the stones to circumnavigate the periphery.

Max thinks that he should head round the opposite way and shorten little Maxi's journey to save some of his energy. It strikes him that he should have made Max walk on the way over, and then just carried him back.

Max engineers a head on collision with his lad and lifts him high.

Bel sees her colourful little bundle lifted in the air and smiles from her distant perch. She feels that this place will always be a sort of home, or somewhere to return to with Maxi as he grows. But she cannot for a moment imagine that he will still be coming here when she is long dead, and he himself has almost run his time.

The Max's have sat down puffing on the grassy tundra.

"If they didn't have cars Dad… then why did they make a roundabout?"

In a flash of inspiration, and keen not to be told again that he is mean to his boy:

"Well they were probably built for their children to go running around Max."

"Oh I see Dad… were they running around here before I went to bed?"

"You mean were they here yesterday Maxi don't you. No Max, it's a long time before you were in Mummy's tummy; it's even before I was small like you."

"I want a wee Dad."

"Okay Maxi, and as it happens, so do I. Hey look right in the middle there, a big flat stone; come on let's both go on that."

Maxi likes the idea of that and they scramble up and race to the middle of the circle. Two released jets of piss douse the slab of granite and Maxi thinks this is a great game.

As Max finishes and sorts his trousers, and his boy's, he lifts his eye and sees a procession of strangely dressed figures approaching them from a fairly short way across the scruffy hillside. Now too there are staffs jerking angrily in the air and a rising collective voice of agitation and resentment.

The group has long everything *(that is visible)*: Beards, gowns, hair, toes sticking from their flappy sandals, and these long old staffs with heavy clubby lumps or something on their ends.

The immediate impression that you get is that they were on their way here to do or perform something. Something that they seem from their approaching steaming appearance to feel has had its ambience ruined by two hippies hosing the stone that they were going to do it on.

It has taken Max five point seven seconds to realise that he and his boy 'are in the wrong place and at the wrong time'.

"Okay Maxi, quickly onto my back, we've got a Druid problem, and it's one that I think can best be solved by us being somewhere else, so up you come."

They are off like Highwaymen back towards the outcrop, where the girls who have already twigged that all is not well have clambered down from the rocks to be ready to make a swift exit.

Bel lifts Maxi from his dad's back and Max looks back askance to the ring of stones and sees the first man stamp around in a small circle with cries of frustration, flinging his apparently now wasted and useless ceremonial staff to the floor.

Then turning across the moor towards the hippie clan, howls something about...

"All day... all day to process from the southern tumuli to here... and you vandals have driven the spirits out for another ten years... we'll get you back for this."

Then he goes loopy and starts a frantic rush towards them, but his sandals run up the inside of his sack-cloth gown and drag it off his shoulders till he launches like a space rocket with his arms pinned to his sides by the neck-hole, and wallops face down in the bog. Like a ricochet, a stupendous ripping fart belches viciously from his arse in the impact of his landing.

Worming his shoulders back down into the neck of his gown and making his arms free again, the spitting Druid raises himself up on his elbows and gets a fix on the hippie group. He sees that the eyes of the child are directly on his own, and wearing a curious smile.

The Druid smarts inwardly, and steams in his bog; he thinks the child may be of all this more guilty than his drugged up hippie dad. Children he knows are closer to their origins both of birth and other lives.

Still this boy smiles quietly at him, but he wonders if the rules of time allow him to construct a spell to curse his little life with; yet feels as well these eyes would have no fear of his spells, and are speaking to him.

He drags himself up from the bog and squelches back towards his fellow priests… a couple of them are grinning quietly at their feet.

Max looks a little nervous, but is able to speak more confidently to his womenfolk, like an ancient tribal leader might have done in times of stress.

"Well I reckon we've seen the best of today's entertainment, shall we head back to the van now girls?"

"Why did that man be singing at us Mum… why was he wearing a nightie… and why did he jump onto his tummy with a splash?"

"I'll tell you as we go along Maxi; hold my hand love, or would you like to be carried back."

"Can I run around the stones again with you and Dad?"

"Yes we will love… but not right now of course, that funny man with the big nightie who jumped into the water will probably like to sit quietly there for a while Maxi."

The hippie clan sets off quietly, and at first all are too concerned with sorting their own thoughts about the last few minutes to say much to each other. But as time passes, one will find a thought that one more also had, and soon the word of all is common currency again.

On the way back Max is the only one who does much rubber-necking for pursuing Druids. It is after all him who they would want if they did come.

He toys with the naughty thought of offering them Anita for ritual sacrifice, and wonders if they would just follow the previous example of High Priest Maximus and roger her ceremoniously or even unceremoniously? No he thinks, these guys seem to take things far too seriously with regard to doing it all properly for them to be diverted by or tempted into any hanky-panky.

They would say *'no thank you, that's just not the sort of thing we like doing; we much prefer to be muttering spells and incantations to a lump of rock, than wasting our energy on a comely slave-girl.'*

But if Max carried her out to them in her grass skirt and trussed at the ankles and wrists, would it be... *'well, just leave her down there for the moment, and we'll take a closer look at her later.'*

"Well they'll have to fight me for her... she's in the Turner clan now,"

He glances a little guiltily at Bel as he surfaces from his naughty thoughts and plods across the moor. He can feel himself beginning to become a little possessive over his womenfolk.

"Blimey, I've got to try and loosen up on this a bit. What will happen if there is a night of free love at the camp; I will become an excommunicated hippie if I'm too possessive to play along with things. Mind you: I'm buggered if I'm going to watch anyone else having a crack at Bel and just offer to look after his trousers for him while he's busy.

"I suppose if I was giving Anita one at the same time it might be OK. There again it could be like one of those dinner parties Mum and Dad go to where you have to sit with someone else rather than your spouse. It works fine with that because they all hate being married to whoever it is and can't get far enough away from them. If this was going to be my only good chance

to have a crack at Anita, it would be a bugger if someone came up and said: 'Come on mate, house rules, you can't have one you brought with you.'

"Yeah now that's another thing: What if Bel is slipped a length here and there, and a month later we find she's 'up the duff'; I'm all for free love but babies cost a lifetime and a lot of money!"

With these sundry passing thoughts he ambles but rather briskly on; and thirty minutes finds them at the van again.

Behind them the moor seems to ring with a disconsolate wailing and gnashing of teeth from Druids who will have to wait another ten years to evoke some deity or other; but if it can only be bothered to turn up every ten years is it worth the trouble. Tragic perhaps, but small beer in the wider scheme of things.

Wide green slopes lead their feet back across the face of Roughtor, nor does he see any resentful druids sculking behinds its giant mushroom rocks… though he is still alert to what might be on either flank or crept along behind?

Has been thinking what best to do as the moor and the Druids recede behind and they get nearer to the van… speaks now manfully to his womenfolk:

"I don't really fancy going straight to the camp and getting tangled up in some new scene before we've had time to wind down properly: Does anyone fancy going back into Camelford or somewhere for a beer to chill-out first?"

"Sounds Okay Max, but we should ask if Anita was due to be anywhere or see anyone else today?"

"Oh nothing guys… it's my day off and I was just stooging about looking for a bit of life in a beautiful but otherwise rather desolate wilderness.

"But hey, perhaps you want some time to be alone as a family… or as the time is getting on, maybe to be getting Maxi settled in the van: what time does he mostly want to sleep?"

"When he's ready Anita, he just puts his head down where ever we are and he's gone… but that's hours away yet."

"Well, in case I never do find Marlo tonight I am going to buy you lot a beer."

"And me be drinking beer as well?"

"Yes of course Maxi; they even do a special beer for little boys at the pub where Marlo bought me beer the other night. Yeah, that's somewhere that you guys might like to go while you're down here. It's 'The Rising Sun' and it's a few miles down off the other side of the aerodrome. It's a bit dead at lunchtime, but I am told it can be pretty wild of an evening."

"Anita, you are describing the pub we seek. What we can still see of each other now are in fact just our astral remains. We are already in the Something Sun drinking beer."

"It was the Rising Sun Max. So all aboard if anyone fancies a beer; unless of course you believe Max that we are already there, and this is just our astral remains, then you can just stay where you are and enjoy your astral beer."

This moorland car park is pretty much chokka with cars of all types: Morris, Ford, and Vauxhall; and even quite a number of foreign ones. Most of course are families who have come to climb up to the mushroom rocks on the peak. Others are less obviously a statement of their owner's type of aspiration, and at least a couple have a rather unusual and suspiciously religious or occultist looking sticker in the window.
But these hippie dudes we see are off and firing out along the lane.
Fields to silvered grey dissolve, till lines of green we would suppose be firs that cloak the airfield's flanks; now rumbling cattle-grid throws sucking rattle at the wheels and speedo slumps.
Then onto causeway long and straight, where in forty years about from now, a grown-up little Maxi will be riding when two big custom bikes will come the other way; and but that he will not remember, yet being faced again this way he will subconsciously recall this line of sight.

He then will raise his now just little fist, that then will be a bunch of fives, and will not know that these two bikes have Germans at the helm, nor that one will later prove to be a touchy beggar!

But that enthusiastic raised arm will shape his world, resulting in the arrival of Anna; and that lead in turn to the birth of Milo, Ulla, and Francesca.

About halfway along the causeway on the left side is an amorphous circling clump of white; with two black streaks that circumnavigate. A few flakes still split off and curve away and cross the road. As the campervan approaches they decide to cross back, then change their mind and veer away again, as a glancing Anita exclaims wide eyed:

"Hey, that was Marlo… that guy directing the dogs there; can we stop in that lay-by and I'll see if he's coming down to 'The Sun' as well."

They anchor up, … so Anita can run across to see if he's coming to 'The Sun'.

The Turner family sit in their van and wait. Max looks up into his rear view mirror to watch Anita run attractively back along the road and across the grass to Marlo.

He is watching her body language… when you have spent the whole afternoon watching somebody's body, you may as well see if it's got anything to say.

He wants not to see her approaching someone that she has much previous knowledge of or commitment to. He feels a pang of envy because she is smiling up into the shepherd's eyes as she waits for a response to something she has just asked. He gets a twinge when Anita laughs and squeezes Marlo's shoulder before standing back with her head tipped on one side.

Her arms fold beneath and lift her breasts like she is making an offer for Marlo to try one of her home-made cakes!

But Max knows also that this is no good, and he turns and looks back at his own woman: hmm… hardly in Anita's league looks wise it is true, but still a tidy bit of kit; but more than that she's the mother of his son.

With this he feels old; he has never contemplated the closure of his life of chance before, but sees that now he is no longer listed in the run of young male flesh: he is already marked down by evolution as having reproduced his genes and further spawn will be a bonus but not vital.

As Anita ran away back down the road she was also retreating from his already copied genes towards a virgin male whose offspring will be unique to the wider clan.

But the worst bit of this is that it means accepting… that once you could challenge any situation that was not how you would have it be; now simply the arrival of his offspring tells the world that he is hardly there in any way that once he was; and in an eerie way has him marked down… for death?

Anita has come bouncing back to the window like an angelic fleshly blessing from the gods, and Max squints to try and stop his pupils from dilating as she throws pheromones across for him to inhale.

"Ah that's really brilliant guys… Marlo will be down as soon as he's separated off a couple of his sheep that shouldn't be with the others. I'm so pleased you guys will be able to meet him, he was so kind to give me a lift home the other night. You'll see what the hill would've been like if I had cycled back up from 'The Sun'."

"And I don't suppose for one moment that the warmth and silky smoothness of your inner thigh had 'sod-all' to do with his kind offer."
Max feels like a misplaced pickle in a jar of olives, all spiced up but prepared for the wrong dish, and wishing that his immediate future lay elsewhere just now.

"Yeah he sounds like a really nice kind of guy Anita. It will be good to chat with him and find out about his life out here on the moor. Though I expect there are lots of things we have in common… I mean like music maybe; I could let him have a look through my stack of cassettes, but being a shepherd, it's more likely that he's into folk music, you know with penny whistles and skin drums and all that traditional stuff."

"All he talked about whenever any mention of music came up was Jimi Hendrix, and he said it was his ambition to in some way follow in Jimi's footsteps… oh yes, but as he hasn't got time to learn the guitar right now all he can do is, I think he called it, 'echo his memory' or something like that."

"Right that's great Anita, we'll have that to share as well."
Anita has climbed back into the van and settled and smoothed her little cotton skirt like a mother smoothing butter icing on her child's birthday cake.

"You said 'as well', what was the other thing you'll both have that you can share Max?"

(Who spoke then, can you say; for doubtless both had wondered what 'the other thing' was on his mind. Yet maybe one at least has got an inkling; is it from the object of his fantasy, or the mother of his child?)
He quickly redirects his thoughts, and answers;

"Share…? Well just being blokes I suppose. You know, we can talk about our sort of things can't we."
And no one will pursue him down the alleyway of doubt so now he drives away along the causeway, and prompting Anita,

"Just tell me if we need to turn off anywhere."

"No Max, it's just one road all the way; you'll see it on the right in a few miles. But watch out as we get further down because the lane gets quite narrow and windy."

'*As where road gets single, and Landrover and dozy shepherd arguing with his dog comes blasting through, and Max's sidecar has to climb the bank.*'

Yes that glimpse ahead is Maxi in his forties, and riding on what is going to be his motorbike and sidecar, and encountering an ageing Marlo when they are both ten years into the next century.
We can forget that just for now, as they cruise along the long thin strip of the causeway, a pool cue pointing at the horizon. The onboard atmosphere is like a British Railways mini-bus that has collected stranded passengers who were held up and detrained by a points failure or a derailment; and now after half an hour of doubt as to their homeward journey are on their way once more.

Maxi sits up on Bel's lap and craning his neck to see over the dash board and further out in front asks,

"Were we here before I went to bed Mum?"

But Bel explains that they just came down to Cornwall today, and tonight will be their first bedtime here. It's often hard to tell what Maxi means or what he's thinking, and often he just gets smiled at or thrown a few words by his mum or dad.

So sailing on the brow of open air, another rattled cattle-grid they leave the moor and slide through fields rough hedged and pockmarked like the moon. Here and there the pasture top soil is so thin that grey slabs lift from greeny growth, as bald men's scalps ascend through hair.

Then further on where trees begin, and a million years of peat and silt that washed in tumbled streams has cloaked the valley floor, the road sinks in.

In hazel hedgy khaki dimness, lanes run deep and fields ascend, until like a metal four-wheeled mole we drive blindly closed by fern hung banks; and wormy leafmould beds the fragrant loam of scrumpled floor both sides, above our heads.

Not long it will be…

"It's not far now Max… there you go, at the end of this straight!"

"Yep got you Anita… hey I reckon I've deserved this pint for all that I've been through today."

"Yeah that pissed off Druid was a bit of a drag I guess."

"And I've driven all the way from the south-east today Anita!"

"Of course Max… yes, I was forgetting you'd just arrived today; now you've driven best part of ten miles back the way you came because of my suggestion."

"Make it worth my while chic and I won't hold it against you."
"Oh it was good that we came across each other Anita, it's been nice for Bel to have another girl in the camp."

In the car-park is to swung, and as they park Maxi remembers and gets well excited at the prospect of his special little boy's beer. As Maxi jumps out and runs across the stones towards a swing in the garden Bel asks Anita quickly:

"Yes Anita, what did you have in mind for Maxi's special beer?"

"Yes I know Bel, and I'd forgotten totally. It just came into my head at the time. Hmm… what about if we get a half pint glass of water then tip half of it away and top it up with beer, that's hardly going to hurt him is it?"

"It will make him sleep I should think, but what is it going to taste like Anita?

"Complete piss-water I should think, but if he can get himself psyched up enough to start with he'll probably love it."

"Yeah that's true I suppose, but you're a nasty mean thing Anita, I pity your kids; isn't there some way we can make it taste nice as well for him."

"We could put some coke in it Bel."

"Look we may be hippies, but I think that spiking Maxi's drink with cocaine is going too far!"
As they stand there chuckling in the late sun and watching Maxi swing, Bel puts the arm of friendship round her comrade's shoulder and gives her a hug; then a sudden kiss on her face.
Max glances up from the engine door bay as he tops-up the ever sinking oil level, and muses on how easily girls embrace and it mean nothing. Well not nothing he thinks, it must be touch and companionship, but to mean nothing sexual. He supposes that it begins at their mother's breast and just goes on from there.
Thinking about Anita and breasts he feels suddenly hungry now, and goes in search of the second lot of pasties that they bought and never ate as they rumbled along the A30.

His search bears fruit. Munching contentedly he wanders to the garden and calls to his little man. Maxi is fast to come and rewarded by a good chunk torn off for him.

Sitting cross-legged in the sun, with his lump of pasty in his lap Maxi is perhaps not unlike a small primate; or an early Hominid, gorging itself in the late moorland sun, and his appearance says that right now there is nothing else in the world worth noticing: to be eating is to be doing everything he wants.

A pleasant singing tone of femininity rings as from the morning throstle, its exhalting question non-specific but as clear as the lifting daylight, and yes Max signals that they should go on in and he will follow when him and he have done with the food and the oscillation of the swing.

There are pleasant though strange feelings for Max: Feelings like that very little about this journey west has reached any sort of, well platform perhaps; so therefore he feels they are still waiting for the arrival of their arrival to arrive.

There is something else that he also feels in this place: maybe that it is not foreign, with no implied urgency to continue away from it. Maxi goes back and forth on the swing, not like a child who goes back and forth on someone's swing, but as if it is his own swing that back and forth he goes on.

He seems very here.

Maxi looks very established beneath these larches and these serried ranks of shifting twittering linnets overhead.

Maxi is not swinging like a small boy swings, with frantic swinging legs and flailing chains. He goes back and forth, and back and forth, and his face is upturned into the ascending larches.
The tisking linnets nip through the twigs and needles as would airborne mice as he watches their quick jumping and catching feet go twig to twig, with their microsecond advance of wings opening, and then delay at next twig they land on. With his acute young eyes Maxi swings to and fro and now will know how little birds move through trees.

He knows also that there will be special beer inside for him. Maxi knows that it is something new and grown-up; and because he sees big men want always to be drinking it, thinks it must be something like the sweetest chocolate ever eaten, but crimson and glowing like the caramel coating on a toffee-apple. He wonders why something that would be so perfect for children to drink is kept from them for so long. Is it because children are always naughty?

The firs above him sweep and slow, and sweep and slow, and he feels loath to stop this riding wave and lulled dream of branches and light. A yawn makes him quickly check that mum or dad did not see it and start making his bed.

Maxi hears familiar voices near and drags his feet to slow and turn to see what's what:

Bel and Anita have come back out with two drinks apiece and words that it was just too nice to stay inside. There are three straight pint glasses, and one half-pint proper tankard glass with a handle and circular dents on the outside.

There is the atmosphere of a celebration, or an initiation for Maxi into imbibing the nectar of life.

Max leans conspiratorially to Bel to ask what's in the special beer and learns it's fifty fifty beer and water. Bel says to Maxi,

"But if you want it a bit sweeter Maxi we can drink some of it off and put some of my coke in it."

Maxi cannot understand why they should think he will want it even sweeter than it already is; that could even make it sweet enough to make him sick. No he is quite sure that beer is going to be quite sweet enough for him.

"There you are Maxi, is it too heavy for you to hold?"

It wouldn't have mattered if they had given him a solid lead German litre glass, somehow he would have wrestled it to his lips.

He wants the first taste to be so mind blowingly orgasmicaly perfect that it has to be a huge swig.

The tankard meets his lips at last and he tilts to imbibe his future.

All eyes are on him as he gulps. For one point two seconds his taste buds and neurones rush together and fill their lungs to burst into a hallelujah chorus… but all must halt, the unswallowed second half of his huge gulp occupies the cavern of his mouth, bitter, and dry, and unsweet, like the dirtiest trick ever. His brain is almost dragged in half by the desperate yearning to love his beer, and the almost unstoppable urge to blurt it back into the glass.

All eyes are on him and which way will the beer go, back to glass or down gullet: The options sit on ridge of roof and which way will they slide.

His little face is a picture of screwed up concentration but his eyes look suddenly much older; we see trust that Bel would not be poisoning him and determination not to be beaten in life if at all possible.

Gulp… and it's gone. Now his eyes have changed to triumph as Bel and Anita and Max cheer and applaud. In his second swig the shock of it not being sweet has gone and though the bitterness dries his mouth rather it is fighting a losing battle against his determination to like beer.

So later when they're in the pub he can clamber up at the bar and ask for,

(A pint of fifty fifty please landlord)

Bel tells Maxi that they won't be able to let him drink beer in the pub which he accepts well enough. In his mind it just confirms how grown up he was being for his age.

At three years old you don't have much control of your status in the world: but drinking beer is a pretty good start.

The campers now from the garden decamp, and after Bel has opened a tin of cat-food for Frank and sorted his litter tray they head from the sombre settling tones of evening into the clamorous light of the bar: a wheeze of interest lifts as they come in.

Sure, people already knew that the 'welcome girl' in the little cotton skirt had reappeared, and was outside with a hippie family.

As they come inside people refocus and recall, and refix on image of some days ago; as many who are here were here that day.

Joe smiles at Anita's re-arrival and confers with Old William. He wonders if it will be long before Marlo turns up too.

They troop with their glasses to a table at the east end, but Maxi drags his feet and trips them up because he is transfixed by the head of a fox who looks resentful, yet defiantly down from a wretched nailing on the beam at centre of the bar.

His beady eye has eagerness: *'Just give me another chance out there in the bracken you bastards, and I would've broken right up that little river valley and not thrown it away in the gorse on the slopes of 'Brown Willy*

Maxi is actually quite scared: is the rest of the fox up in the ceiling? Is it made to sit with its head out of the hole all the time?

Bel sees his thoughts and goes back to touch it and show him that it's just the shell of a broken life, and no longer a living creature.

Joe grins at Maxi and tells him he can remember the day that fox was caught, and a few weeks on that head being brought in here and fixed up on the beam. Bel tells Joe that Maxi thought it was a real one up in the ceiling.

As they make themselves comfortable Bel sees Maxi only has a tee-shirt on, and comments that after a day in the sun and the wind he will be feeling chilled soon.

"I'll pop back out to get his wooly jumper Bel, I'll get some more drinks when I get back ladies."

Max re-crosses to the half-deserted stony car-park; with sun now gone behind the moor and sinking to the sea no doubt.

He hears the squeal of bald tyres taking a bend not far along the lane and turns to watch.

A motor's clatter opens and increases as it nears the bend, when you would think to hear it throttle back; a big old Oxford lunges round and aims diagonally across the yard. But sailing past it all goes quiet and door swings open as if a body is being thrown out.

It's the driver who has vaulted out and walking towards the pub while his abandoned car squeals hand-brake dragging to a gentle thud on further bank.

Max's first thought is that it must be some drug crazed hippie from the camp and starts to wonder if they should be taking Maxi there. He is aware that sometimes he thinks like his old-man rather than a hippie.

The dark haired striding lad sees his open mouth and calls hello, and something about Anita, and a push-bike and his boot.

Of course Max knows it's Marlo then, and glad to lose the clutter of the bike he pulls it out and offers it.

He sees how eagerly Marlo takes it, and thinks it seems to be a link to an aspiration of some sort: Not being a 'Gripper', Max is pretty fast to twig that it must give Marlo promise of a crack at Anita; as Marlo is, he would be too.

"I guess you're Marlo, well I'm Max and I was just about to get a round in. What do you fancy Marlo? (*"Apart from Anita."*)

"Yeah thanks Max, I'll have a pint of 'Doom' if it's on… though you may find Anita wants to get mine; she says she still wants to say thanks for her lift back to The Vicarage the other night."

Max ponders momentarily,

"Ah, so it's true that you didn't get to exact payment in kind then Marlo… hmm, yes she did say about a beer, but what to think: Does that leave the field more open, or suggest she keeps it all to herself?"

"Yes I remember her saying earlier about you giving her a lift with her bike the other night."

Marlo hauls the door open for Max to be first to the bar. They enter to a muted chorus of 'heyo boy' and 'it's that wanker Marlo', and he in return hugs Old William kisses his crown and fondly polishes his bald patch with his sleeve.

Marlo passes a wink and a nod to Joe, then spots Anita up the end with Bel and Maxi and like a bee to a honey-pot is drawn to the stool beside her.

"Hello Anita… and while I think of it, your bike's in my boot."
Anita sounds already a little bit tiddly in her giggled response:

"For a minute Marlo, I thought you had said 'your boot's on my foot!' But thanks Marlo, that's really kind. Yes let me get out to the bar and I can pay for that beer that Max is getting for you. Before I go, This is Bel and Maxi… oh and Bel, we may get another chance to talk more together about it later on perhaps."

Marlo turns to redirect his attention to Bel and he asks the usual stuff about where they are from and what they've done so far. He is of course quite genuinely surprised to hear that they were chased from the moor by embittered Druids.

Anita gets to Max and gives him thirty new-pence to cover Marlo's pint.

Bel hears all about Marlo's flock and his daily routine on the moor and his plans to get a place in Launceston where he can live more in the style of his hero Jimi Hendrix. And Bel finds it hard to picture anywhere down here that you could live in the style of Hendrix, but she keeps that to herself.

"Have you got a wife or girlfriend Marlo?"

"Christ no Bel… well I suppose unless you count Ginny, as we see each other now and then, but it's really nothing serious Bel."

"How long have you been seeing her Marlo?"

"A little over three years now."

"Blimey Marlo, when you got to three I thought you would say months. Three years is as long as I've been living with Max. Are you quite sure that Ginny wouldn't think it was a serious relationship Marlo?"

"Oh I shouldn't think so Bel, she must know that I'm planning to be a rock musician soon. Everyone knows that you have to hang pretty loose in that kind of a life."

Bel has already picked up that Marlo has not learned the guitar yet; her next question is far more aimed at striking a blow for the sister she has never met and who she assumes is being strung along to be at some point dumped when he is ready to shoot to stardom.

Clearly stardom isn't going to happen, but the picture of Ginny discarded and alone fires Bel up a little.

"I really admire the life you've chosen Marlo… do you play a Fender or a Gibson?"

"Oh yes well… what right now you mean?"

"Yes, at any time, like just when you play your stuff of course!"

"Well just at the moment it's neither Bel… until now the flock has taken so much of my time and energy that it's not really been very easy, if you know what I mean."

"Oh yes, hard to get enough practice in I suppose. Have you ever played anything to Anita or Ginny Marlo?"

"At this very moment in time Bel...? I mean I might well be playing to one of them very soon… but right now, I haven't em… haven't started learning the guitar yet Bel… nor even bought one."

"Oh I misunderstood you Marlo, I'm sorry; I had thought this new life as a rock musician was something that you were just about to go off and do any time now?"

"No not in the next couple of months Bel."

Bel steps back from her somewhat partizan attack as she knows she has used the situation and information she held unknown, to take advantage of someone who is really not a sinner in any great sense.
She brings her ship across the wind and says more softly:

"Look, good luck Marlo, I really hope you get things together and get a chance to start learning the guitar sometime soon."

"Yea thanks Bel, I know it can happen if I can just get myself into the right frame of mind. But sometimes I think: Blimey, it's nineteen seventy-one already, Jimi's dead, and is the music scene just going to fade away before I can get going. Will I get my guitar and head on to London and find that everyone's gone home to be plumbers and… well shepherds I suppose. I am so scared that I will just miss it all.
You know Bel, I was just too remote here to be part of the start of the hippie thing. I wanted to do the 'free love' thing. I didn't want to jump straight into some mid-terrace in Camelford with
nothing except children and sheep to look forward to for the next forty years.
Look Bel… between you and me alright… I've only ever been with one girl in my life, that's Ginny. Even then it's not been proper no holds barred sex sort of stuff; she says she'll take no risks until we're, well at least engaged.
So all this free love and stuff Bel, it must be really fantastic, I mean have you two done much of it, you know with other hippies and friends and so on?"

"No Marlo, never… oh yes sometimes we've been doped up with friends and lying around with our heads on other people's legs, and when I know Max isn't looking I've kissed a boy's bulge to be a bit flirty. Once I let a bloke I knew 'tit me up' inside my shirt for a few minutes. But no, no I've never had another bloke inside me if I can put it like that to you Marlo, not in the last three years that is: And we won't talk about the one I was going out with before that because I was only fifteen."

"Oh Jesus Bel, that's just it you see, I've been standing behind the door all this time. I'm twenty-eight now, and when I sort of lost my cherry I was more or less ten years older than you were when you lost yours."

"Oh Marlo, this would be probably be better left unsaid but when I actually lost my virginity I was twelve!"

He was about to go on and point out that although he is about ten years older than Bel she had had sex…

"Sorry we took so long getting back with your drinks guys, Old William was telling us all about Marlo and what to avoid and watch out for with him."
Little Maxi looks up eagerly as they enstool.

"Have you got me special beer again; I like it because it makes my head move funny."
Max says that he's got orange juice this time, and that the vitamins will make him big and strong so that tomorrow he can carry him across the moor on his back!
Anita remarks to Marlo that there is a nice pool table through the other half of the bar, and wonders if he or Max are any good at pool. Both the boys are pretty keen on having a game with Anita and make enthusiastic noises about the game. Anita says they should play each other and that she would rather sit with Bel and Maxi.
She asks Marlo what coin the table takes and then finds three in her purse:

"There guys, now you can play the best of three!"

Max and Marlo file away with their coins and their beer. Going with a look and thought that this was not exactly what their dreams were made of in respect of the evening. They look a little bit sent: Like children told to go and play outside.

The best of it will be made and displayed of course, nor show they will disappointment; in fact Max can imagine that the women folk will get a bit lonely back there, and be extra receptive when the lads get back from hunting in the forest.

So *'up the balls are racked and war begins'* but it's not really a war that pounds at the walls of anyone's castle. Often they will have paused between shots while Max may ask what Marlo knows of Anita, or Marlo what Max might choose if he could summon up his most desired free love situation.

Max has no idea that Marlo has already been told by Bel that they have never done any real free love stuff. He is quite happy to let Marlo believe that he's seen some action now and then; and Marlo quite happy to believe him.

Max can tell as they speak that Marlo is not some woman killing swarthy Thomas Hardy type shepherd, but just some chap who has spent too many years chasing his sheep and his dreams around a moor.

Increasingly he likes this chap. He sees he's not a threat to his own ample ego, 'the leader of the tribe'. Max would never think he's got an ample ego; he would just see it as if he has been chosen to bestow calming authority and sexual acquirement on more than one female, and that they can *(the females)* all benefit by their joint association.

Well, that's vaguely the gist of how he would see things working out.

Now Max has vague wonderings. He wonders if while they play pool, the girls are chewing over the thought of a love in, and because Marlo is one of the group tonight it will not just be as Max had conjectured, a three-way show, but four-way.

Of course Max doesn't like the thought of any one else getting their todger into Bel's belly really, Free love or not; but he isn't half keen for the chance to lay some pipe on Anita.

If free love is in the air, this is his chance while they are playing pool to strike some deal with Marlo, get some ground rules agreed, like about where the vinegar stroke can actually be struck for example.

Max decides to sound Marlo out about all this. He begins throwing a few thoughts across the table between shots. His questions reveal that Marlo is certainly up for some free-love.

First Max needs to ascertain if Marlo has only got eyes for Anita: If he has, that would scupper everything; you can hardly have a proper love-in with your own woman.

A few carefully worded questions reveal that Marlo has got burning loins for Anita, but wouldn't turn his nose up at anything half reasonable that came along if it seemed receptive. A secondary, but more direct question as to what he reckons to Bel, brings a politely careful but enthusiastic enough verbal appreciation. So all that is left to do now, is for Max to reveal his desire to get to grips with Anita for there to be smoke issuing from the chimney of the Vatican.

The lads have chosen a Pope without even shaking hands.

"Well Max, it's one game apiece; should we play a decider to see who comes out on top? All things being equal we should both end up on top!"

"Yes I'll drink to that one Marlo, except as I said not to another baby; but don't worry Marlo, Bel gives really good head. But with regard to another game, it's up to you Marlo, but I don't think we really need to; I think it would be cool to get back round to the girls and see what if anything they've been cooking up."

"When I went round to the 'bogs' ten minutes back, I glanced across the bar to their table and they both seemed to be in very close discussion about something Max. So you think maybe…"

"…Well absolutely Marlo, they must have been saying something that they didn't want the next table to hear. It was a husband and wife beside them so they wouldn't have much to talk about and will be ear-wigging like fury to try and relieve the monotony."

"Thinking about it Max, Maxi was on Bel's lap and she had a hand over one of his ears. Mind you, he looked half asleep anyway."

"So whatever happens he'll have to be taken to the van soon by the sound of it Marlo."

The would-be free love hippy dudes pick up their beer and pullovers and eager as soon as possible to be wearing as little as needed they weave back through the tangle of the bar.

The table wears the mood of love and the atmosphere of celebration.

Maxi is all dreamy eyed and almost gone, but now on Anita's lap side-saddle, and with the side of his face against the cushion of her breast.

What are his dreams?
There's none to say…
But dream he certainly does,
And what will be will be.

The guys sort their places round the table and both swig their beers. They sit reclined and nonchalant, wanting not to disclose their cunning deductions about the likely fruitful progress of the evening. Or their devilish treaty that should get them each more quickly on top of the right woman.

Max is pretty eager to get to the bottom line but plays it cool. He might as well let them open the batting then he has the upper hand in steering it the way he wants it to go.

He has asked about getting Maxi to bed and Bel says she'll be sorting him quite soon.

Anita adds that she wants to be helping with that too, and Max hears a tone of physical inclusion creeping in that he is happy about.

As they chat and laugh about the Druids, and what if they turn up tonight, and whether to get some more beers in, Bel brings things round to what she loves about life as a hippie.

"Yeah guys… I was telling Anita how we love our world and all we find in it. And how that extends to physical love in lots of ways; you know, like with our children, and our friends children;

and sharing love with our friends as well, physical love I mean of course… we both agree on that don't we Max?"

"That's all cool… yes you know I dig it, and I was playing pool just now with Marlo and telling him how we feel about life and the world wasn't I Marlo."

"Yeah that's it. It was amazing just how close we were on lots of things *especially the overriding desire to grapple with female flesh*… like em… thinking there should be more love in the world and so on?"

"That's really good guys, so at least we all want the same sort of life then."

"Yeah, not half *oops, that might have sounded a bit desperate, never mind we know where it's all going now* with more free love there would be fewer wars."

"And we can all drink to that one can't we? …Well, we could if most of our glasses weren't empty."

"Anyway, so me and Anita were thinking, that we would take Maxi across to the van in a few minutes and stay over there for quite a while. That's okay isn't it?"

"Yeah that's great Bel… he'll be asleep over in the back in next to no time. That will leave the whole of the middle bit clear won't it."

"Well yes, but space is no great issue for us."

"Fine Bel… then em… er shall we come across when we've had our beers?"

"Ah… I see Max. Yes I was beginning to think maybe I hadn't been quite clear: no Anita and myself want to put Maxi to bed and be there on our own… you know Max, sisters together and all that?"

"Ah yeah okay I dig it Bel… and… well of course that's cool with us. Yeah it's world love, and that's what we're all here for man isn't it."

"And I can thrash Max in another game of pool while you're em… while you're in the van."

Anita has stood up while cradling the nearly sleeping little Max Turner. Bel kisses Max senior and says they'll see him soon. He nearly asks if they have any idea what time it's likely to be but stops himself.
Bel remembers she wants the van keys, and they're gone.

Well… what to think… what not to think?
You've got two guys with all the equipment… and eager to see it pressed into service. Then you've got these two girls, apparently ripe for some attention, but who want to attend to each other.

The man and wife on the next table smile sideways at each other with a, if you live long enough, you'll see everything sort of look.
It feels a little pointless and a little public to stay at the table where they all were, so another beer and another game of pool offers them the escape they need.
Chris is behind the bar tonight.
Old William is on this side of the bar tonight with his beady hawk-like eyes.

"Two pints of Doom please landlord."
Chris grins at Marlo's implied promotion.

"One day Marlo, but a while off yet!"
And William is already waiting open-mouthed to interject.

"So the girls have gone then boys?"

"Yeah they're getting Maxi settled down for the night."

"Funny they went out at the same time as those two beefy young lads off the building site on the Polyphant road."

"I knew you'd come out with something like that William you shit stirring old goat."

The beers arrive and they head off to the pool table.

Then once more 'up the balls are racked' and Marlo breaks. This time though, the fervent crack of optimism is not there; the stroke is solid but the ring is dull and disconsolate… under the loss of what is he labouring?

Thirty minutes back he thought he was finally about to be part of a scene. He would be both doing some of the things that were utterly vital to his self-esteem as a young rock-star male, and correspondingly would be linking himself to the hippie world.

When he arrives in London it was going to be: 'Yeah sure mate; down in Cornwall we have festivals and I've done free love with dudes I hardly know. It's a good scene down there and now I've come up here to write and sing about all that cool stuff.'

Alright, saying it straight out that sounds a bit naff, but it could come out something vaguely like that.

But now that vital little toe in the door of coolness has been taken away from him. He must face swinging London without having romped naked with a hippie mum while her man got his teeth into the well fleshed Au pair that works for the Vicar and his wife.

He needs that story of them all being in one van and that he was top to tail with Bel, while her old-mans arse was pumping on the other girl not two feet away.

In London it is going to be this sort of stuff morning noon and night.

Now with them back in the van alone he'll have none of that to take with him.

Max too looks rather down at heel. He takes his next shot, then as it bounces harmlessly away from the pocket bangs the butt of his cue on the floor and says:

"What flipping good is it really going to do them…. okay, free love and sisters and all that shit… but they can't really do anything can they?"

"I wouldn't have thought there was very much Max… I suppose I don't really know, but no, I wouldn't have thought there was much worth doing."

"They may just get bored with it and come back in to get us so there's something worth doing."

The dying coal of the sun is sunk to a fleck of glimmered ashes on the distant sea.

In their curtained wheeled home Bel lounges with a smile and one arm draped over the cushioned rear bench seat to stroke Maxi's head as he breathes and sighs in the back of the van.

Anita faces her with her leg up across Bel's knee, and asks what little Max's birth was like as she loosens Bel's clothes with warm hands. The account she hears does not alarm her, and Anita's warm hands do not alarm Bel. She holds Bel's waist as if she was picking up Maxi, then pulls herself up towards her and settles her mouth onto her friend's warm mouth.

To Bel this kiss feels strange, yet strangely too, exciting. She wants to do this well; she's talked to hippie friends who gave themselves to other girls for an hour or so to find their sister spirit, but she is quite relieved that Anita seems to be taking the lead in the main and making the running.

Bel doubts that she would be able to open Anita's clothes as she has done to her, though not because of envy for her more succulent form, just for simple shyness.

Bel feels like she is clinging onto Maxi with one hand for support, and wonders also what the guys are thinking.

"I reckon you'll be lucky to get that ball in from there Marlo… cor flipin heck you almost did 'n all."

"Hey Max… what do you reckon they're actually doing at the moment? I suppose it would be wrong to creep out there to have a peep."

"Probably not a lot going on anyway Marlo. I suppose they can kiss a bit, and suckle each other a bit, and… well they haven't got any strap-on's or any tackle like vibrators so there isn't that much else really."

"Well, one could go down between the other's legs couldn't she?"

"I suppose yes, but how long for I don't know: Bel hasn't had a bath for about three days."

For now they've kissed enough, and it was nice, though Anita was certainly 'the man' if we can say that.
They hold a little open and Anita says how lovely Bel looks in this half-light and how she hopes that it is all nice for Bel.
Bel asks if she was ever with a girl before and remembers that Anita is about five years older than herself. Anita tells her about a girl she was sometimes naked and intimate with when she was about Bel's age.
Bel tries to be more active in this role and puts a hand behind Anita's neck either to caress or to move her a little, mainly just that she feels a bit of a spectator at the moment. Anita is eased forward but moves down to breast and curls her tongue around a nipple.
It is both pleasant and starts to feel like the point of no return… Bel has flashes of remembering Maxi close against her and also other times Max sneaking a taste as he did.
Is Max really fine about her seeking pleasure and worldly experience with this girl?

"I don't know about you Marlo: but I feel like a bit of a 'pork pie at a Jewish orgy stuck in this pub'."

"No I'm sure that should be 'wedding' Max. You mean 'a spare prick at an orgy maybe?'

"Okay Marlo whatever… but it wouldn't be so bad if there were a couple of girls that we could make a move on… hey but perhaps I'm being blind Marlo…?"

"What do you mean Max… hang on, I must just take this shot… Yeah, alright carry on, what do you mean by blind?"

"Well Marlo, you're a nice looking chap, I was just thinking free love etc… that perhaps you'd like to…!"

"I tell you now Max; the only action you'll get out of me is the invitation to naff-off; now get on with your shot you silly tosser!"

Bel is pretty much a tingle now, and feeling much less the spectator. When she feels Anita moving down she pushes her across and rolls instead, and down she slips.. she lifts her eyes though tongue continues. A sleepy sigh climbs up to join another's satisfied sigh and sees a little lifted arm raise in the back of the van, then fall to Anita's neck who smiles and holds it with her other hand.

Outside a sudden blinding light of multifarious song: Bel gasps 'and stops abruptly at the first note heard'.

"What is that astounding sound, or bird? Can it be a Nightingale?"

But at Anita's urgently whispered request…

…and slipping into night, and dreams, all beasts and people take their paths and roads to a little safe sleep…

… just a few days on the moor is smudged and stroked by clinging stratus cloud.

Drizzle simmers in the warm wind.

The sun not far above is strong and makes the damp shroud bright translucent to the wincing eye: it means the promise of a not bad day, so no one minds.

In the un-euphoric hippie camp, Max's mate's friend sits on a box outside his van… it is a box that sadly has no friendly and easily serviceable noose dangling above it.

He scrubs dolefully at an acoustic guitar, and nods solemnly and admiringly as he watches the fingers of his left   hand clamber crab-like from chord to chord. Sometimes they clamp optimistically and unadvisedly up the neck on what should be a barre-chord, but badly fumbled so hardly a note rings clear, and he pretends he's just doing that rhythmic Hendrix style muted strumming thing.

Each time he does successfully land on a chord, he glances up as if this suddenly were revealing a new glimpse of genius to the camp.

This gifted hippie moans as though he were afflicted by gastro-enteritis. The words you can make out are platitudes of tedium and emotional cliché.

Max slumps in the back of their van and fantasises about striding across there, snatching away his instrument of torture, and bringing it down hard onto his welcoming skull. He sees it shattered to matchwood on the offender's shoulders, with his head sprouting bulb-like through the back and out the sound-hole; and the strings retentioned and twanging over his lug-holes.

Maxi and Frank are across the slope of turf and bog grass, and not far from the stream. There are other small children and one of them has got a puppy not a lot larger than Frank, and quite probably younger.

The puppy seems to prefer to play with the kids, but Frank is so attached to this little dog that he gambles along beside it everywhere it goes.

A mum sits just away from the group twiddling grasses and with half an eye on the gang's proximity to the stream. The splashing burble runs across stones and rocks and after little rain there are no deep bits so it's pretty safe.

Having another mum on watch allows Bel to fiddle around and sort a few bits in and around their van.

She glances in at Max once or twice. She can see he has a halo of glumness today, and thinks she knows a couple of possible causes but wants to know which one it is.

"Hey tell me Max... you've seemed a bit at odds with things for the last couple of days, what's been up with you?"

"There's nothing up with me Bel... why do you say that anyway?"

"Because I can tell that you're not right; I mean can you really say that you've been happy just lately?"

"What me not been happy lately Bel? I've been totally delirious!"

"There you are Max, I said something was wrong. I think you haven't been okay since the other night when I was close with Anita. Are you sure that it didn't upset you in some way Max. It was important for me to be close with her that evening, but I suppose these things can have a different effect on your partner."

"No I was fine about all that stuff Bel… *'mind you, it's me who should have been in the van 'giving her one', or doing whatever you two did. I'm sure I could have given her a better seeing to than any woman can'*… no I think it is really important that we hold the values of free love, and for Maxi to have been near when you girls were together, even if he was asleep."
'I just want to know when I will get to do some',

"Ah, so that's okay then Max; but I have been a bit worried that you might have found some of our hippie ideals hard to live with."

"Not if I had got to slip some plump breasted horny bitch a length I would have been with it all the way; but even a game of pool is not much fun when there are 'going's on' in your van that you are not a part of.
" No I dig it all Bel, and everything that happened is just what I wanted to see happen. We have come all this way to be part of other hippies and world love and stuff; it would be un-cool to have pushed your sister away from you that night.
"Mind you Bel, between you me and those rocks over there, you wait till some spare hippie girl turns up with an eye for me; I'll be in there like a rat up a drain-pipe!"

All thoughts of the other night must drift to find their place in 'things done'. There will be fewer returns to it in the coming days. Max feels like some of it has been got out of his system and been replaced by that reassuring thought that it gives him the right to take opportunity with a clear conscience should it come, though with his luck doubtless it will not.

The gifted hippie had been silent for some time while he went off either for a crap, or to find fresh inspiration: by the dismal sound of it, a homogenous mixture of the two!

He's back now.

He takes up his position and his instrument of torture and his verbal platitudes, like someone returning to deep truths that must be spoken… or at the very least, groaned!

"Yeah people oh people, you've got to stand up for what you believe"

"Oh my giddy aunt, will someone give that guy an honorary degree in the bleeding obvious!"

"Hush Max, keep it down!"

It sounds as he gets going again like he probably went off to write his own song about something, and has returned ready to make a gift of it to everyone. Max we see is clearly not drawn to empathise with the projected spirit; though from the back of the next van a hippie girl that they chatted with the night before lets out a sort of confirmation yelp and a flabby arm flags two 'peace' fingers at him.

The songster heard nothing of Max's words above his turgid scrubbing at the strings. He lifts his eyes to fix on Bel and Max, and throws them the lifeline of his superior vision:

"Because when you need to know who you really are… *Chingka ching ching ching,* no one else will stand there for you… no they won't… nope"

And aims a huge swipe at a chord to give him a few seconds in which he can pump a palm forwards V sign at Bel and Max with sagely oscillating head. Max's swivel on it minge finger is ascending, but Bel sees its rise and throws herself across him with two arms up and flailing sympathetic 'V's' at our man and mouthing something.

Before his hugely swiped chord has died away he renews his assault on all things pleasant.

Max shoots his hand up Bel's tee-shirt to grapple with her breast and says in her ear,

"I couldn't quite hear what you were saying as you were waving peace signs at him; was it something like, 'put a sock in it after this one will you?'"

"No it wasn't Max. It would be mean to let him think we didn't like his singing."

"His singing is a crock of shit, and would be an abomination even to the ear of a deaf Philistine."

"Maybe Max, but it's what he's got that he can give the world… or this camp!"

"Well why can't he keep the sodding lot for himself and do us all a favour eh!"

Bel can see that there is black-humour in Max's complaints; but sees also a general grouchiness with things round here,

"I think Max, that it would be nice to get out of the camp for a day; perhaps even have a night elsewhere… maybe find somewhere we can park out on a beach. It would make a nice change for Maxi… and for us as well."

"Hey, you know for you Bel, that's a really cool idea."
And to show his appreciation, she is rewarded by the ascent of his other hand to join the grapple.

"I'll check the oil, which I doubt will have gone down that much, while you pack the cupboard and find Maxi."

Only Bel packs the bed away and is pretty quick to gather up food and things into the van's cupboard.
The mist is burning off to hazy warm sun, with all drizzle long since ceased. The scattered light across the slope translucent, where it falls seems now to light a route of past; or showing that it feels some past returning.

But not the rocks: The rocks are far too old and set in their ways. No one's past is old enough for them to notice.

Mitch and Sandra have seen movements that speak of departure in the Turner camp: Mitch is sent across to see.

"No Mitch... not home, just a day by the sea or somewhere. It was Bel's idea; thinks Maxi will enjoy a day out."

"Yeah that's cool Max: Sandra was worried that you were off home I think."

"No this place is perfect... except for the wandering minstrel."

"Yes you're right Max, if he would just wander off and stop fouling up the atmosphere we would all be a lot happier."

"So then it's not just me who doesn't dig his tedious groaning Mitch?"

"Of that we are blood-brothers Max!"

Bel and Maxi skip across the slope in parallel. The little dog runs too so there comes Frank galloping and pouncing at his heels.
And getting near they wave to Max who is embarrassed and pretends in front of Mitch he hasn't seen. But even so a secret pride creeps up his leg and lifts his hand.
A few further words of explanation from Bel that she could have kept are thrown across and soon they're gone.

Chugging out along the lane Max feels how big the world is and how small their hippie camp beside it. Expansion in his head pulls in horizons to be assumed then included in possibility.
Only now does it strike him just how static the last few days have seemed. The three of them have hung suspended in the lives of others; pulled into positions and procedures that it is

assumed they have adherence to… well that was the idea of course?

He knows their hippie life involves a dream of inclusion. You shouldn't do it if you are at odds with feeling one of a huge family. But he doesn't like people expecting that he will enjoy or do certain things: like when as a child of nine, although a nifty mover and the favourite to win, he didn't want to enter the Rock'n Roll dancing competition at Butlin's holiday camp.

Never mind those thoughts or doubts of hippie life, it doesn't matter now. Now the only thing ahead is the open road, and the passage of a family of four… including the cat.

An azure blue haze lifts and curls behind where they have gone. It could be that the last remnants of early mist are cut and lifted as if a voluminous white kite were being flown and swirled against god's blue ceiling. It could also be that Max's van's valve-guides are so worn that oil pump's past them all the time and that's your blue swirling haze.

It clatters on, and sounds like it will carry on its clatter for a while if all stays well.

The sucking rattle of the cattle grid says they are leaving the moor and their road joins the old airfield perimeter track. Once the peri-track was open to all wind and weather, and pilots who steered their growling birds on freezing gusty dawn patrols would think 'abandon hope all ye who exit here'; and some would later find that it was true.

Now the airfield is part grown with firs, and runways cut like avenues across.

But of 'abandon hope all ye' it is not now: Here is creeping faster clatter as the old girl winds herself up for the big road.

In the back of the van Maxi sings out that he is going to take Frank swimming with him, then sulks at being told he won't by Max. Of course Bel saves things by a softer explanation about Frank's fur soaking up so much water that he will get heavy and sink.

"Why doesn't Clapton's fur soak up so much water Mum; he was jumping in the water all the time to run away from Frank, and he didn't sink?"

And settles with Bel's description of how dogs have different fur and like to swim. So Frank will be allowed to lounge in the van while Maxi is down on the beach.

A couple of miles on along the lane they join the road from Bude but turn towards Camelford to get some food and stuff.

There are increasingly more trees as you head down, giving a feeling of falling onto a sort of valley softness. Perhaps you subconsciously know that the depth of top-soil is protecting you from the background radiation of granite.

Whatever it is from, you feel less vulnerable to the ancient elements of the moor.

Sweeping round a curve to another straight Max pulls away from the verge to give safe room for a small well loaded figure who walks ahead of them in the edge of the road.

Bel notices it is a female, and with a large ruck-sack. She remarks on its size to Max, and speculates on just how far she could have walked with it, being fairly small herself.

As they steer carefully round her Bel glances back and says,

"Christ Max, and she's no spring-chicken either."

Max points out a lay-by just ahead saying quickly,

"Shall I stop for her?"

A quick confirmation from Bel and they have slowed into this off-shoot lay-by of the old road. Max says that she of course may not want to be given a lift into Camelford, but as they both look back to her approaching form the knees have a slight wobble to them that suggests they are not hiker's knees.

"I'll wander out to the edge of the road Max."

"I'll come with you Mum."

She's still a hundred yards or so away but Bel gets out to open Maxi's door and put his wellies on his bare feet.

"When the lady gets to us we'll ask her if she wants a ride with her heavy bag down into Camelford Maxi."

Max sits in his van. He feels glad to have got away from the camp and the expectations of the others. It is nice to be just here in this lay-by and just a bloke and his family. He has stopped pretending how cool everything seems; now things just are, or they are not.

He wants at the end of their day out to just stay away if they fancy, or head home to the camp if they fancy: secretly he hopes they will feel drawn to stay away.

His eye is taken back over the climbing ground sweeping up to the moor. Max knows he will with Maxi always come here. He wonders if when Maxi gets to his great age, he will be bringing his own kids here?

He cannot know, and if he could, could not visualise that Maxi will be more than twice his age before he has kids of his own: or any as far as he knows!

Glancing back to the road he sees the walker has arrived and is crouching down un-bagged as she listens to something Maxi is besetting her with.

And standing again her head nods in grateful acceptance as Bel's mouth moves because the nodding and laughing at whatever it was Maxi regaled her with sent ebony grey curls bobbing around her small face as her chuckle lit dark smiling eyes.

Now Bel grabs one strap as the lady bends for her ruck-sack. Between them they carry it across to the van.

Max sees they will manage the doors okay so stays inside.

"That's all right Max, you don't have to help us lift things in we can do all that!"

"I'm sorry Bel, I would have come out if I thought you weren't up to it!"

The lady is laughing because she can see it is only being said in jest. And now too she addresses Max to thank him for his kindness in saving her legs and her back.

She says that she had been about to cross the road to walk facing the traffic, it's habit to walk on that side where she comes from. She had in fact not long before been dropped off by someone who gave her a lift all the way from the coach station in Plymouth. They dropped her and headed north to Bude a few miles back.

Max says he is sorry that they are only going to Camelford, but as the road gets very windy and narrow a mile ahead, it will at least get her safely through that bit. She says that that will be fine, because she is going to be looking for somewhere to stay in Camelford.

Bel announces that with what they already know of the town, and with their contacts it should be easy to find her somewhere both pleasant and cheap. The lady admits she would be grateful for any sort of help.

Driving on down the main road Max calls back to Bel and the woman, that when they get to the car park they will put the kettle on... meaning that when they get to the car park Bel should put the kettle on.

All in the rear-view mirror nod: Nods of gratitude and nods of acquiescence, and a little rapid nod for anything that smacks of something that could lead to having fun.

Minutes on they are dropping into the outskirts of Camelford and the woman is leaning forward and peering out in a most intent and interested manner with her grey tinged curls swinging and bobbing about. It is quite hard to say what things engage her most; it is almost as if she is trying to look at everything at the same time: the people, the streets, the shops, the river.

Max who glancing inquisitively back at her in his mirror, wonders with a smirk if he should offer to go back out and drive in again for her to have another look. As they approach the car park there is still as much she seems enthralled with so he carries on in.

Finding and reversing into a spot where it rises high and there is a nice view onto the street he parks on the steep slope. Bel jumps quickly out with their block of wood while Max holds it on the foot-brake and explains that the van has a very dodgy hand-brake.

Bel comes round to the side door and adds that this way round, at least the kettle won't slide off the cooker.

Max might be feeling a tiny bit guilty at having not got out to help them into the van just now. Or maybe not, but either way he volunteers to take Maxi to the shop and buy some bread and bits while the kettle boils.

Away they stomp, Max in old army boots, and Maxi in blue wellies, hand held and running a pace to left then tugged back like a Springer-Spaniel on a lead.

"Your little boy is really sweet; he must I would think be less than four years old. I have two girls, and girls grow up so much faster but I should imagine I am about right am I?"

"Yes, he's not that long turned three in fact. How old are your girls?"

"Oh yes… one's twenty-four, and one's twenty-six, but both of them have left home and are married now; that makes the house seem very quiet these days."

"Are you married… I mean do you still have a man to look after in the evening or are you living on your own?"

"Yes now I'm on my own. I became separated over a year ago so that's why I was able to come over here; which I had been wanting to do for the last… nearly thirty years."
Bel can hear she is not from England, though her accent is strangely indefinable. She speaks as if she is part French and part American. Bel can feel also that some strong impulse must lie behind her journey.
Bel wants to have covered any difficult stuff that the woman wants to speak of before the boys get back. It is not because she is eager to pry… alright, she does want to know what's what: But she also feels there is something that this woman has got bottled up: Something that she has come here from wherever it is to find some release for, or closure of.
Bel lights on a thought that without her prying may give her sister a chance to bring other life into her story.

"Have you ever been to England before… or is this your first time down in Cornwall… or well, anywhere else I suppose?"

"Ah… now that's a question: And you will think it was another life. For me it feels almost like another life, except that one part of it has been with me almost every day since that time.

"Yes it seems hard to say, though should not be… except perhaps I should be thoughtful if you live in Camelford, and may be connected… do you?"

"No it's okay, we're from across the country, and until the last few days knew no one from around here."

"Well that's fine then I would think. You see my dear, I was here thirty years ago."

"What in some way connected with the war?"

"That's it completely… I worked up there on the airfield as a kitchen girl because my boy was away in the Canadian army.
At the end of the war he went home from North Africa somewhere, and I went home, and we started our life and our family… it was all fine… except that I had left a boy behind."

"Is that a boyfriend you mean?"

"Oh no my dear… I mean that I left a son here. Yes of course there had been a father, and one I really liked… who in another life would have been just as good, or as it's turned out, possibly even better than my Darren. But that didn't matter so much… I left my son."

"I hardly know what to say… was it some sort of accident?"

"Not really an accident, though I wish of course that I could tell you it was. Of course in another time, or in another life, I would have avoided it and gone in another direction. It was an accident for me in the sense that I thought I was taking the right road… doing the right thing for him.
"Look, I was very young and far from home, and told there were couples around who wanted kids and if I took him

home it was going to screw my life up with Darren… and that he, the baby would never know and be much happier staying here.

"It seemed to make sense.

"I gave him to a local authority, who said they would give him to a childless couple in Camelford.

"Thirty years later… and I still yearn to see him, if he's still alive. In all that time he has always been in my thoughts."

"I still hardly know what to say er… yes, I'm Bel, what can I call you."

"Hello Bel, I'm just Anne.

"The most important bit of my life in terms of its effect on me started here, and I suppose I have come to set the record straight; or find what perhaps it should have been."

"Once you've got a bed sorted, I suppose the next thing is to find your boy Anne."

"Well yes Bel, but I have to decide also if the right thing is to see him… I mean see him to speak to, or should I just see what he looks like, maybe get to where I can hear him talk… then take myself away again.

"There again Bel, for all I know he and his parents may have emigrated to somewhere… perhaps even Canada, years ago!"

"But assuming him to still be around, he may be happier left to continue with his life and parents here."

"I suppose that is a question only you can answer Anne. I know what I… that is, I think I know what I would want after coming from somewhere across the sea thirty years later."

"From Canada Bel."

"So there you go Anne; It's a hell of a long way to go home again with just a brief glimpse to carry with you the rest of your days I would think."

"Yes I know Bel, but after deserting my boy, it will be right to do what's best for him won't it?"

"Yes absolutely Anne. At least to do what you decide is the best thing for him. Of course it would be almost impossible to ever know without asking, I mean what was actually the best from his point of view… You know, what he would want himself.

"As I see it now that I have thought about it, the important thing is for you to convince yourself that he would want to know who his real mother is!"

"Oh Bel you're dreadful; it's going to be much harder to take the right course of action under your influence… but I am still really glad for your words and thoughts."

As they laugh the boys come tramping across the tarmac to the door with milk and bread.

"We've seen big fishes in the river Mum. Dad says we could eat them if we could catch them."

"That would be nice for our tea Maxi… but Max; I was right in the middle of something with… well, this is Anne; could you take Maxi to play on the swings for a while?"

"Oh blimey Bel, not more sex with your sisters is it?"

"Push off Max, we were just in the middle of a conversation about something really important."
With a knowing oh yes!, and looking askance into the van as if he were checking their state of dress, he turns to Maxi with,

"Who wants to play on the swings?"
And knowing he will receive a resounding vote of approval from the little chap they go.
Bel says to Anne that seeing as the boys have gone off they should have that cup of tea that was intended when they stopped here. Anne smiles gratefully at this and wonders if she should ask if her arrival has broken their day or their plans. She senses this is probably not the case, and can see the relish Bel is showing at meeting someone who had a little boy like her own, but lost him.

"So tell me Anne…"

Her words float a moment on the air as she strikes a match for the gas.

"What do you think you'll do now?"

"Oh, just wander round the town a bit, see what I can find by way of a room. Maybe see if there is a bus or something that will take me out to the coast this evening to find a little bistro perhaps, for a meal: I expect the fresh fish is as good as you can find anywhere in the world.

Bel was not expecting a list of potential social engagements, more a resolve towards some course of action.

"No Anne, not that sort of 'what are you going to do now'; I was meaning with regard to finding where your boy lives. Though fair enough, perhaps you won't actually start till the morning."

"Yes I see Bel… but you never know, I may in fact begin talking to a few people tonight."

"Well look Anne… I really don't want to interfere in your life; but can I play some small part in helping you get started in your search?"

"Yes I would love that Bel; I have no contacts or starting point. Sitting here now, I cannot think for one minute where to begin. How do you think I would best get started Bel?"

"So you weren't told the names of the couple who brought him up I suppose?"

"No I have no idea about that,"

"What about the name of the father. You've mentioned him, but not his name… you must remember him!"

"Yes definitely Bel; though I have no surname, I only knew him like it seemed everybody knew him, as 'Joe the farrier'. It was all very secret because he had a long term but rather love-less thing with a girl he was engaged to. He was a lot older than me so could even be dead by now after such a hard life.

"But certainly she is likely to still be around so I must be careful for their sakes."

"And I presume we're assuming that he never revealed his true identity to his son. I suppose that would have eventually got back to his wife; and then eventually the boy might have got in touch with you Anne. So what sort of age would you say he was Anne?"

"Let's think now… he seemed a lot older than me; but that's because I was only twenty-two. But if I reckon he would have been thirty, no, thirty-five perhaps, I guess he may in fact not be more than seventy yet."

"It's a shame it's such a common name Anne. I was talking just a few words with a Joe a couple of nights back in a pub on the other side of the moor; and roundabout that age I would say: But I don't suppose for one minute it was him."

"No it's not going to be as easy as that is it."

"But I'm meeting my em, sort of hippie sister… Anita there tomorrow on her day off. If I see him I can easily ask him what he did for a living can't I?"

"Yeah Bel, but tell me, what's a hippie sister? You mean just another hippie that you came here with."

"No Anne, and she's not even really a hippie. We were… very close a couple of nights ago. We shared sister spirit… and stuff. That's what Max was teasing me about when I asked him to get lost for a while longer."

"Right Bel, I think I see... anyway, then if this Joe says he was a bank-manager, that's him crossed off and out the way."

So the women seem to have some rather vague yet plausible starting point sketched out. To ever achieve success it would in the normal run of things involve the inclusion of a lot more thought and accumulated inspiration as they go on.

We can see of course that chance has bowled them an easy swipe.

Even as we speak he sits in his red car just where he likes to sit. Where he looks at the ruined buildings; where he sees still the cookhouse and the mess-room where his love was born that sadly never really was to be.

Does that lifting curlew's 'tloo tloo roo roo roo... throw a song against the wind that is to sing of that time... the song it sang those thirty years ago was just the same.

Joe taps the rim of his steering wheel and his heart ache's though his old bones seem as if they always ache; today his distant and persistent memories seem to ache as well.

He wants the chance to do it all again. He doesn't want to be here now, with so much time expired on the clock.

In his red car he sits, and in his mind he is telling a young Canadian girl that he has a good income; he is telling her that he will one day have his granny's house across the moor, as now he has though for Claire he lives in Camelford.

He is telling her to keep their child and to let him sort things to finish with Claire; he will make his life with her instead... but there was also Darren pulling her the other way.

She went.

She went though to where and to what.

He knows of course which continent, but not her life.

Joe sees her at this minute with small children in some dark pine forest. Sometimes these children are theirs, and sometimes just hers; but always just out of Joe's reach.

They never grow old *'as we who are left grow old, age will not weary them or the years condemn; at the going down of the sun and in the morning...* he will remember them'.

She is forever sultry, and succulent, and her warm mouth laughs through ebony curls that always… always, will frame a young face.

And as she walks away forever, her bum-cheeks dance sideways beneath her kitchen overalls and pinafore.

"I can't just sit here pondering all day… I could, but it doesn't change things. And it feels like time's… a glance at watch, his dreaming stops, and life and yearning courses through his veins… *yeah it is; time's getting on, so I doubt that Marlo is coming past this way now.*

"At least it keeps me out of the way up here; Claire doesn't want me under her feet all day. It would just be nice if one day I suddenly knew why it all had to be the way it is. Nice if I could suddenly say OK, fair enough, at last I can see that this is all as it should be… perhaps then I could close the book on what might have been.

"Right now it feels increasingly like the time to go down to 'The Sun' for a beer. I bet Marlo went straight down off the back of the moor. So that little blighter's given me the slip again!"

"Come on Joe, fire the old 'red devil' up and get yourself a beer."

He goes. He goes in his shiny red car towards his daily beer and chin-wag.

As he drives away the wind comes back across the old peri-track; fresh it flows, and freshly scented too, as if some fresh word of change floated on its breath.

In the town two women have found a man and boy on a swing and conferred with them, then left. Now one is in 'The Darlington', and one is in 'The Masons Arms'; then both will meet and see which was the cheapest or had rooms vacant.

With a room sorted and her afternoon mapped out, one will relax and begin to think her way into the days ahead. It will suddenly occur to the other that they should take her with them the following night to the pub across the moor where they know more people to ask about it, like their shepherd friend Marlo.

A pub from where it is less likely that word will get back to Camelford or Joe's wife, assuming he is the right Joe, and from where Anne can be sure if that Joe is her farrier or a bank-manager.

A plan is made to find each other again the next day…
then with Anne finally settled they drive away seeking to

park up by the sea for the night and so get Max away from his talented minstrel in the hippy camp, and Maxi to some sand and seaweed for a swim.

Sliding quietly down a seaward track Max drives the bus behind some dunes and well screened from the road, so there they make their camp and boil the kettle on their stove for tea and a packet of instant cocoa for the little man.

Later, and back from an evening walk along the beach to search for crabs and fishing net floats they settle down as dusk slides in across the sand dunes, and a coolness off the water makes a dew form on the campervan's roof.

A little man is snoring sweetly inside over the engine bay all snuggled in after a final before bed piss into the sand... what dreams might he traverse this night? Where might his magic carpet night bed carry him away to in those dreams?

Now gulls and Fulmars as with kittiwakes are all bedded on the rocky cliffe or far out floating dozing on the sea as it is so calm; here too the hippy family are all finally in the land of nod, but just the cat seems up for action with head pushed under curtain tail twitches side to side in anticipation... but little stirs outside so he's not missing much, therefore finally climbs into the very back to join the boy for a kip.

Much later as the night is halfway from the dawn and sunset, the surface of the water stirs in the bay as a fin protrudes, then a second joins to cruise across and soon returns; is it shark or maybe dolphin, who can say in dark with just sporadic moonlight from the ragtag sky of dying stratus cloud cut here and there with stars.

The night sea air is cool but calm, perhaps set fair the day to come but we must wait a while to see.

All feels to sleep in this dead hour of the night when it is thought that souls slip silently away from folk in the final hour of all the rest that was their life.

Another hour on and we are seeing a lighter blackness to the east where all days start, though we will have to wait a while, and sleep a bit, till it arrives.

Time indeed has moved a fair way on as we were sleeping, and the gold of growing day is here with gulls crying urgently and heading out to sea so you rouse early and indeed there is a female nose thrust under a curtain by the bed to snuff the air and see what's what.

In the dunes it soon gets warm.

You rouse and take a butchers out, but you lie there half-awake and listening for movement from your little boy.

Though Bel would not say 'half-awake' that she lay:

"I am lying here half asleep, but it is really just that bit too hot to stay here and stay comfortable… though not quite certain I can get myself to wake-up and do something about it. At least there's no movement from Maxi yet."

As your hand slides up the glass outside the familiar velvety cloth of the curtain, the touch of the glass is cool but charged with static. Though it is uncommon to have early moments without Maxi climbing in, you discard any thought of coaxing the big boy beside you to play games as you take a large gulp of the heated moist air, nor are you really that much in the mood for lurve.

Your head is hot and heavy; you try to decide if you have a headache or not. You feel too dulled to really say if there is.

Lift away the bedding and lower your legs. Feel the fablon floor tiles cool on the night-soaked metal van floor beneath the soles of your feet. Cool where from below the dark breeze has all night passed below.

You stoop forward so your head dips under and lifts the door-side curtain this time.

The whispering dunes and beach are deserted.

So quietly now as not to stir a soul, you lift a pale grey banana shaped plastic German door handle and push: A wheeze of often squeezed rubber speaks for half a second, then air carrying the aromatic scent from pampas-like dune grass filters through.

You slip outside, and leave it open for the boys to breathe.

"I will sit with the morning sun on my skin, and warm sand under my bare bum. I might still get half an hour of peace before Maxi wakes up.

"If Max finds I am not there and calls out, I can pretend I'm doing something and tell him to get up and put the kettle on.

"There's no point sitting right beside our van, I shall climb that little sandy lump to have a view… but first things first, I need a piss.

"Oops, I thought it would be easy crouching on sand: No danger I thought of piss flowing over my feet; but suddenly your heels sink in and you start to fall backwards.

"Now that's a thought, why don't I just sit down on the sand, and do it in comfort... ah now that's beautiful. Even if someone walked past I could just smile and say good morning and they would never know, unless it makes me fart at the same time perhaps.

"They might I suppose even if they twig nothing, think I was being a bit daring out here without a stitch on but that's another matter. "Actually, sitting up here with our van just there below, I think my life is just about as perfect as it can be. To be honest, if I just had a cup of tea there would be nothing else in the world left to desire.

"I could be tempted to creep back in to my stove and make one, but that could blow the whole thing. Everyone would suddenly wake up and want something: Maxi would want to get up and go for a swim; and Max would try to pull me under the bedclothes to service him or something.

"Best thing is to keep quiet and enjoy the sun... hmm, and maybe even enjoy myself alone for once.

"It feels wrong to say it but it's true, that this morning and being here would only be more perfect... if I was here alone: But with a cup of tea of course.

"Though apart from here now, I wouldn't want to be without Maxi. I suppose I could probably get by without Max quite well if push came to shove.

"Fair enough, if you need a man you will do a lot worse than him: He's fun, and he's sexy, yes with big hands, which I like. But if he ran off, he wouldn't be too hard to replace. That's the beauty of men, they're like cars: All subtly different but provide the same basic functions, so therefore all very interchangeable.

"I wonder if this sand was ever beneath the sea? I suppose that's a stupid question, it must have been at some time. I mean that was this mound I'm sitting on ever part of a beach, and did it have waves lapping over it.

"I have this feeling that it is as if I might be living on a tiny Greek island in the Aegean.

"I imagine myself with my children on the beach, and have waded out till the waves kiss the tops of my legs with their cool searching tongues; but this dune grass would of course be flowing seaweed around me. If I then sit down, what would it feel like? As the waves come will I feel my softness moving up and down and up and down, in the water's cool caress, as if perhaps I have been entered by the motion of the earth: Hmm... and that's not at all unpleasant either!

"I can hear Maxi laughing and splashing in the shallows as he chases fish and searches out small crabs. He will make a wonderful little sand urchin.

"Phew... all those earthy thoughts of sand and sea are a little too stimulating for a simple hippie girl... more to the point, or at least as a means of getting my mind onto other things: Tonight how best to help Anne to make some progress in her search.

"It's lucky she's a rather attractive fifty something and not sixty or seventy, it will make it so much easier to get men to take an interest and listen.

"It can't be that hard to find the old blacksmith, or at least his grave; though that can't tell us much I suppose. But in 'The Sun', someone's bound to have known him. Even if he was Camelford's final farrier, someone will know where he retired to surely.

"Hmm... that sun is getting so lovely and warm. I shall... yes that feels nice, I shall stretch out on my back like a sea otter. But instead of eating raw fish off my chest! I will just check that none of my bits that are not so used to the sun are getting too hot or going to burn: or I'll be fighting to keep Max off me for the rest of our time here.

Bel closes her eyes as if wanting suddenly to focus her thoughts on something distant in time or miles.

You see how open her eyes are beneath their lids. They are starring hard or deeply; but if not forwards, then back into the depth of her consciousness, and their movement below her translucent skin is because she is looking rapidly, almost earnestly through the fast accumulating layers of her life.

A staccato chuckle breaks the air, 'caccabab', or something not dissimilar. From cliffs that end the undulation of dunes have sailed a pair of Fulmar Petrels. They glide on straight white wings with dihedral, and to our hippie girl would look like gulls.

But she lies on, nor eyes do open, and they fly on, nor wings do close. They, like two parallel white crosses of aerial flow; she, like a warm living sculpture that would no doubt delight the surprised discoverer at least as much, or even more than would parting foliage to find a secret Henry Moore in the 'Yorkshire Sculpture Park'.

Our marble girl shows little movement. But there... Bad luck you missed it, a toe twitched.

If you look closely, though not too close, her left thigh muscle has a tiny sporadic flutter, just where the slope becomes really steep... toward the other, then minutely curves away to make a sudden gap.

Put your face against her face now: If not too distracted by the softness of her skin, can you think you feel what she is feeling. Do you feel you think what are her thoughts?

Bel ponders further:

"I hear the sea roll lazily back and forth 'with Cornish haste', and speaking with the voice of Greece... What were... I couldn't be bothered to open my eyes, but what were those chuckling birds who sailed across? Obviously some sort of seagull I presume.

(There you go!)

"Strange that I am lying here without a stitch. If I opened my eyes I might find that all the time someone has been standing there above me. Once or twice I thought I felt a touch, or was it maybe someone's breath on my skin... in several places. Or was it just the love-child of a vivid imagination?

"The most likely watcher would be my Maxi. If it was I would just grab him and cuddle him.

"If it were Max... well he would probably be all steamed up and needing action. Which would have its compensations I suppose!

Quickly and almost without forethought she sits up. Sand falls from her still sleep tangled hair. Now Bel's eyes are wide. She looks out at the blue of the sea and the yellow sun speaks to her.

Her thoughts speak too.

"I will never be here like this again. Perhaps I will be here, but not like this; or be like this but somewhere else: But never here like this again. Any moment Maxi could wake and call me to come and help him get up. Well Max can do it, I fancy a swim.

"And my best bet is to make my getaway here and now.

That was easy… and almost out of earshot already. Now mum is hardly in the picture, and down in these dunes already the van is lost from view.

"Hey this feels so cool… just trotting through the dunes like a sea-nymph. Now I feel like more than just a hippie, I'm a spirit; I bring the women who lived thousands of years ago on this beach, to fish, and give birth, and collect seaweed; I bring them all together… Ouch, my toe…! There was a rock in the sand… but the distant sisters, I bring them alive again in me being here today and my naked presence proves it.

"I suppose they were probably only naked once in a blue moon: Most of the time in Cornwall you would have been 'freezing your bits off', so generally well wrapped up in home-spun wool and skins I expect.

"But let's not let the truth spoil a good story! Hey… that's the dunes finished with, so now the beach… and they certainly would have left their bear-skins on the rocks when they got out this far. So from here on I reckon my suit is pretty authentic.

"Hang on, before I get too far away from the dunes: My head may be starting to feel nice and free and clear, but I am increasingly aware that my arse is full of shit.

"I shall just have a nice crap before I go out to the water.

"This will do nicely… in the deep soft sand at the foot of this dune. I can scrape a nice hole to squat over.

"Hmm… is there anything as wonderful… now I will be really ready to face the day… Oy bird, who are you beak'ing down at?

"Okay… cover it all up and head for the sea again.

"This is the first time in my life that I have had a mile of distance that way… a mile that way… quite a bit back that way; and at least several thousand miles that way: And above all not been wearing a stitch of clothing. Yes, and I missed above me: Which would be a big number of miles that if I began to recite it now, I would not even be halfway through before I was old and grey.

Actually, that's bollocks; both space and the number of miles are infinite so there's no point even bothering to try that one.

"There should with me doing all this naked stuff, be someone out here to sign me off as a proper fully paid up hippie dude.

"Between his snores, does Max I wonder realise that his woman is a mile away and without a stitch on. He tries to play the dead cool hippie dude but he's really quite old-fashioned. Sure he bangs on about free love and stuff, but he'd do his nut if I really did any.

"I suppose there was Anita… but, I don't think he sees that as being sex, because in his mind we were just two girls so it's no threat to him. And I know he thinks that if he had been there, the two of us would have been gagging for his body… I suppose we might have found one or two jobs that he could have got on with.

"Mind you, if I ever said: I've just met this really cool hippie guy: He wants me and him to wander off across the moor so he can slip me a length with his enormous 'free love' todger; and so we can feel at one with the spirits of the rocks and the grass or whatever… Max would say through gritted teeth: that's fine, but I hope you don't have too much trouble hitching home!"

"If I'm honest… Yeah, if I'm Honest, I wouldn't want him not to care about what I got up to. I want us to be a mum and dad for Maxi that will still be there for him for quite a few years yet. This free-love stuff is really nice, but I wouldn't let it get in the way of what was going to be right for our little boy."

She's a sweet chick isn't she, Bel.

She's like a banana that you have taken out of its skin and begun to eat it, but as you do so you realise there is another even sweeter banana inside the whole thing.

She deserves some time away from her boys. She deserves some time to relate the objectives of her hippie life to the needs of her job as a mum.

Few would want her not to dabble freely in the shallows of what else might be for her in life, except maybe Max.

As she reaches water, the shock that water does not heat to your romantic expectations makes her gasp.

She gasps, but that is all she does. As water meets her shins she picks her knees up determined that having trotted this far she will run into water as if it were both mild and alluring: Water the pleasantness of which makes you quicken your stride eager to get into it as soon as possible.

You don't play this sort of game just to stop when anything cold reaches your 'bits'. To help her in, her ancient sisters take an arm on each side when she gasps and decelerates a little. You don't get to swim for your school and county by being scared of cold water.

Two more laboured steps as the level passes her waist and with half a lung to make her not too buoyant she launches head down to swim to the sandy bottom.

It is easy to know when you are just off the bottom: In this water her nipples shoot out like chapel hat-pegs, or the extended eyes of garden snails, and though they don't see too well they are the first bit to brush the sand as she gets near.

Twenty or so reaches and kicks of perfect breast-stroke and Bel can feel from the pressure that the sea bed has sloped steeply. She rotates into the vertical to kick up to the sun. One, two, three, and four! Then woosh, that blast of air and sun, and grateful lungs gulp deeply in the softly lifted breeze.

Treading water while the early waft crazes the surface of the smooth sea, she bathes herself and cleanses every nook and cranny: Even does behind her ears. Bel feels kissed by the sun through the lips of the ocean.

"What heaven… yes just to be able to do that, I would give up Max, and give Maxi back. It's lucky for those buggers I can be out here anyway.

"Now I've been down quite deep the surface feels almost bath-like. I shall have a good hard swim along the top and when I'm really puffed, which won't take long now I'm not in training, I shall float on my back and doze in the sun."

Head down Bel pounds her way out across the bay; beneath her sea hangs luminously green and deep.

Octopus looks up from deep, sees perhaps a giant hungry squid against the sky that could see him as dinner, and wriggles bulbous under rock, flushing shrimp whom he gratefully eats.

As if on coastal command two fulmars pass yet other way and chuckle dolefully. Are these the same pair again, if so they are returning. So where did they go, and why together? Unless they were both female of course; yes that could explain it!

She really is the most superb swimmer. Watching her go you cannot believe that she was not Olympic class. It is hard to imagine that this Cornish bay has ever seen someone who can travel so far through the water in so little time.

She deserves a breather. By the time we get to her she has rolled onto her back to float with her eyes closed.

She's quite right about being out of condition: for a one time County swimmer she is really having to puff very hard. It is as she grabs great lung-full's of air a reasonably attractive sight, so we should not perhaps be too critical of her!

Now she floats. She floats buoyant and bonny in the brine; and each normally thought average size breast looks like it wears a thrusting German pickelhaube helmet: though the warm sun will soon make things subside!

You can in your mind see a pre-Raphaelite painting of Ophelia floating drowned down the river amongst flowers and water-weed. But it spoils it to remember that she was painted in a bath with candles underneath to keep the chill off it. Or of Burn-Jones. That one where water-nymphs are trying to beguile a young lad who is just about as pretty as they are to come into the river. It could be either.

It is hard to say she is alive as she floats. She is, *'the lady with the skin so white, like something out of Blake or Burn-Jones* and her paleness seems incongruously foreign to the chemistry of the ocean: A chemistry in which you can only survive as a relevant part or you are soon recycled.

It would be quite good wouldn't it.

Quite good if a yacht left Penzance several days ago to sail round Lands End, then up the west-coast of Wales and England to South Uist in the Outer Hebrides.

Having the best part of the summer to get there and back, or even on over the top and back down the east coast if the weather seems set fair, they would be in no great rush.

With just a gentle waft of sea-breeze but having to stay out beyond it to miss this rocky coastline, even with your copious spinnaker out, you're fairly much becalmed today.

If a leisurely coffee in a bay is mooted by one of the chaps on board, I doubt if any of the lads would resent the suggestion.

So if all that were the case you would choose a nice little bay that your chart shows not to be cursed by underwater obstructions, and you might coast gently in with your sails falling slack as cliffs surround and dunes approach.

Of the five lads *(averaging fifty-six)* Simon *(sixty-three)* is less gung-ho and more keen to eschew un-charted rocks. He hangs nervously off the bowsprit rail and all agog as first blurred dismal forms below darken perilously in his eyes and lour into his imagination.

The rest however have got the brandy out while kettle boils, and with scarcely a creeping knot tickling the needle talk is of *'when to dump the anchor'*, and *'might as well get as far in as we can, then it's not so far to pull it back up when we go'*.

Simon is almost mesmerised by the blurred and gradually climbing sea bed; so relaxing now he lifts his eyes... sees, no it cannot be... not a dead body!

Scrambling round and back he threads between deck wires and ropes to the cockpit and the boys, who see him come and joke about *'any sign of land yet Simon!'*, and he with hushed reverence:

"There's a dead body in the water ahead!"

And skipper drawls like some seasoned salt *(retired Civil-Servant)*,

"Oh Jesus, why do we have to pick the only bay with some rotting corpse. It's probably some old fisherman washed off rocks ages back; and now we must deal with it!"

"No it's a girl, just ahead on our left. You can see it's a girl because she's on her back... and em, naked as a babe."

"Then I suppose we'd better take a look... em, John can you steer us that way while I get the boat hook and some rope."

They all who are not detailed to drive the boat then crowd the port rail like the playground fence when 'Big Jim' was knocking the shit out of one hated fascist prefect years before.

And leaning out with voices hushed and *'what a shame'* and *'pretty young'* and *'pretty too'* though nothing lewd or disrespectful.

When you doze with ears submerged you hear the creaking sand and moan of weed and hum of distant depths but not these voices in the air.

So when with:

"I'll try to slip the rope on her arm gently. If I jab her much the police may think we murdered her."

With no words heard you feel a sudden rough noose above your elbow. It could be the cruel tentacle of a giant squid and you scream like final breath of a witch at the flaming stake; and hear in echo a crew bellow in horror as they fall backwards onto the deck. By rights, at least two should have died through heart failure. But all survive.

"Flippin' eck, what are you guys after?

Which might sound a risky phrase for a naked girl to use with a handful of fairly active middle-aged men. Bel is panting and incongruously sweating in cool water.

"I'm dozing on my back and then suddenly a load of mad old men are trying to take me prisoner or something; but where have they gone?"

These first ten seconds are a little confused. It takes fifteen to twenty seconds for a body that was dozing to come to terms with the sudden shock of being roped up to a ship.

It takes around the same length of time, or even slightly longer for elderly chaps who were carefully and respectfully attaching a line to a tragic corpse that suddenly came alive and howled at them… for them to get back on their feet and arrest their storming heart rates.

The skipper crawls to rail and says,

"Young lady, I am so dreadfully sorry… I really don't know how to apologise enough."

"That's because you wouldn't be able to."

"But we thought you were a corpse my dear."

"Oh thanks, so I'm really that foul and bloated am I?"

"No, not at all not at all… our bow-man came astern saying there was a dead body in the sea ahead, but I am so sorry… look my dear, our kettle is just boiling for coffee, would you like to come aboard."

"Oh that's such a flipping brilliant idea, half a dozen randy old men and me without stitch on."

"I have a towelling dressing gown you can wear."

"Have you got any tea-bags?"

"Earl-Grey' or ordinary?"

"That's a deal then, either or both!"

So the skipper heads for his cabin below, and the rest apart from Roger make polite conversation with their sea-nymph and try manfully not to scan her shape or lumpy bits below the surface.

Bel retrieves the floating boat hook that the skipper had let go of as he gasped and fell backwards.

He is back with a huge white beach gown and a whimsical grin:

"I think I already know the answer to this my dear; but would you like two of us to lift you bodily from the waves, or shall we turn our backs and let you struggle up as best you can?"

"Oh don't worry about me getting up there, I swam for my county, and did a little bit of gymnastics too."

"Well I didn't know any of that, but I guessed you might prefer to get yourself up here… okay men, about turn."

They hear just a slight splash, and a few drips land on them from behind, then a moment's muffled flapping and,

"It's alright to look now."
And there she stands; their very own tame sea-nymph.
Roger had been sorting the kettle and cups down below; it meant he had a secret look through the galley window as she came on board. She would probably allow him that one because he is now emerging with her dreamed of cup of tea, and a pot of coffee for the boys.
Now they lounge in deck-chairs on the deck. Well some just perch on bulkheads some have chairs, and Bel is given pride of place on the skipper's sun-lounger… with her cup of tea!

"Ah now thanks for having me up for tea guys, it's really cool."

"I'm so sorry dear, we'll make you a fresh cup, it won't take a minute."

"No don't be silly, it's not that sort of cool, no it's really nice and hot thanks."
But several have got children or grandchildren who use that sort of expression so are able to nod and grin knowingly.
There are many with the same question in their mind, but one voice asks:

"So how do you come to be floating right out in the bay, and at this early hour young lady?"

"Well that's… and I'm Bel by the way,"
At which nods and smiles tilt round the crew, and skipper gives a quick-fire list of who's who.

"Hello everyone… but as I started to say, that's much more straight forward to answer than you all may imagine.
"I'm a hippie, and if you look about a mile up there in the dunes you can probably see the mauve roof of a van. Well in it is

my bloke Max who may still be asleep, or may be up and making tea by now. Also there is my little boy Maxi."

"Your little boy! But you're hardly more than a child yourself Bel. How old are you and your lad?"

"I am nineteen you know…! But he's only three. I had just turned sixteen when I had him. And Max is a couple of years older than me."

"So is your stuff left at the water's edge Bel… it's just that I think the tide is on its way back in now. Yes and while were all sitting, can someone do a few shots for the album?"

"No it's not a problem, there aren't any clothes or stuff to worry about. I woke up rather warm and sneaked off without waking them up… or without clothes, and that's how you found me."

Bel can feel she is a bit of a mascot to these guys, or a muse perhaps.
One of the stories that will be told and re-told of their trip for years to come will be the one about Simon spotting a corpse in the sea ahead, and probably it will end up after many years and telling's, as where they roped it up and were towing it in to port before it woke up and became a very vocal 'she' again.

All that will depend on the company, and the number of empty Brandy bottles.

But here and now the tale is still being born and Roger the galley slave is down below and shouting up about who wants what etc. and Bel is definitely up for more tea.

Roger re-emerges like the patron saint of sorting things, and Bel lounges like the Queen of Sheba with her second perfect mug of tea.

She asks them where they were heading, and gets a rundown on their proposed route and schedule. Then asks if they have room for another crew-member, which of course gets an enthusiastic *'no problem'* from these over-grown schoolboys.

"I would leave Max behind… but would have to bring my little boy."

And that has all the one-time dads smiling on behalf of their wives… and all the bachelors wondering if they have missed out on something. This girl who they might have passed a thousand times and thought was just a low-life: Now brings them a little insight of a mother's love.

And that's pretty much it really. Bel laughs again and they smile like sudden dads for her, and she soon is set to move away, and they to set their course again. And time and other closes round this passing.

"Look inland on the beach there guys… that must be my little Maxi with his dad. They must be wondering where I went. Look, thank you all so much for my tea today, it was all really cool. And have a great trip up the coast but watch out for storms."

She probably shouldn't… but when you spend a little while with some bunch of guys, and have posed amongst them for the photo's of their voyage, you want to leave a fond image of you for their memories.

She stands up: Bel stands up from her sun-lounger… and her gown, and walks between their flushed farewells kissing her palm and anointing shoulders and bald heads. Then as if there were some invisible springboard she clears the side-rail and goes in like a cormorant.

And that's it! They were already turned so they might enjoy on parting what they missed on arrival, and now they wait to see her head bob up and call goodbye… and it does not.

"Oh shit boys! Has Bel got tangled with our anchor chain or something!"

They rush and stumble to the rail and stare with horror into the depths that have robbed them. Has the earlier horror that was not, now come for real?

They hear as gulped moments stretch another cormorant dive, or a big fish leap perhaps not thirty yards away and,

"Cheerio guys!"

A grinning Bel gulps grateful air and waves a fond farewell before she turns to steam competently off towards her beach and her boy.

"She swims very well doesn't she Roger?"

"Yes, very nicely I'd say."

"What did you think Simon, after all, you saw her first."

"What do I think…? Well it's all a bit too late for me now lads… but I think… 'if only life could be like that'."

Which speaks for most of them as they clear up things and haul up the anchor.

Bel is back in her depth and stands waist deep in the sea. She calls and waves at her boys, then turns to face the sea again and waves to the yacht as its sail's fill in the gentle breeze.

Skipper lifts their aerosol fog siren and gives Bel a salute that echo's from the distant cliffs as they turn slowly and creep towards the open sea.

Bel rotates waist deep to wade towards her boys and a naked Maxi comes running into the sea to be picked up and kissed and hugged in the gentle waves.

"Ah that's really sweet, Bel's cuddling her little boy in the waves."

"Well yes I see that… but is it really the thing to be looking at her through a telescope?"

"She's a child of the earth: she's not shy about being naked."

"I suppose not."

"Would you like the telescope?"

"Well, perhaps just a quick glimpse to remember her by then... hmm yes, that boy's a lucky little blighter."

"Mummy?"

"Yes Maxi"

"When I waked up I climbed into your bed. And when Daddy turned over he cuddled me and rubbed me, then he shouted out and jumped up: why did Daddy shout out Mum?"

"Well... probably because he thought you were me in bed. You know Maxi, it's like those times you wake up at night, and me and Dad are tickling each other and kissing lots... do you remember being scared the first time, thinking that we were fighting?"

"I thought Dad was hurting you Mum."

"Well I think Dad was wanting to kiss and tickle me... Like he doesn't do to you."

"Why doesn't Dad like to kiss and tickle me Mum... doesn't he like me as much as you?"

"It's not that Maxi, he likes you even more... it's a different sort of tickling. Only mums and dads do it... yes, because it's how they make brothers and sisters for you."

"Why haven't I got a brother and sister Mum?"

"Well... maybe in quite a long time from now there will be; shall we ask Dad if he knows when?"
Bel carries Maxi up the sandy beach.

"Hi Bel, we guessed you would have gone for a swim; but em, was that a hippie yacht or something Bel: We saw you dive back in... you know, without clothes."

"No, not hippies Max… just a middle-aged group who are on their way to the Hebrides from Penzance."

"Ah right then. But didn't the wives mind there being a nineteen year-old girl naked in their midst?"

"No that wasn't a problem Max, as it was only a load of blokes on the boat…!"

Somehow even the boy seems to get the joke and chuckles as one who knows this kind of stuff quite well now; big Max does his best to play it cool like this is what he wants to hear and all in the cool scheme of things, but later after breakfast when they fire the old bus up and head inland he starts to wonder if he is really fully up for all this pass your woman out and free love thing… alright of course if it was all coming his way instead.

The old VW chugs back up the valley towards the higher moor and the town it cradles, as Bel tells him as much as is needed for a bloke to know of the general plan she and Anne had for meeting up again this following day.

Soon rolling into Camelford the rendezvous with Anne goes well, enjoying her pastie and tea in the sun by the river and she is nervous with anticipation of their plan to seek old Joe and if it's the right one, then from him to find her long lost boy.

Anne is safe on board and they are off towards the moor and a hot climb for the old air-cooled chugger till across the rumbled cattle grid onto the old airfield then straight across and down the lane towards The Sun to see who is in down there?

We get there first when they are still some miles away and see a new face and hear a European accent that will cause some consternation by and by:

Hello er, mate… my English was not ever very good…, but I have not been here for serty years now. Can I have a pint I remember you say, of English beer please; not of German lager!

"Yeah good on ya mate… you fancy 'Doom Bar'?"

"Sure, if people drink this, I go for this."

A foreigner in The Sun: It's good to see, and gives the locals something to speculate about.

This one is between fifty and sixty years old with a small scar on the side of his face.

Old William, who could not quite catch any of the words from along the bar, could however hear that the voice was sort of mid European. He leans across to Rocky with a definitive look on his wizened old face: Rocky knows he is about to be given the ultimate truth, or the usual total bollocks.

"I remember him quite well Rocky…"

"Oh here we go!"

"I mean I remember seeing his face a couple of times. You remember hearing about when bombs landed in that farmyard outside the village of Advent Church… yep? Look are you listening Rocky!"

"Course I am William."

"Yeah you better listen mate because he may have come back to finish what he started."

"Go on then, enlighten me."

"Well at least twice I was up on the peaks as a Focke-Wolf came in low and fast across the moor to hit the airfield or whatever nearby. The low sun was behind me and I could look straight into the cockpit.

"That day the farm was hit he was banking left around Roughtor and I swear our eyes met as he straightened up and went for the farm across the valley."

"Blimey William, what are you going to do about it now he's here. Call the police before he gets nasty you reckon?"

There is still a teasing tone in Rocky's voice.

"I think we should bide our time to start with, though don't think I haven't clocked that you're taking the piss Rocky. First of all, you get some beers in Rocky while I go for a slash, and we'll talk about what's best to do; I mean there's no way of telling if he's armed or not!"

"Was it really my… oh never mind, s'that 'Doom'?"

They like a bit of intrigue almost more than they enjoy anything else there is. When your own life is pretty routine, something that has even the least hint of trouble is welcome.
Today, with the added hint of personal danger too, it's doubly good.
And it all adds up: Why else would a German airman travel hundreds of miles to the land where he will be viewed as a pariah if anyone twigs him, except to settle old scores, or finish his business.
Rocky is a little circumspect, but not as quick thinking as William. How, he cannot quite remember was the deduction made that the chap was an airman at all. Was it instant facial recognition, or after hearing the accent?
He wonders as he gets their beer if Old William could just be making it up as he goes along; though there seems little doubt he was German, and around the right age.

The assumed and therefore potentially terrifying Luftwaffe pilot is chatting with the barman, and after counting off the fingers of one hand has passed a wedge of money over to him. Could be gaining information about his targets. They both seem to be laughing happily enough, but that's what he would try to do isn't it!
Chris sees Rocky waiting and comes along. Old William steps forward to alert and question him, but the kraut takes a swig of his beer and comes along too with:

"Can I have this stool okay?"

Even Rocky gulps a little now as with that scar and his iron grey crew cut he looks a pretty tough assailant, so if William is telling the truth, could this mean they're being picked out for a hit!

Or it could mean they've been chosen as some sort of informers, and may be quite safe themselves.

"Yeah okay, it's free mate."
He throws back, and tilting his chin down to try to make his own voice sound more deep and gravely.
The pilot turns and speaks to them:

"This beer, is the best beer in the world I believe… our beer is good, but not like this."
Old William knows he should speak, or Rocky will think he is scared to say anything. But it's all feeling a bit more real than he was expecting.

"So em, my friend… have you seen very much of Cornwall?"

"Not at all since the war comrade."

"You saw Cornwall in the war William gulps?"

"Yes but mostly from the air."
Both Rocky and William feel a bit thunder-struck: William because he thought he himself had been making it all up, and Rocky because he had doubted William's story, and also because as the younger fitter one, he will be expected to defend the pub when the shit hits the fan'.
William starts to dread what he now feels he must ask, but can think of no means to duck it.

"Did you em…
He hesitates to take a swig at his pint,

…did you do any bombing in the war?"

"Yes comrade… I did my share."

Then the door opens and Joe walks in with jovial *'how-do's'* to left and right, and a fleeting nod at this new face as he heads for the bar.

William starts again, but feeling now as if by some fluke of cruel fate he might be signing his own death warrant.

"Machine guns too, or only bombs?"

"Oh yes friend, we do all and make a pretty good mess of towns I think."

They are almost speechless; this guy is proud of what he did. He is almost crowing about it.

Is this the point where if they jump him he pulls a Luger and they both have to die for the pub and England.

Now he puts his English beer down and silently mouths a few words before speaking.

Is this his moment? Perhaps he will challenge one of them to fight to the death for the honour of Cornwall. Rocky knows that as the younger stronger one it must be him.

Fritz looks up again as if he had just been searching for the right words and names.

"Do you know Joe… Joe the farrier, I look for him."

With dull dread and realisation, Old William knows why this man wants Joe, though it almost seems too fantastic. Everyone knows Joe saved a Polish crew from a flaming plane: So this must be the resentful Luftwaffe pilot who was ultimately cheated of his kill by Joe.

"No, no I don't know any Joe round here mate"

Then William wonders whether to give Joe up might be the only way to save their own skins. But the airman continues:

"No, oh sorry, the barman said Joe will be in soon and you can point him out for me then… in the war he save my life. Perhaps I will know his face, but lot older now."

"Eh... so, so are you German mate?"

"German yuk... no please!"
He pretends to spit on the floor.

"I was a Polish rear-gunner fighting with the RAF."

"So... you are the one who Joe saved up on the moor in '42'?"

Relieved that they will not be required to soak up bullets for England and St George both grippers take very large swigs of their beer and feel distinctly stupid.
But never one to miss a trick, as the Pole calls to the barman for beers all round, William turns to Rocky with a triumphant grin saying.

"There you go you great twat, I had you stitched up a kipper that time didn't I!"

"You rotten old sod William, did you set me up?"
Rocky never was the brightest candle in the church, but William still was not expecting to pass it off so easily that he had known all along.

Joe who had gone back outside to look at Jim and Marni's Brand new MkII Cortina, reappears holding back the door for the other two, and saying nice things about how good it will be to take on a run with its comfy seats and all.
Rocky throws a *'heyup Joe'* and at Joe's lifted eye throws his hand out and back towards his own chest like a policeman bringing traffic on.
You come across. Most of the time in life you are reasonably well loved, but you come in, and later you go again, and no one really wants you. When someone's arm enfolds your astral body to their chest, you come across.
Sometimes you can feel you may be walking into an ambush, it matters not, as it feels so pleasant to be called across.

And he is come:

"Do you remember Joe… about a hundred years ago, back when you could still get an erection… there was this war going on?"

"Course I can you gripper, what of it?"

"That there was this plane that had a rubbish flight crew and didn't know how to aim at the runway so they landed on the moor."

"Hey… this is not right comrade, our captain was an ace… we had no engines!"

"Don't worry mate, it's just how we tell things in England."

"So you may remember helping some bloke who was a bit slow getting to the emergency exit?"

"Well yes, as if it was yesterday… but why"

"Cos this is that bloke, that's why!"

"What Petr…! It really is… I never thought to see you again in this life, and here you stand! It's so good to see you friend… or comrade; and to see that you survived the war. Then what brings you here after so long?"

"Well I love to be in England again… but also just you Joe… How can I get old and die happy in Poland with my family; and never know again the man who me, and all my children, and all my grandchildren are here because of… my life is really yours Joe."

Joe was pretty stunned in 1942.

When someone comes from Poland because they feel their life is owed to you, you do not just brush it off and buy them a beer for their trouble, and ask about their children, or if their mother is still alive etc.

You feel instead that something has been poured into the depth of your life, which nothing in your day to day existence has prepared you for. Then you raise your hand to welcome his. He takes it. He starts again as years before to lift it to his lips; but though retired from the forge your arm is still strong.

You smile like you might have done in '42' had you not been overcome and overawed. You lift his hand to your mouth and kiss it.

Petr hears exactly what you've said. He senses exactly how often men in Cornwall kiss each others hands.

"Thank you my friend... now where are those beers I was calling for?"

"Oh Chris will be watching our glasses to come when they are almost down the bottom. But I want to get this one Petr.

"It has been a day that when I woke up this morning, I had no idea what would be waiting for me. Claire will be so happy that we have met again... now that's a thought Petr, we have a spare room, would you like to stay with us?"

"It is so kind Joe but I am all paid up here for my stay; but thank you all the same. And while I think of it Joe, the factory where my son works as a draughtsman has a big contract starting next year with English firm. He says to tell you that he will come to meet you then to say thank you."

"Then I will try to live long enough to see him Petr!"

Again the barman starts his travels to the pump and back for next empty glass. Chink and tinkle reflects upwards from the stone slab floor and tones like you hear below the polar ice-cap vibrate the air without conveying the actual words.

The beam-nailed fox with drawn back jowls pokes eagerly towards the door. It is as if he wants always to be seeing the arrival of shock to others. He likes it best if someone peens their crown on his burnt sultana nose, then he chalks one up against his lousy day on the slopes of Brown-Willy when he was hounded out of reach of hole, and wound up on this wooden plaque.

Today his once eager ear receives tones that though it cannot hear them now are rattled past the window and the door and into car-park.

A few *who's this now* heads turn, and turn back and all continues.

Joe is getting hearty thanks for his round as if no one else ever did that sort of thing. When Petr does the same he will be thanked as if they really weren't expecting him to. And Rocky much the same. Then Old William; well more likely he will remember someone that he must speak to at the other end and suddenly be off so forget that one.

The door opens.

Is it more people who have been on the guided tour of Jim's new 'MkII', or people from the vehicle that went past the window moments back?

The first in is a stunning girl, her eyes somewhere between grey and yellow, and apparently translucent so you cannot say if she is she close to you, or further away. She holds the hand of a chap who turns heads at the first table inside the door, but is half as tall as people sitting down.

Next is a tall young male hippie, and behind him a young hippie girl holding the hand of an older woman with dark curls tinged with grey.

The tiny man is pointing upwards at the fox and telling his hand holder something about it, and she smiles down like a vision of life and loveliness that he is too young yet fully to appreciate; except that he can tell he is being held by a hand that is the hand of a girl who loves him.

The older lady looks not left or right, though Petr two 'Dooms' down feels very nice inside… he feels so far from home and open to other life. To him she looks uneasy so not like a local… or someone's wife.

Might she be far from home like him he wonders. He studies her, and notices her disinclination to gaze around the bar; and still she is holding the hand of her young companion.

Petr watches.

The young companion removes her hand and gives the older woman a reassuring hug as if setting her on her own two feet: can it be her first time in a pub?

As he looks at her and speculates whether she might spice up his time in Cornwall, he finds also it is as if he is re-meeting a cousin not seen since childhood, or an old School girlfriend.

Joe notices Petr's dreamy far-away yet aspiring look.

"Petr my old comrade, are you tired, or thinking of your family. Maybe the Doom is getting the better of you after your long journey across here?"

"Thanks, but I feel fine Joe. Between the two of us Joe, that lady caught my eye as being maybe single, and not too many years younger than myself. I was imagining myself seeing some of Cornwall with her... and maybe some of her with Cornwall, you get my drift Joe!"

"Yes of course Petr... you are far from home and seeking other life that you will not have when you get back to the family... is that the sort of thing?"

"That's it Joe. But as I was looking I found she was seeming, er... do you say a bit family?"

"Ah yes I know Petr, it's familiar... like perhaps you had already seen her somewhere."

"That's it Joe... do you see her in here quite often Joe?"

Joe looks across the sea of heads. He has to lean around a bit because she is so small and there are a few big guys, and now some big women in the way.

He holds Rocky to one side to sight along the bar. She stands in profile as a drink is being passed to her.

Joe looks, and knows for ten seconds that he has seen her before. Then leaning along the bar, he knows that she is Anne.

He is frozen by delight and horror. He is frozen by all the things he knows, and all the things he doesn't know.

Is she just over for a holiday with Darren, to show him where she was in the war? No, that idea is crazy, she would never take that sort of risk.

There is no man who is obviously with her, as Petr said she looks alone… then is she here to search for someone… someone who she left behind. He wants so much to think that it is him but fears it will not be.

Now the hippie girl with her beer is craning round the bar; her eyes stop as they get to him. He smiles though rather feebly and Bel lifts her hand, he nods his head.

Joe looks away but keeps them in his peripheral vision. As soon as his eyes leave her she turns and speaks quickly to Anne:

"Just look at him Anne and see if it's your Joe… or shall I go and ask if he was a farrier for you. He's already nodded hello at me.

"I know, we can just go and sit at that table along there. I expect Anita's friend Marlo will be in soon and he can help break the ice a bit."

"Okay we'll go and sit Bel. But I'm so terrified that I'm nearly wetting myself."

Bel leads her handed as a child, and Max picks up Maxi who wants to go too. Plus this might be his best chance to get closer to Anita now Bel has another 'sister' to concentrate on.

"Shall we have a game of pool Maxi, with Auntie Anita"

Which is added deliberately before she gets any ideas that a third spirit sister might be useful up the end of the bar.

Anne feels too scared to look up as she is led to the table. They sit down side by side on the wall bench leaving a stool vacant on the bar side.

Joe is still in a state of shock being so suddenly confronted after all these years, but knows he must go to them. He steps forward through the lads to sit on the spare stool. So too does someone else and they nearly do that ending up on the floor either side of the stool trick that you see in old films.

It was Petr, and on seeing Joe must have fancied this woman for himself, though he thinks perhaps a little too advanced in years to really do it justice; even so, he without hesitation defers to Joe and is steering him by both shoulders onto the stool.

After all the years sat pondering her loss he is in front of her.
His mouth can find no words.
His head has nothing to say.
No relevant thought flows through his brain.
The woman who he sits and sees in his head every day of his life, is in front of him… and shaking visibly. A tear runs down her nose.
Joe lifts his hand from his lap and offers it across the table.
Only at this movement do her eyes lift.
A shy girlish smile flirts across her eyes and she puts her hand out to him. Anyone you might ask would know what he does to it:
Does he pump it manfully… of course not;
As he holds it against his lips he thinks how warm and soft it feels after Petr's hand; yet he has to look up at her again to be sure this is not all simply some trick of the light.

"Hello Anne of Green Gables"

"Hello Joe the farrier"

"Is Darren somewhere here with you Anne?"

"We are not still together Joe."

"Have you come to find your son Anne?"

"Or perhaps Joe, just to see what he looks like, maybe hear him speak."
Though Bel adds.

Anne doesn't want to mess his life up… but she's come so far to see him."

"Whether you want to see or speak to him: Both will be as easy Anne,"

"Yes Joe… and Bel… it is something that I have thought about for thirty years. But I don't know if I can see him but not speak to him. Does he know that you Joe…"

"No Anne… nor anyone."

The bar had been starting to thin out somewhat. The sound of a few more cars turning in across the gravel comes. It's a group of the lads from football practice and after slamming doors and lolloping across the road they pile in full of optimism for tomorrow's match.

"We've just got to keep passing it around to wear them out."

"Yeah, they're big strong blokes I gather, but they all carry too much weight. If we can just try and keep possession they'll be shagged out in the first half hour."

"Okay Marlo, but we've got to get some shots in too; a nil nil draw gets us nowhere."

So they swan in like stars still mud-smeared and glorious, and head for the bar and their well earned beer.

"Four lagers Chris you namby pamby tosser!"

"Alright Marlo don't start on me, you know there was no way I could get to the practice."

Joe wonders what he is going to do. What to say. What not to say. So much of so many years has ganged up on him today. It's all stuff he has been thinking his way through all his life: But now it's arrived like some deranged *'hunchback of emotion'* and it sits on his every moment demanding attention and instant knowledge of what he should be doing next. After thirty years of pondering, he has it seems little more than thirty seconds to know what best to do.

Joe looks up from his cumbersome hands; his eyes are lifting, but with no spark of where to go from here. How can he suddenly present Anne to her son, or him to her, and by implication, himself to Marlo also. He feels a total dullard as he looks again to Anne: Who seems transfixed. She is starring straight past Joe and up to the bar.

"Joe… you must please tell me… is that?"
And guessing Joe replies,

"Is he tall, with dark curly hair Anne?"
Joe speaks those words, more as if confessing to a murder than confirming the arrival of her life's dream.

Anne leaves her seat and walks quietly up to the bar with her drink. She stands by the group but starring straight ahead and listens.

Just to hear his speaking voice come alive to her for the first time in her life is like some miracle. It has the same pace and intonation of the cries he uttered as he came out of her body. It feels like some sudden birth of new life to her, though she knows he has been speaking for more than twenty years.

The heroes banter on as she drinks in the sound; but they are gradually aware that someone has chosen to stand close by them who is not holding out a glass to be served.

Anne starts to feel the harm that she might do. Not just to him, but 'his parents' who all these years have nurtured him, and given their life to him; and are waiting now for their son to get home with his mud and scars from his day of football practise and friends.

Anne knows at last that she must just drink his voice… then go back to her other life, and girls so far away.

Taking one last breath of their shared air she straightens her back to walk away, though does she see the nudge that was met with,

"Wa's that then Steve?"

She lifts her glass to turn and go and glancing sideways… finds that talk has stopped for now. And he has turned to fix her in his gaze: Two dark eyes down below now meet two dark eyes higher up and she halts; though not sure if they maybe thought she was there to get herself a young stud or something, or that they were just wondering why she came to stand there.

Momentarily the two hover and you might think that only like two humming-birds who thought they were both heading to feed from the same flower.

Marlo smiles a little apologetically at Anne before he says,

"Hello…"
then after a few more seconds looking down at her,

"and excuse me, but I feel I know you from somewhere, though I cannot for the life of me think from where. Have you been in here before… em, madam."

Here she laughs. And some distant spirit of resolve then takes her by the hand:

"In which sense do you feel you know me, and thank you for the madam bit… I think I caught your name as being Marlo… do you mean you think you know me like you have met me before, or
that even without us having met you feel you have some previous knowledge of me?"

"I would say em…?"

"Oh yes sorry Marlo I'm Anne, but you may soon have an extra name for me!"
Anne cannot resist adding.

"Well Anne, that sounds intriguing, but I think it was more the second one of the two… you know, without prior knowledge of you, but perhaps like finding I have a big sister… though that's unlikely because your accent sounds like you come from a long way off."

"I am from Quebec in Canada. And a big sister, yes I like that idea Marlo, but twenty-eight years would be one hell of a gap between siblings I think!"

"But at least it would stop us suffering too much sibling rivalry!"

He throws in, and feeling by it that he looks rather more confident and intelligent in whoever's eyes her's turn out to be. Then he returns:

"But you know more about me than I realised: That was my age you just said... that twenty-eight years."

"Yes it was Marlo, but no... you have never seen me before in your life...

"You may have felt me around you perhaps... look Marlo, I don't really know if I should say all this, because it will throw everything in life you have come to accept as real into the corner; then again... I've gone too far already, and geographically too I have come too far to turn back now!"

His mates begin to wonder what the hell all this is. What is this old bird going to come out with next; one of them somewhat perplexed, and too dim to contemplate anything this complex, calls Chris for another round of lagers.

"When you say *'around you'* Anne, is it like for some reason you have thought about me sometimes, or that you've been around me during my life or living near here without me knowing you?"

Certainly the first Marlo; I've thought about you at least once every day for the last twenty-eight years; and physically? Well yes, because at one time... I was all around you Marlo."

"So... er, so... I know there's something, but I just can't put my finger on it."

"Then let's try the palm of your hand Marlo."
Anne takes his hand and holds it low on her tummy.

"Does that bring back any memories Marlo?"

"What are you saying Anne?"

"You were in there."

"What... but how was I... not like a baby or something?"

"There's only one alternative Marlo, and we both know it wasn't that!"

"So... you're my...?"
At which Anne giggles girlishly back at him,

"Yes and you're my... and you know old Joe...!"

I am glad you came along, Mark P..........

And to conclude:

Bel and Max have no more children.
They split up in the long hot summer of 1976; a summer when Bel often wants to take the growing Maxi to Cornwall on her own.
Bel dies of cancer in her late twenties.

Anita moves to Camelford and becomes a popular barmaid in 'The Masons Arms', and often alongside and somewhat eclipsing the ageing Marilyn: Which seems to feel like history repeating itself.
She is blessed by several children in the coming years, by more than one father.

Marlo is so happy to suddenly have two mothers that he decides not to become a rock star in the metropolis; but he never forgets or loses his dream, and for the rest of his life a part of what he is, is Jimi.

Chris the Kiwi barman inherits the 'Rising Sun', and is still serving 'Maxi' pints of 'fifty-fifty' at a great age in 2032.

Ginny learns to do a lot more than just stroke Marlo's balls and look *'set to do her worst'*. She falls pregnant in 1972 and they get a place together. A year beyond that she even gets him to the Altar.

The non-believing vicar Mr Hennacy is de-frocked in 1973: a reporter from the Truro Gazette photographs him naked and having sex, and as if that wasn't enough, from behind with a druid altar girl in beads and a grass skirt. All this was shot at the stone circle on the moor as he cavorted with a coven of Druids and white witches.

Petr visits Joe again in 1974. He stays in Joe's, by then, cottage on the moor at the same time as Anne, who is there whenever she can be to see her boy, and Cornwall.

Petr loves Cornwall; a passion grows for the county, Anne, and the beer; and he is blessed by seeing a lot more of all three!

When Frank the kitten is a year old they decide to let him stay at home when they go to Cornwall: he gets run over and killed while they are away. Years and years later, the grown up Maxi (by then a Max) and his German wife Anna get a very similar looking kitten that they call Fritz.

hot summer of 1976; a summer when Bel often wants to take the growing Maxi to Cornwall on her own.

Bel dies of cancer in her late twenties.

Joe is a new man. Released from the gagged years of his double life he finally starts to feel confident in and around Camelford. In 1975 he gets elected Mayor. He lives to be ninety-seven years old… same as my Great Uncle Billy the blacksmith of Stiffkey in Norfolk, who saved a Polish rear gunner exactly as the story here tells.

Bel had wondered all those years before, if herself and Anne would find Joe still alive in 1971: He outlives Bel by over twenty years.

Claire is understanding about the earlier years and likes to take on the role of a sort of joint second or third mother to Marlo when Anne is in Quebec with her grandchildren.

Si 'joins up' in 1942, and later is lost in the D-day landings; 'missing presumed dead'.

Maxi, though soon called Max, grows up in Sussex but with a love of Cornwall and his moor. He wants to be a novelist, but for most of his life writes operating manuals for household gadgets.

In 2009 he is back as he frequently is in 'The Rising Sun' where he meets his German wife to be Anna. Soon they have a son called Milo, and two daughters, (oder zwei toechter) Ulla, and Francesca.

In 2032 when he is getting on a bit, and has not called home to his family in Sussex for a few weeks while he is writing a novel on the moor; his doting son Meelo begins a journey to find and check his old-man out.

Meelo's route takes him to Cornwall via Greece… but that's quite another story!

Others who lent words, and glossary of terms

'Time is a thief' p.33 and 'the lady with the skin so white etc.' p.143 and 'Hunchback of emotion' p.159 and 'Time elapses' p.22 or 'A dog upon a lead' p.62 all: Peter Hammill.

'Hey Joe, *(where are you going with that gun in your hand)* p. 25 31 34 41 45, and 'Foxy Lady' p.15, are songs by: Jimi Hendrix.

'Remembering, *Joe* forgets' p.35: has to be Siegfried Sassoon. As is, 'queer blots of colour etc.' p.51 and 'the quiet no-mans-land of daybreak' p.57 and 'a red sleepy sun' p.57 and 'Sunday morning peace' p.66 or 'as time ticks blank and busy' p.83 or 'Tins boxes bottles etc.' p.83 or any 'hearts' being 'hurt' is all SS.

'Snuffs the air' p.45 and 'around the angled doorway etc.' p.75 like Sergeant Hoad in 'The Dugout' and 'lagging loath' p.64 from 'Concert party' all by: Edmund Blunden.

'When we are' p.57: from John Cleese in 'Clockwise'.

'There could be no mistaking the nightingale' p.60 and 61 and 'stops abruptly etc.' p.125: Edgar Phillips *(the authors granddad)*.

'Summer's lease' p.62: Will Shakespeare.

'Little Lady' p.15,16,59, keeps cropping up as attributed to Jimi Hendrix; I actually picked it up from Leonard Cohen who used it to greet Janice Joplin when he met her in a lift and not knowing who she was. She and he were staying in the 'Chelsea Hotel' New York; and if you know the song you will know what she subsequently did to him. Anyway, it's a hotel where Jimi I gather, liked to stay as well. I bet that Jimi used 'Little lady' (*the expression*) too. And, 'In the wrong place, and at the wrong time' p.104, is to paraphrase 'I am in the wrong room, and I am with the wrong woman': Leonard Cohen.

'The wind comes posting by in gusts' p.89 and I recall that it confused their memories of the 'salient' (*a curve or bulge in the front line that was a bastard to defend*). I have at the moment no idea which 'Great War' salient it was; or whose memories were confused. It might even I think have been the snow that blew on the wind that did the 'confusing', but 'remembering, we forget'.

'Gripper' p.116, 155 : A Cornish term to describe someone even lower down the scale than a 'wanker'; without even the intelligence to move his hand up and down!

'As where the road gets single etc.' p.110; is from Chapter 7 page 53 in 'Two Birds Over'.
'So up the balls are racked and war begins' p.118 The same phrase occurs in 'Meelo' chapter 6 page 79. It is from a habit of Winston Churchill, as with 'It is a situation up with which we will not put'.

'As we who are left grow old etc.' p.137: I haven't got the faintest idea who it was first said it! I just know they were not my words. **Brian Burnett now tells me it was by Laurence Binyon 1869-1945 'For the Fallen' 1914.**

'Freezing your bits off' p.141: From Tina Parker.

'If only life could be like that' p.148: By the author… he believes.